EVIL ASCENDANT - DELIVERANCE

WITHIN & WITHOUT TIME - BOOK IV

D. I. HENNESSEY

arkHarbor press

www.arkharbor.press

This is a work of fiction. Names, characters, businesses, places, events, and incidents are either the products of the author's imagination or used in a fictitious manner. Any resemblance to actual persons, living or dead, or actual events is purely coincidental.

EVIL ASCENDANT - DELIVERANCE © 2022, by D. I. Hennessey, (WITHIN & WITHOUT TIME - BOOK 4). You have been granted the nonexclusive, nontransferable right to access and read the text of this book. Unless otherwise stated, biblical quotations are based on the American Standard Version of the Bible, 1885 by the English Revision Companies. At least one Scripture reference is taken from THE MESSAGE. ©1993, 1994, 1995, 1996, 2000, 2001, 2002. Used by permission of Nav-Press Publishing Group.

ISBN 979-8-9859336-0-4 (Paperback Edition)

ISBN 979-8-9859336-1-1 (Hardcover Edition)

Version 006252025

Dedicated with love
To GREYSON, HUDSON, CORRENA, ESTHER GRACE, BRYSON, ISLA,
ELEANOR, AND JOSEPHINE

CONTENTS

Jezebel sent a messenger to Elijah, saying, So let the gods do to me, and more also, if I do not make your life as the life of one of them by tomorrow about this time.

~ 1 Kings 19:2

EVIL ASCENDANT

"That's when all Hell breaks loose."
~ Amos

The colossal glass cathedral stood in stark contrast to the surrounding architecture in the capital's old quarter. Its modern glass structure rose more than sixty feet high with a forest of pointed spires that jutted upward like flames from a star.

Inside, a vast audience wrapped around a large stage surrounded by the auditorium's seating on three sides. The large forum was filled with thousands of awestruck worshipers.

Unbeknownst to them, the air above them contained an untold number of sinister, shadowy figures — they eyed the crowds beneath them like hungry predators in a restless dance.

I had witnessed the ominous scene once before, in a foreshadowing of these events. Now Chozeq and I were watching them together, unseen by the crowds and shadowy figures around us.

At the front of the auditorium, I recognized the cathedral's strange wall of religious symbols atop the central platform, rising like a great tower of Babel, thirty or forty feet high.

AT ITS FOUNDATION were the quotes:

"**Nothing is, but you are... there is nothing other than your Self.**
"**The less you know, the closer to being truth-realized you become.**
"**All states of mind are a delusion — transcend them all.**" - Zen.

FURTHER UP, the quotes became more ideological...

"**The people, and the people alone, are the motive force in the making of world history.**" - Mao Zedong.
"**One must be a revolutionary, not a reformist.**" - Joseph Stalin.

FINALLY, the quotes became less obscure and more terrifying...

"**When everything under heaven is in utter chaos, the situation is excellent.**" - Mao Zedong.
"**Death is the solution to all problems.**" - Joseph Stalin.

SCATTERED upon the tower's heights at different levels were statues of ancient Hindu deities, Egyptian gods, and occult symbols. A giant statue of Buddha was prominently displayed near the center. Above that was a large 3D Peace Symbol formed from a broken cross turned upside-down, and above that a golden Qubba — the Islamic Vault of Heaven. At the tower's peak is the goddess Anath of the Phoenicians, the ancient Canaan goddess of love and war... sister to the god Baal.

I recognized Athaliah among a group of religious dignitaries seated across the stage. They were dressed in the ceremonial robes of the world's major religions — absent any representation of Christian or Jewish forms. They all rose to their feet as Athaliah walked to the podium with her hands raised.

The dignitaries behind her raised their hands in unison, symbolizing their union — united in a rite of worship from which God was conspicuously absent.

A large cadre of reporters and TV camera crews were gathered in front of the stage. Athaliah focused her attention on the cameras as she spoke in flowery words that masked the deadly venom within them.

"Today, we dedicate this beautiful temple to the people of America. The gorgeous structure you see around you was built by my father as a gift to all of the people of this great nation. It is a cathedral, not of division and exclusion, but unity. Today, we unify all religions in the single essence of inspiration they embody. Together they reflect the human spirit — a spirit that reaches and aspires to attain the greatest longing of our hearts. Peace... acceptance... and the freedom to be what we choose to be."

She raised her arms high as she lifted her voice in a near-shout. "Today, we dedicate this hallowed place as the National Temple of Human Enlightenment!"

The crowds erupted in wild cheering — so loud that it drowned out any further attempts to speak. Athaliah waved to the crowd triumphantly and then turned to the other religious leaders behind her and bowed. They bowed towards her in return and then turned to congratulate one another.

While the loud celebration continued, a large contingent of 'ushers' wearing holstered handguns suddenly gathered around the reporters and directed them toward the doors. With the temple dedication's public relations formalities out of the way, there was no longer a need for members of the Press. They were ushered away from the building as an even larger group of armed guards outside formed a barrier to prevent any re-entry.

Inside the temple, anticipation was building as the driving beat of loud music hinted at the events to come. The adoring crowds quickly filled the area where the Press Corps had been standing, gathering in a large mob that pressed against the stage and wrapped around it. Invisible dark masses and leather winged creatures in the air above them grew more excited, moving impatiently in expectation.

Suddenly, the crowd became eerily quiet as the music abruptly stopped, and the auditorium lights dimmed. Spotlights shined on Athaliah, now alone on the stage in a dramatic stance, with her eyes closed and arms outstretched to her sides — her head was tilted back as if basking in sunlight. However, it was not light that she basked in, but darkness.

Her eyes suddenly opened, briefly flashing yellow and catlike before turning completely black. All of those around her bowed low with their hands raised as Athaliah turned toward the tower and reached for it with both hands, her fingers spreading wide. As she drew her hands apart, a large central section of the tower structure — the section that contained the peace symbol made from a broken, upside-down cross — seemed to melt away. Behind it was revealed a giant golden statue of a man-like creature with the head of a bull. It was seated on a golden throne and held in its arms an infant child made of gold. It filled the center of the tower prominently as bright lights were directed toward it, reflecting in golden beams onto the audience. A chill ran through me as I recognized the image — it was Ba'al, the ancient Phoenician-Canaan god of eroticism, war, rain, and thunder. The god of infant human sacrifice.

As the entire audience dropped to their knees, Athaliah's voice cried out over the throng.

> "Great Ba'al-Melqart, the ancient lord of the earth, ruler of the gods.
> "You are Ba'al Qarnaim, Lord of the Two Horns, who rules with thunder.
> "Lo, it is the time of his reign!
> "The season of the great Baal!
> "Whose voice speaks in thunder from the clouds.

"He flashes lightning to the earth.
"We call you now to rain upon the earth with the mighty rain
*   of your power. Send upon us your indwelling energy.*
"Take us now to be your loyal servants — we empty ourselves
*   and invite you to fill us!"*

While she was still speaking, I watched the sinister, shadowy figures in the air above descend upon the crowd. They swarmed like sharks devouring minnows in a frenzy of cries and smoky mist until thousands of kneeling worshipers suddenly reared upward as their heads snapped back, and they peered at Baal's image with the red snake-like eyes of their new demonic masters.

Athaliah looked out over the crowd — her own yellow catlike eyes were revealed as she surveyed the scene. A sly smile curled the edges of her mouth with a look of sinister cruelty as she welcomed her newly enslaved minions. Standing beside her was Devlon — his own eyes glowing red as the pendant of Molech glowed brightly on his chest.

They turned to welcome a familiar figure, who appeared vibrant and infused with mysterious power. He was dressed in a golden robe that flowed to his feet and wore on his head a golden-horned crown. His eyes glowed with the appearance of fire. It was her father... Bahal. The consul of Ba'al.

THE SURROUNDING crowds fell on their faces before the tower's golden image. A chant rose from among them, growing louder and louder as it was repeated again and again....

"GREAT IS Ba'al-Melqart - lord of the earth!"

THE TEMPLE CRIES CONTINUED for some time as Bahal, and the others stood soaking in the crowd's adoration. Devlon and Athaliah stood beside him as he placed his hands on their shoulders and nodded approvingly. The three of them stood god-like above the worshiping crowds, an unholy trinity.

THE REPORTERS HEARD the rumbling of the loud chants but could not decipher the words from outside, while the small army of guards kept them at bay.

———

IT WAS after sundown when the crowds began to emerge from the cathedral. A light rain was falling, and reporters stood under a tent of black umbrellas.

Many of the religious leaders who had been on the platform proudly agreed to be interviewed by the waiting news teams. They spoke of a dawn of world unity and praised Bahal for gifting the nation with such a beautiful cathedral.

A great commotion swept the crowd outside when Athaliah finally emerged, accompanying her husband and father. Secret Service agents held large umbrellas above the trio's heads as they made their way into the open and paused at the landing above a flight of steps. News teams and cameras quickly gathered below them and were held back by agents in a wide arc. Questions were shouted to them from a distance while scores of microphones were aimed upward as far as their bearers' arms could stretch.

"PRESIDENT SHEEN... You have spoken a great deal about the importance of separating religion from government and even from public life. Do you support your wife and father-in-law in the dedication of this new cathedral?"

"Yes, of course! It is a great and generous act on the part of Athaliah's esteemed father. A gift to our entire nation. Religion in and of itself is not objectionable. Only when it is pursued discordantly and with prejudice does it become a great cause of suffering in the world."

. . .

ANOTHER REPORTER SHOUTED TO HIM... "Christianity and Judaism are notably absent from the religions included in today's ceremony. Why is that?"

Athaliah quickly answered for Devlon while he nodded to her gratefully. "They were invited, of course, but unfortunately declined to join us. It is, sadly, a tribute to how divisive those particular faiths have been throughout history. They are responsible for so much of the world's conflict and intolerance."

Several reporters began to challenge that remark but were interrupted by someone who quickly shouted from the crowd, changing the subject. "Are you going to introduce your father?"

Athaliah beamed and welcomed Bahal to her side. "This is my father, Bahal Ebezej, the generous benefactor who is responsible for this great cathedral."

"Mr. Ebezej... What made you want to donate something so magnificent? This must have cost you a great fortune."

Bahal stepped forward, clearly relishing the fawning attention. "It is my honor to give back to this country a small part of what it has given me. America is on the verge of a great achievement under President Sheen — the unifying of all religions and soon the unity of all nations under a common purpose. For the good of all people."

Devlon thanked his father-in-law with a grateful bow of his head and then spoke to the crowd of reporters — continuing the theme. "Unity, as you know, has been the theme of my Administration and will continue to be the goal that I strive for. For far too long, the world has been held hostage by those who hide behind religious and moral doctrines to oppress and control others.

"I promise you here today that their God will have no place in my government or in the United States of America. This is the land of 'We the People.' A nation that does not bow down to any power except the power of our own will. We will choose to build our own future — a future without the crippling oversight of an overbearing God. We are determined to shake off His hold on us, and we reject his sovereignty in our affairs.

"Beginning today, we are not 'One nation under God,' we are a nation *free* of God! We are: *'We the People!'* and we make our own choices. We, and we alone will govern ourselves!"

THE SURROUNDING crowds broke into wild cheers, drowning out any further questions.

———

CHOZEQ and I watched the scene from our vantage point in the air above, invisible to the throngs of demonic hosts who still hovered above and around us. I was not surprised by Devlon's shocking remarks but felt great despair, nonetheless. His act of defiance was leading the nation into a great and terrible darkness.

As I was watching, I suddenly heard the Lord's voice. Not in a still, small whisper, but loudly — He spoke in a powerful tone that shook my very soul.

You ARE my witness to this defiant generation. Speak the words I give you boldly and without fear. No harm can touch you....

HE HAD NO SOONER SPOKEN than I found myself instantly transported into their midst, appearing in a brilliant flash of light that nearly blinded those around me. I stood atop the stairs a short distance from Devlon and the others, in front of the reporters and cameras. Chozeq was standing at my right hand, and Ardent stood at my left, with swords drawn in my defense.

I quickly discerned that Bahal and the demon-filled hosts could see Chozeq and Ardent clearly, but the reporters and secret service agents could not. My angelic protectors were a powerful deterrence against any thought of attack that might have entered the enemy's mind.

Those standing all around stood paralyzed in stunned amazement at my sudden appearance, including the armed guards who seemed unable to move, even though they surrounded the area where we were all standing. Words filled my thoughts, and I used the advantage of surprise to capture their attention. I turned to Devlon and the others, surprised at how loudly my voice seemed to thunder when I spoke to them. I shouted as loudly as I could....

"The God you have rejected has sent me with a message for you and the nation.

"Since you have rejected Him, He has also rejected you. Beginning tonight, your government will cease to abide under His wings and is no longer kept under His holy protection. The hearts of citizens will be divided against one another and will not submit to your authority. Nor will your people hold brotherly affection and love for one another. Since you have corrupted justice and rejected mercy, He will likewise show no mercy upon your nation.

"As you have chosen for today to be the day of rejection, so will today be the beginning of His judgment upon you. From this night forward, no rain will fall on any possession of your land, so you will know that there is a God in Heaven.

"Everyone who is listening, hear this! God's heart is not turned against you for evil but to turn you back from your defiance. Remember, on the day that you turn back to Him, he will accept you, as a loving father welcomes his child. Then He will open the Heavens and refresh your land and will have mercy upon your nation and heal your hearts.

"Tonight, God has spoken to you."

THE LIGHT STEADY rain that had been falling stopped suddenly, and a dry breeze swept over the crowd.

Then, with a flash as bright and sudden as before, I was gone from there.

⌘

2

NATION DESCENDING

"... it's all part of the plan that God is fulfilling."
~ Jimmy

The airwaves were abuzz with talk of the *glass temple*. That's what I'd decided to call it. 'The Temple of Human Enlightenment' sounded dangerously presumptuous, not to mention being unnecessarily long for a name.

The real story that should have been reported was the message that God had delivered, but instead, the focus was on the means of transportation that God had used to get me there. The profound importance of that message couldn't be overstated. The lifting of God's favor from the nation was a calamity of earthshaking consequence.

Regardless, the event certainly made an impact. My appearance had overshadowed the dedication of Bahal's cathedral. That fact by itself had probably been the greatest irritant to him. Devlon and Athaliah seemed stung by it as well; they could barely find words to express their outrage each time they were asked about it. The very fact that they were asked about it was itself an outrage.

Sheen's Vice President, Bo Strident, condemned the media focus, which, he said, diverted well-deserved attention from an epic act of generosity on the part of Bahal. Perhaps Bo was thinking of the thirty million dollar 'gift' that Bahal had given *him*.

"You've been quiet today," I said to Anna as we stood together watching the goats eat.

I was pretty sure that I knew what was bothering her. She had acted the same after the events on New Year's Eve when I made that unexplainable appearance at the tent. That had only been a mile away, and the message that night had been encouraging for the most part. This time was different in just about every way. I took her hand and waited for her to work out what she wanted to say.

She stammered slightly as she tried to put her thoughts into words... "H-how?... Why-why you?"

She had succeeded in putting her finger on the two most difficult questions — the two questions that I was least able to explain. I gently squeezed her hand a little tighter and looked her in the eye.

"Anna, we've known all along that God is doing something different here. None of this has been normal...."

She searched my face like she was trying to see if I was still the same person. I pressed forward, hoping that I'd say something that made sense to her.

"Look at everything that's happened. The crowds, the miracles... my being shot, all the people who've been saved.... Look what happened at mom's memorial!

"Amos' journal talks about all of it — it's all part of the plan that God is fulfilling."

A hopeful look in her eyes seemed to be fighting an equal amount of fear and sadness. Her voice wavered as she spoke... "I'm scared. I'm afraid of what will happen to all of us... to the whole world. I'm worried that you'll be arrested or... who knows... taken up in a whirlwind or something!" She did her best to smile about her remark, which sounded more like a joke once it was expressed out loud, rather than the honest concern that it really was.

I held her hands with both of mine. "I'm not going anywhere. At least that's one thing I know for sure — I'm in this right up until the end. You and I are in it together."

Her eyes searched mine seriously, scanning back and forth for a moment until she finally accepted what I was saying. In her battle between hope and fear, hope seemed to prevail for now. She leaned toward me and squeezed her arms around my neck, holding onto me as if she didn't dare let go.

AMOS WAS right about the effect that the events at the temple would have on the country. Unfortunately, *Hell breaking loose* seemed to be far too accurate a description for it. Thousands of the pagan adherents who had bowed to Baal suddenly began exhibiting remarkable and dangerous abilities. The combination of their unloosed demonic powers, along with the withdrawal of God's protecting grace, soon resulted in the country being overrun with catastrophes. Unexplainable events were commonly reported — everything from people being mysteriously stricken dead to entire buildings suddenly bursting into flame. Hatred and rioting were rampant throughout the country.

Despite all that, people continued to dismiss the threat of judgment for as long as they could, denying even the possibility of a drought. However, by June — after almost two months in which no rain had fallen, there began to be an increasing buzz about it. Especially since those were usually the rainiest months of the year. What puzzled meteorologists the most was that even Alaska and Hawaii had been rainless — an unheard-of amount of time for those regions. Even the US territories, like Puerto Rico and Guam, were drought-stricken. More perplexing, however, was the fact that Canada, Mexico, and the rest of the South Pacific had remained unaffected.

The one part of God's judgment decree that Sheen's Administration seemed to take to heart the most was the warning that *'citizens will...not submit to your government.'* They were cracking down on challenges fiercely. Yet, the more they tightened control, the further the country descended into chaos.

MID-JUNE - GRADUATION...

CENTER SPRINGS SEEMED ODDLY INSULATED from the worst of this chaos, at least for now. It was hard to believe that the time for our High School Graduation had finally arrived. After everything we'd been through in the past year, it felt anticlimactic, to be honest. Still, it was a welcome milestone, and I felt incredibly grateful for all the efforts of the school's faculty this year that made it possible for me to finish.

The AV crew streamed the outdoor graduation ceremony so I could watch it.

"At least there's no chance of rain," I commented to Anna. She thought my joke was in poor taste, so I kept it to myself after that.

Nyle and Uncle Mike banded together to get a new flat-screen TV for the farmhouse, and Nyle wired it up so Uncle Jim and I could watch the ceremony together.

In a gesture that I thought was pretty cool, the school arranged for a seat to be reserved for me among the graduates and placed my folded graduation gown and cap on it. When my name was read, there was a cheer from my classmates and the audience at large. It brought a lump to my throat. I knew it was more than a friendly gesture — nearly all of them had become believers thanks to the year's extraordinary move of God and were cheering in solidarity. I offered a prayer of thanks and thought of Kelly, whose prayers had been the catalyst that touched off the whole thing.

Uncle Jim placed his hand on my shoulder and gripped it supportively when they cheered. Mom's absence felt palpable as I thought about her... I had the sense that he understood what I was feeling.

. . .

ANNA and her mom stopped in after the ceremony ended, careful not to draw attention to where they were going. Anna handed me a rolled-up diploma with my name on the outside.

"That one's fake," she revealed. "They're sending us the real ones later."

"Great. I wonder what they'll use for an address when they send mine."

"...I gave 'em my name as the next 'o kin," Uncle Mike answered as he walked in the front door, catching the conversation. "That works for diplomas as well as Last Wills 'n Testaments."

He winked at Anna and greeted her mom with a quick kiss.

"Can't think of anyone I'd rather leave it to," I offered.

"Hey!..." Anna challenged, pretending to act offended.

"Oh wait, that's true," I quickly admitted. "You probably deserve that diploma more than I do after all your help this year."

"You're welcome," she said as she wrapped her arms around my neck with a smile. There was no resisting her kiss. I realized when it finished that it was the first time we had ever kissed in front of the others. Uncle Mike and Anna's mom teased us with applause, and Uncle Jim nodded approvingly.

As THE WEATHER had grown warmer, the meetings at the tent again became a daily phenomenon. By mid-June, they were in full force.

Now that school had ended, time seemed to slow down a little. Anna was able to spend more time with Rosie and Elroy, and she also let *me* hang around with her while she was here.

Pete had been recruited to help plow the fields, but it became apparent that there wouldn't be much hope for a full harvest this year due to the dry weather. To conserve irrigation Uncle Jim decided to sow just one of the fields, watering it for just a few hours at night.

Like Anna, Pete didn't know quite what to make of me right after the events on Easter. It wasn't until we spent time together that he finally started to feel comfortable around me again.

"Dude! I can't believe you're like a real, honest-to-goodness prophet! You're like Moses or that Elijah guy. What did it feel like when God transported ya like that? It musta been like Star Trek — can you ask God t' beam ya up whenever ya want?"

I laughed at his joke. "It's not quite like that." The topic still made me uncomfortable; I nudged the conversation to a different subject.

"How's Radison doing? Have you heard anything about his new foster family?

"PJ and I have been trying to contact him, but no luck. I don't suppose you could do what ya did before and locate him for us?"

"That wasn't me exactly," I admitted, "...but I'll pray about it."

I couldn't help feeling that an ominous darkness was gathering over Rad. It was clear that Pete and PJ would have a part to play in helping him, but the enemy was doing all he could to prevent it.

Pete and I were still talking when the sound of a car pulling up the drive drew our attention. I was surprised to see PJ as he parked and stepped out — it had been a few months since he'd been to the farm-house. The last time was on the day when he and Pete first searched for Radison, in fact.

"You're here about Radison, aren't you," I guessed as he came nearer.

PJ shrugged with a certain irony, not appearing to be surprised by my comment.

"He doesn't answer my calls anymore," PJ explained. "I think he was moved to a different foster family, but Social Services won't give me any information. I was hoping that maybe you could... you know — like you did before."

I felt my forehead wrinkling as I looked at both of them uncomfortably. How was I supposed to explain how I had traveled to the boy's grandmother's bedside? It had been as much of a surprise for me as it was for them. All I could offer was a suggestion that we pray together about it.

We gathered in the living room, kneeling together around the old coffee table. PJ began to lead us as we lifted Radison before the throne. I couldn't help thinking of how the boy looked the last time I saw him — it was in a visit to his future. I recalled his broken and hopeless condition after his father's execution... the memory haunted me. Hearing PJ's voice as he led us in prayer only reinforced those shocking scenes.

"Lord, we lift Radison to you now, understanding that You have laid him on our hearts today for a reason. Whatever the need is that he faces now, we pray that You would intervene for his good. May those circumstances help him to see his need for You. Whatever it takes, Lord, draw him to Yourself — until the day that he can claim You as his personal savior."

I waited for a change in the scene around me — bracing for the flash that would signal my arrival in another place and time. However, no flash came, only the echo of Radison's cries on that coming night when he will mourn over his future condition.

PJ prayed more earnestly: "Help us to find him, Lord! Lead us to him, just as You have led our hearts to seek Your face on his behalf. Show us what You need us to do!"

The sudden revelation that came over me was not a trip through time or space. It wasn't a voice from Heaven or a dream-like vision. It was simply a thought... an idea that entered my head. Yet it was so fully formed and lucent that it was more like a vivid memory. I pondered it as PJ and Pete finished praying, looking at them quietly as we finally knelt together.

"You need to call someone named Bea Goodall," I said to PJ. "She works in Social Services. She'll help you find Radison."

PJ gratefully placed his hand on my shoulder and added a prayer of thanks before we all stood.

"I don't suppose you know how to *find* Bea Goodall, do you?" He asked as we walked toward the door.

"I'm not sure, but something tells me you should start with Rev. Jerome at Calvary Hill Church. He might know how to reach her. It's just a hunch."

PJ put his arm around my shoulders. "I'll go with one of your hunches any time. I'll give Jerome a call."

"I hope you find Radison," I added sincerely. "I think he really needs our help."

The two of them promised to make it a priority as they headed for their cars.

. . .

BEFORE I HAD much time to think about it further, my phone chimed with a text message — it was from a name I hadn't seen in months... Agent DeMassi.

- Can we meet? -

⌘

3

MOONLIT GRAVEYARD

For the weapons of our warfare are not of the flesh, but mighty before God to
the casting down of strongholds.
~ 2 Corinthians 10:4

The idea to meet at the Old Hill Church had entered my mind the moment I saw Agent DeMassi's text. It was nearly midnight when I used the mausoleum key to let myself out and closed its gate behind me. Frank wouldn't be arriving for another half-hour.

I'd never been to the old church before and had to feel my way carefully through the graveyard by the light of a waning moon. I made my way to the back of the church, finally finding the back steps where we'd agreed to meet.

The dim moonlight cast a gray pale over the unfamiliar church-yard around me as I sat alone in the darkness. I suppose the experi-ence might have been terrifying to me a year earlier; it helped that I didn't have to imagine what types of spiritual visitors lurked in the darkness — I could clearly see the angelic presence that accompanied me. The air was pleasantly cool — a relief from the increasingly hot drought conditions that had become common during the day.

In the quiet of the night, I felt my heart turn toward the amazing protector of my soul who had been with me constantly, especially in the past year. It was the Lord Himself who had shepherded me. He had even provided Heavenly guardians without reservation. A silent prayer of thanks swelled my heart.

Second Corinthians 4:7 came to mind once more — it had become a constant reminder of the reality of what was happening.

"But we have this treasure in earthen vessels, that the exceeding greatness of the power may be of God, not of ourselves."

I recalled Chozeq's words from late last summer when I struggled with the calling placed on me....

"Bear in thy heart a constant memory of thy weakness; it is good for thee to do so. Remember that ye are but an earthen vessel in which is contained an infinite power and the riches of Heaven itself. It is not the vessel that is strong but the power within it. Draw ever nearer to the source of that wellspring and leave not thy gaze from Him."

If there was one thing I'd been forced to learn in the past year, it was that I had nothing to fear. No matter how frightening my situation had been or might become, there was nothing that could harm *me* — the *real* me — the *me* that would last forever. Even if my body were killed, it would never kill *me*.

The truth of that epiphany was liberating. I was truly in God's hands, and He was supremely good. Whatever happened would be for both my good and the greater good. I whispered the Apostle Paul's words aloud to myself as they came to mind:

"FOR ME TO LIVE IS CHRIST, AND to die is gain.[1]"

"THAT'S some philosophy you have there," Frank DeMassi said unexpectedly as he quietly arrived beside me. "I guess that explains some of your reckless shenanigans lately."

He took a seat on the step beside me.

"You surprised me; I was expecting to see a flashlight or some-thing," I noted, reacting to the way he snuck up on me in the dark.

"Two tours of duty," he said in explanation. "Guys with flashlights don't live very long on Special Ops. missions."

"I think I know how you felt on some of those missions," I admitted.

"I'll bet you do. I've gotta hand it to ya, kid; you have more guts than most of the guys I fought with."

I glanced over at the vigilant angel warrior standing a dozen feet away with his sword drawn in our defense and smiled to myself. "It helps to be on the winning side," I answered.

Frank's voice grew more serious. "I have to say; I don't know how you keep so positive. It doesn't look like your side is winning at the moment."

"It may look that way, I'll admit, but don't count God out yet. He has a way of getting the last word."

I heard Frank exhale sharply and could tell that I'd managed to put my finger on a sensitive topic. He spoke quietly....

"Fair point. I guess that's kind of what I wanted to talk to you about." He paused silently, and I could tell he was gathering his thoughts for an important question. "I've been watching everything that's happened this year — especially in the past few months, and it's never been clearer. Things are happening that can't be explained in natural terms.

"First, there were all those miracles with people being healed..., and those lightning strikes when people were after you. Then I saw what happened with that reporter, Trudi Staring — with that demon-thing. All of that was pretty crazy, but now with these last two times when you did your appearing and disappearing act on live TV. I'll admit there's no natural explanation for any of that."

He sat quietly for a minute as if he was struggling with something that had him seriously rattled.

"I guess I've always believed in God — I was never an atheist or anything like that. I just never gave Him much thought, ya know?

"Sure," I said reassuringly. It was pretty easy to imagine how he was feeling.

"Look, I've done a lot of things I'm not proud of. I've also seen stuff... in the war... and back here... stuff you wouldn't believe that people could do to each other. It makes ya pretty jaded after a while — I guess that's the only way to cope with it. I always prided myself on bein' tough and not letting it get to me.

"The thing is, the stuff this year has been different. The crimes lately are more... evil."

He paused and hung his head for a moment before continuing.

"I-I just don't know if I can do it anymore. I just don't have the strength emotionally, ya know? It's a lot like this drought... that's how dry I feel in my soul." After a short pause, he kept on....

"There was something you said when you appeared at the temple that I can't get out of my head — it keeps repeating constantly. You said...

'...ON the day that you turn back to Him, he'll accept you, the way a father loves his child.' You said that He'd *'have mercy and heal our hearts.'*

"I BELIEVE those words were from God — I honestly believe it. Do you think they could apply to one person the same way they did for the whole country? Could it be true even for somebody like me?"

The sense of God's presence was growing stronger as he talked. I could feel the Spirit interceding on Frank's behalf from deep within me. As I answered him, I felt like the words were being spoken by God's Spirit into my heart, specifically for him.

"As a matter of fact, they can *only* apply to one person at a time. Every one of us has to give his own account to God, and the relationship He wants with us is deeply personal. Yes, they apply to you — they absolutely do.

"Jesus said, 'Come to me all who labor and are heavy laden, and I will give you rest.[2]'

"The only qualification needed for God to make us strong is to have a sense of our own weakness. In the same way, the only thing that qualifies us for His forgiveness is a genuine awareness of our own guilt. When we lay our lives down in surrender to Him, we find the truest freedom."

Frank released a deep breath, "Phew…. that's profound, kid." He was silent as he considered my words before adding: "I'll be honest; I haven't got a clue how to do that. Surrender is something I've never been good at — they don't teach that in boot camp."

I chuckled at his comment. "Surrendering to God isn't what you might be thinking — it's not throwing in the towel or quitting. It's a conscious act of obedience — surrendering our right to call the shots — giving that control to God and letting Him give the orders. It means making Him the Lord of your life."

He sighed painfully. "I've got a lot of baggage. There are things I'm not sure I can ever forgive *myself* for. How could He accept a guy like me after the things I've done?"

"I don't know all the things you've done, but He does. He's seen them already, and He loves you despite it. The fact that you're here tonight having this conversation is proof that that's true. The Bible says: 'In him, we have redemption through his blood, the forgiveness of sins, … it's according to the riches of God's grace.[3]'

"It doesn't have anything to do with what we deserve. There's not a person who ever lived that deserved it, except Jesus himself, and he's the one who gave his own life as the ransom for yours. He already took the blame for all of your sins — God won't judge the same sin twice; that debt is paid when we trust in Christ.

"The thing is… you have to trust Him as your substitute. Jesus is offering to give you *His* righteousness in exchange for your sin."

Frank's head was hanging lower now. I couldn't see him very well in the dark, but the sound of a sniff and a quick wipe of his face with his shirtsleeve let me know that he was struggling to stifle a tear or two. The sense of Divine presence around us was growing stronger every minute. It was clear that God had his sights set on Frank and was bringing the full power of His Spirit to bear in his heart. Frank was soon bent over and holding his head in his hands as the realization of his need for Christ became overwhelming.

"What you're feeling right now is the call of God on your heart. No education on earth can reveal Christ to a man's heart — only the

Spirit of God can do that. It's when God Himself overshadows us with his wings, and we suddenly sense the holy of holies of His presence; that's when Jesus is truly revealed to the spirit of a man. Only when the Holy Spirit has touched our eyes to open their blindness and quickened our hearts with the awareness of divine life — then we can see Jesus in all His majesty.

"It's that awareness of His presence that reveals our own sin to us. In His presence, we understand how far we are from His perfection — how unworthy we are. That's a tremendous gift! It's a divine act when God stirs repentance in a human heart. He is wounding your heart in order to open it — so He can wash it. So He can take all the guilt away.

"Jesus said, 'I stand at the door and knock: if any man hears my voice and opens the door, I will come in to him.'

"He's knocking, Frank. I know you feel Him knocking, don't you?"

He wasn't able to speak. I saw him nod his head anxiously as this rugged warrior's shoulders shook with a sudden sob.

I turned to kneel on the old church's stone steps, inviting him to join me. He didn't hesitate. As soon as he knelt, the floodgates of his remorse broke loose — he shook with the pent-up emotion of a man suddenly confronted with the full weight of all his sins in the presence of God's holiness. But it wasn't guilt that overwhelmed him; it was the feeling of God's unconditional love and acceptance.

I prayed silently for him as I waited for this wave of emotion to slowly ebb, then led him in a prayer of repentance that he anxiously repeated.

It didn't take long for his wrenching remorse to turn to tears of joy. I gratefully joined him as we rejoiced together, losing track of time as we basked in the incredible manifestation of the Lord's presence that seemed to permeate the entire churchyard. When our hearts finally became quiet again, I put my hand on his shoulder and began to pray for him.

As soon as I began, I was stopped short by the sound of *THAT* voice — the voice that I'd heard before on five occasions. From Frank's gasp and the way he raised his head to look around, I could tell that he was hearing it too.

Franklin James... you are my servant — today I have chosen you. I have anointed you to go from here in the power of my Spirit. You will no longer war according to the flesh, for the weapons of your warfare are not of the flesh, but mighty before God to the casting down of strongholds. My Spirit goes before you, casting down imaginations and every high thing that is exalted against the knowledge of God. In my power, you will bring every evil spirit and every wicked thought into captivity to the obedience of Christ, and no enemy will be able to resist you.

*Rise and go in the power of **my** might!*

⌘

4

DROUGHT

"From this day forward, no rain will fall... so you will know that there is a God in Heaven."

The Forth of July had a different feeling this year. It would be hard to explain the difference other than by saying that it felt like something important was missing. Due to the dry conditions, most fireworks displays were banned, and private celebrations were canceled. But the real difference wasn't due to fireworks — there seemed to be less of a feeling of unity in the nation every day. To be honest, that's putting it mildly; in many cities, people were practically at war in the streets.

By August, the country's farms were struggling with failed crops, and water levels in lakes and reservoirs were well below normal. Shortages of food and basic staples were just beginning to be felt throughout the country, adding to the unrest. Wildfires were already ravaging forests in the West, filling the skies with thick black smog over vast areas of the country.

UNCLE JIM HAD the TV tuned to the local station. The news showed a press conference with Sheen's press secretary, Ermine Pounder.

[Q] A RECOGNIZED reporter from a major network raised his hand. "What is the Administration doing about the worsening drought conditions?"

Ms. Pounder looked out over the sea of reporters with a condescending gaze as she answered. "As I'm sure you realize, the planet's ill health has been in the making for generations. These conditions result from Global Warming and have a clear scientific explanation. It is completely man-made, I'm afraid. Unfortunately, it cannot be corrected overnight."

[Q] The second reporter stayed with the same theme: "You say it's a global problem, but so far Canada, Mexico and the rest of the world have not seen the same drought conditions as the U.S. — what do you make of that? Do you think there's truth to the claim that God is withholding rain from us because of the President's actions?"

The press secretary smirked dismissively. "We prefer to trust in the science and not the fanatical delusions of a ranting teenager."

[Q] A third reporter shouted out her follow-up question: "Still, it is coincidental that the drought can be traced to the same day he made that claim. There hasn't been any rain anywhere in the country since that night."

Ermine's eyes flared momentarily in anger. "We do not entertain superstitious or magical explanations for world events as if they were facts."

[Q] Yet a fourth reporter was heard above the others as she drilled into the

same line of questioning. "In that case, how do you explain the fact that that is true? The rain ended that same night."

Ms. Pounder's annoyance was visible as she gripped the lectern tightly and stood silent, seeming to regain her composure by brute force. "We are investigating all possibilities. As you know, the Moretti boy is a known terrorist who was responsible for the tragic bombing on November 1st. If he is working with a foreign government to use climate-disrupting technology against our country, we will take all necessary steps to counter that threat."

Hands shot up across the crowd of reporters as everyone shouted questions about the shocking revelation that foreign enemies could have climate-disrupting technology. The words 'terrorist' and 'foreign agent' were repeated throughout the chamber. A pleased-looking smirk could be seen on the press secretary's face as she quietly gathered her papers and walked out of the briefing room.

MID-JULY...

PETE AND PJ pulled up to the address on Steinway Street that Social Services had provided. The building was located in an endless row of small storefront shops with apartments overhead. Even with help from Bea Goodall, a senior agency director, it had taken weeks to navigate through red tape and obstacles to locate Radison's foster family.

The small apartment that they approached was upstairs over a bakery. The delicious smell of fresh-baked sweet rolls, bread, and cakes filled the air in the small staircase as they climbed to the single door located at the upstairs landing. PJ knocked on it.

After intermittently knocking and waiting for nearly five minutes — which felt like an intolerably long time in the stuffy stairwell — a woman's voice answered from inside.

"Who's there?"

"Hello… Mrs. Oram? Shirley Oram? I'm Reverend Rodriquez — we spoke on the phone this morning? Social Services sent me."

Through the door, PJ and Pete heard the sound of several latches being unlocked, and then the door opened a few inches — still held by a chain. The plump face of a middle-aged woman peered out.

"Radison ain't here. I ain't seen him since early this mornin'. There ain't nothin' wrong with the child — why is Social Services checkin' up on me?"

"It's nothing like that," PJ reassured her. "I'm here on behalf of his father."

"His father?" she exclaimed in surprise. "I thought his father was a no-good criminal. He's supposed to be in prison."

"Yes, ma'am, he is. I'm his Chaplain — from Stockslock Penitentiary. He's become a committed Christian… he'd like Radison to know that."

"I don't care what he's gone an' become," Mrs. Oram said dismissively. "He's in prison, and that's where he belongs as far as I'm concerned."

PJ and Pete glanced at each other awkwardly, unsure how to answer.

"Any idea where Radison hangs out?" PJ asked. "Are there friends that he hangs with?"

"He's off with the Powis boys, more'n likely. They're good kids, for the most part. They usually hang out up at Ditmars playground playin' basketball or ridin' their skateboards."

"Thanks very much, Mrs. Oram. If you have no objection, we'll check there for him."

"I can't control what you do on a public street, but thanks for asking, just the same."

With that, she unceremoniously pushed her door closed and secured the deadbolts. PJ and Pete looked at each other in surprise and smiled as they shook their heads. Pete checked the map on his phone as they got into the car.

"Ditmars playground is north a few blocks."

The small park was surrounded by tall tenement buildings but seemed clean and relatively well-maintained. Crowds of young mothers roamed the playsets chasing small children. The basketball courts nearby were busy with much older kids. A smaller group of boys around Radison's age were off by themselves riding skateboards on a makeshift track of cement walks that cascaded down several levels. PJ found a parking space on the street a block away.

Pete tapped PJ on the arm as he spotted Radison and opened his mouth to call to him. PJ quickly stopped him.

"Be cool. We don't want to scare him away," he warned.

The two of them took a seat on one of the curbs nearby and watched the boys on their boards. When it was Radison's turn, they were surprised to see him lift off and catch the top of a handrail, riding it with his board to the bottom where he did a two-rotation helicopter and landed wheels-down. PJ applauded as he came to a stop a few feet away from where they sat.

Radison smiled and pumped his fist in the air triumphantly, then realized who was clapping for him. The smile left his face, but he didn't turn away.

"Hi Radison, that was some gnarly gliding, bro. Didn't know you were a skater."

Radison didn't answer but seemed to get more comfortable. He nodded and pointed his skateboard at PJ in a gesture that meant thanks. PJ pointed to Pete.

"You remember Pete... he was here with me the last time." Pete waved his closed fist in a gesture of solidarity. "We were in the neighborhood and thought we'd see how you were doing. Your foster mom told us you'd probably be here."

Radison's friends gathered near him to see what was up. They caught sight of Pete's tattoos and came closer.

"That body suit is big yikes — wicked tats, dude!"

Pete threw PJ a comic glance and stood to his feet, pulling his teeshirt off over his head, then assumed his classic, incredible hulk stance. The kids whistled and raved as they saw his tattoo-covered chest, shoulders, and back. The ink covered every inch of him above the waist like a long-sleeved shirt.

"Rad, man, your friends are Lit. You gonna intro us or what?"

Radison seemed reluctant but pointed to Pete and PJ as he said their names. "That one's Pete, and that's Juan... they call him PJ. He's like a Reverend from the church."

"He's dope for a Reverend," one of them complimented.

"Hey, are you skaters?" another quickly asked.

PJ raised his hand as he declined. "Sorry, no. I'm just an admirer."

With a little relentless begging, they convinced Pete to show them his skills. He admitted that he hadn't skated in years but managed to make it down all five landings without falling, although he didn't attempt any rail-gliding.

PJ nodded toward the hotdog vendor nearby. "Anybody hungry?" Radison's three friends quickly said yes, leaving him no choice but to come along. As they sat down to eat, Pete kept the friends occupied while PJ took the opportunity to talk with Radison one-on-one.

"Your dad says hi and sends his regards. He'd love to meet you."

Radison objected. "Man... I don't even know the dude. I've never even met him in my life!"

"Well, this is your chance to meet him. He really wants to get to know you. He is your father, you know."

"Honest, I don't even know what that means. I ain't never had any kinda father around. What's he gonna do, take me campin' in his prison cell?"

Despite Radison's initial objections, PJ finally got him to agree to a single visit to see Chase and promised to come and get him once the arrangements had been made.

THE TWO MEN felt pretty good about their successful visit. As they drove back to Center Springs, the music on the radio was suddenly interrupted with a news flash. Athaliah was preparing to give a statement.

"I'm taking this opportunity to address the American People directly with an important message of hope and solidarity. While some in this country would have us believe that their faith promotes peace and brotherly love, their actions bring only conflict, division, and hardship for all of us.

I'm talking, of course, about the fanatical Christian sect led by the wanted terrorist, James Moretti. Not only has he opposed the efforts of our administration to bring unity and equality, but he has also continually used inflammatory rhetoric to divide us. As you know, he has now found a way — whether working with foreign enemies or not, we can't be sure — to disrupt and threaten our great country through climate terrorism.

This has hurt all of us, and I'm sorry to say that you, the American people, have borne the worst of his painful assault. I can assure you that our law enforcement agencies are doing all in their power to bring this fugitive to justice. I call on all of you to help in this effort by alerting law enforcement if you see or hear anything that could lead to his apprehension.

In the meantime, I urge citizens of goodwill from all faiths to unite in calling on the universal supreme deity — however named — to end this terrible assault. If you will allow me, I'd like to lead us in a prayer of unity, honoring that common faith.

"Our great spirit-father, we unite our hearts in calling to you for the peace of all people everywhere. We look to you, oh god of the rain and thunder, to whom we ascribe dominion over our earth — send us the rain that our thirsty land requires and bring relief to the people of this great country. I make this plea publicly so that all may know that the god of our mother earth — Ba'al Qarnaim — is our true god."

PJ COULD BARELY BELIEVE his ears! She was literally leading the country in a prayer to Baal! What's next — infant sacrifices?

⌘

5

COMING TOGETHER

God has a plan...

Late August...
"Say hi to Chase for me," I said to Pete and PJ as they stood at the farmhouse's front door. They were preparing to leave for a long-awaited visit to the prison.

After more weeks of red tape with Social Services, PJ finally arranged for Radison to visit his father; they were on their way to go pick him up.

"I wish I could be there when they meet each other for the first time," I said wistfully. The thoughts that rushed through my mind were of a future scene — when Rad will witness his father's execution. I guess the feelings it engendered were visible in my face.

"Don't look so bummed about it," Pete encouraged. "It's gonna be awesome."

I snapped out of my daydream. "You're right... I'm really happy for them." I shook off my distraction and nodded gratefully. "Thanks for taking an interest in Radison; I know it's been a lot to ask."

"Are you kiddin' me? You remember who asked me to do it, right?"

I smiled and nodded my head in acknowledgment. It was pretty hard to say no to an audible voice from God, I had to admit.

"Watch it on the roads — it's getting pretty crazy out there. I'll be keeping you guys in prayer," I promised.

"Thanks, dude, really appreciate it." Pete shook my hand and swung his left arm around my shoulders, slapping me on the back, then offered a casual salute as he spun around and headed down the porch steps. PJ smiled as he waved as well, climbing into the drivers' seat.

I HAD NO SOONER SHUT the front door than my phone rang. Mr. O'Malley's name on the caller ID surprised me.

"Hi, Uncle Ward."

"Hi, Jimmy. How are you? It's been too long since I called to see how you were doing."

"It's only been a few weeks," I pointed out. "I'm fine - still under house arrest." My sullen mood over missing Chase & Rad's reunion was harder to hide than I realized.

"I know it must be tough," Mr. O' sympathized. "You've handled it well — you're doing an incredible job... really incredible."

I appreciated his attempt to encourage me, even if he was over-doing it a little. I took a deep breath and did my best to shake off my temporary slump.

"It's not so bad; I like it here," I admitted. "Uncle Jim has the harder part of the deal — he has to put up with me, 24-7." I smiled at Uncle Jim, sitting across the room, and he winked back.

"You're welcome here as long as ya like!" he hollered loudly enough for Mr. O' to hear.

"How are you guys doing?" I asked, returning my attention to the phone.

"The cabin is great, and the mountains are beautiful. Ed and Marsha... Mr. Johnson and his wife... have been gracious hosts. Work has been as busy as ever, even busier, in fact. That's partly what I was calling about."

"You're calling me about work? What could I do?"

"Well, we've all been praying — the four of us here, and feel strongly that the Lord has laid something on our hearts. With all that's going on around the country, so many pastors and churches are suffering. Many are being jailed and separated from their families. We feel the Lord is calling us to start a legal defense fund to help them."

"That's a great idea!" I agreed. "What is it that you want me to do?"

"It's more about what you've already done — your contribution to our Foundation. How would you feel about some of that money being used to support the new mission?"

"I'd be fine with it — it's a great idea! It's probably not enough to go very far, though. The legal defense mission is a lot bigger!"

"You're right about that — we're trusting the Lord for the rest."

"I can mention it on the podcast," I offered. "I'll bet there are a lot of people who would contribute to help with that."

"That's a generous offer, thank you. We have some things to get set up first — I'll email you a link to the website when it's ready."

I put the call on speakerphone, and Uncle Jim joined in. We spent the rest of the time catching up with Mrs. O' and talking to little Ryan before finally saying our goodbyes. As we were about to end the call, Mr. O' picked up the phone and spoke in an earnest tone:

"I don't have to tell you this, of all people, but I feel like I have to say it anyway… God has a plan. We just have to remember that He has all of this under control."

"Thanks, it does help being reminded of that. We're still in His hands."

———

LATER THAT EVENING, Pete called to report how the prison visit had gone.

"It was touching, man. Chase was pretty busted up when he saw his son. He apologized for not being there for him and asked for his forgiveness."

"What did Radison say? How did he take it?"

"I guess it was a lot for the poor kid to take in, not knowing Chase or ever seeing him before. He just sat kinda quiet, like he wasn't sure what to make of the whole thing. He was quiet like that pretty much the rest of the day — all the way back home."

"Well, at least they got to meet. Maybe it will be the start of something good," I said hopefully. "Thanks for the update."

As I hung up the phone, a prayer for Rad crossed my lips. If only we could do something to reach him before it's too late. Maybe we could save him from the tragic future that I'd already glimpsed. That thought immediately brought to mind a conversation I'd had with Amos a year ago. It was on my last night at home before I moved to the farmhouse. It was the night before Amos went home to be with the Lord.

> "God doesn't see time the way we do — in a series. He
> sees all of it at once. He doesn't see a timeline that's
> changing as it goes along — He sees everything
> happen the way it actually does."

That memory was followed by something else he'd said that night:

> "…use the time you have…prepare God's people for
> what's to come."

MR. O' finished setting up the new legal defense fund within days, and we announced it on the podcast. Within a week, they had dozens of requests for help. Donations came in as well, but not at the level that was needed. The biggest surprise was the number of other legal firms and sympathetic attorneys who called to offer pro bono services. However, the costs for travel, posted bail, and other fees were quickly depleting the fund's reserves.

From reading Amos' journal, I knew that the number of cases would soon grow much larger.

THE LEGAL DEFENSE Fund stayed on my mind for the next several days. The more I thought about it, the more convinced I became that God wanted us to do more. I struggled with what I could do to help; I obviously could not help in a courtroom — that was out of the question. There honestly wasn't much I could do to help financially either. We were already doing all we could to get the word out in our podcasts, but contributions were slow coming. Too many families were now struggling themselves.

I pondered these thoughts while I checked the water level in the secret passage and decided to pay another visit to the underground room and its mysterious trunk. The room's lanterns cast a warm glow and illuminated the space brightly as I sat down to examine the strange vault again. I admired its shape and construction — like an old treasure chest made of heavy bronze, with sides as thick as a cannon barrel. The base of the trunk was set into the floor — embedded in it somehow. It was clearly meant to be immovable. Impregnable as well, from the look of it; there were no latches anywhere, not even visible hinges.

Amos' words replayed in my mind as I stared at it — almost seeming to echo inside the lonely cavern.

> "...you'll find provisions — don't use them until you
>   need to."

While I considered those words, the puzzle of his epitaph ran through my mind once more....

> With angels' wings, provision sown.

I couldn't help feeling that the two phrases were connected somehow, but I remained at a loss to decipher how.

The more I thought about it, the more futile it seemed. Even if I could open the trunk, it wasn't likely that Amos could have filled it with millions of dollars — enough to provide what was needed for the Defense Fund.

Reluctantly, I doused the lanterns and made my way back to the farmhouse.

———————

LATE SEPTEMBER...

"HOW ARE things at the sub shop?" I asked Anna as she poured feed into the goats' bowls.

"It's still really busy. Sheriff Flanagan stopped in yesterday — he and Mike talked for a while in private. Not sure what it was about."

"Yeah, I wonder. Uncle Mike hasn't mentioned it," I said curiously.

"It was about our irrigation," Uncle Jim answered from the barn doorway as he entered. "Sorry, wasn't meanin' t'eavesdrop... jus' happened t'hear what ya said.

"The Sheriff wanted Mike t' give me a heads up 'bout it. There's a new order comin' that says we'll need t' quit waterin' the crops."

"But the aquifer is still full," I started to object. I glanced at Anna for a second, realizing that she didn't know about the secret passage and underground springs. "I mean, the well is still pumping strong," I hurried to explain.

"Well, I reckon our waterin' at night has kept it from evaporatin' away. Lucky fer us, most of it likely seeps back down into the ground-water again."

I thought of Elijah and how God took care of him at the brook Cherith and with the widow at Zarephath. "...I don't think it's luck."

"Well, right you are, son... right you are. It's sure 'nough the Lord's doin' — He's lookin' out fer us without a doubt."

"What are you gonna do?" I asked.

He turned and looked out over the lush green field. It stood in sharp contrast to the dry surrounding landscape. "I reckon we'll quit waterin'. Don't want t'be drawin' any attention our way. It's near ready fer harvest anyway — we'll need to gather it in a mite early, is all."

OCTOBER...

PETE WAS RECRUITED to help with the harvest, and Anna rounded up a dozen other volunteers, who finished the job in record time. The only downside of all the extra help was that I had to stay out of sight and couldn't pitch in.

Despite the earlier harvest, the crops' yield was surprisingly plentiful. Uncle Jim said it was nearly as much corn as he usually got from three fields. He stored enough for chicken feed and seed corn for replanting and quickly sold the rest. Corn was in short supply since most of the larger farms' crops had failed months ago.

MEANWHILE, the drought was worsening at an increasing pace. By November, the water levels in lakes and reservoirs reached a critical stage, and the government seemed to be running out of new restrictions to impose.

The nightly news was beginning to look like a collection of scenes from apocalypse movies.

"Massive forest fires continue to ravage California and the northwest," the news anchor explained as footage showed the devastation. *"New fires have broken out this week in Maine, Vermont, and upstate New York.*

"In other news, the unrest over food shortages rocked more cities with violent protests." The scenes showed angry mobs smashing storefronts. The protests looked more like an excuse for looting and random destruction.

"Riot-sparked fires have reduced another city's commercial district to smoldering ruins," the anchor continued as the screen showed block after block of destroyed buildings.

"Meanwhile, the number of unemployment claims has reached the highest level ever recorded. With employment tax revenues plummeting, some in Congress are proposing an emergency measure that would allow the IRS to seize private assets from large corporations and high net worth individuals. President Sheen has expressed his support for the bill."

"SWITCH off that TV for us, will ya?" Uncle Jim asked as he announced that dinner was ready. Anna was wearing an apron in the kitchen and smiled at my raised eyebrows when I entered the room. Uncle Mike and Lena were already seated with Pete at the table — everyone had been invited to celebrate the recent harvest with a festive meal that included a huge platter of steaming corn on the cob.

Anna hung up her apron and took a seat beside me as I sat down. Then Uncle Jim invited us to hold hands as he bowed his head.

> *"Lord, we're truly grateful to you for your care and for*
> *providing this bounty before us in a time of need. We know*
> *that the true need in the nation is for folks to draw near to*
> *you. You're surely waitin' with open arms. We pray for*
> *that day to come soon.*
> *"Thank you, Lord, for watchin' out fer all of us here. We're*
> *trustin' you t'keep us safe, no matter how rough the times*
> *may get. Bless this food to our bodies and ourselves to your*
> *care."*

Everyone joined in, adding, "Amen."

"God has amazing patience," I felt compelled to say. "But waiting is not all He's doing. He's actively chasing them... that's what this is all about. It's like a father rushing to save his kid from a dangerous fall. If they could only see how hard He's running to save them, it would melt their hearts; I know it would."

⌘

6

VIGILANCE

"God is still on the throne."
~ Ward O'Malley

Thanksgiving...
  Devlon was seated behind The Resolute Desk[1] in the Oval Office as cameras focused on him. The pre-announced telecast was being broadcast nationwide.

"I speak to you today — one week before a holiday that has been called *Thanksgiving*.

  "As you look around you, you may feel as I do that it is difficult to be thankful. The appalling climate attack that has so damaged the nation has hurt all of you. Indeed, there is little to be grateful for.

  "The history of this particular holiday is stained with the crimes and abuses of our forebears. It was even enacted as a national holiday amidst a terrible Civil War. Certainly not an occasion for which to be thankful.

"It is time for us to shake off this soiled legacy and move on to more noble aims. Beginning today, the Federal holiday known until now as Thanksgiving will be renamed "Autumn Feast." It is a time to celebrate family and friends and honor our great earth from which all bounty comes.

"I have instructed all Federal and State agencies to enact this change immediately. Today, I call on private industry, commerce, and all of you — the American people — to do likewise.

"We must stand together in solidarity in this time of need. We stand against tyranny and those who would force their misguided ideals upon the rest of us. We must band together against them! Together we will preserve this great country by our own strength and with the fortitude of our resolve. *We the People* will not bow to any power except ourselves!"

DEVLON'S remarks were not a surprise — Amos had recorded them practically word-for-word in his journal. Even members of the Media saw their irony. Several commentators noted that the move seemed to be inspired more by Devlon's self-proclaimed vendetta against God than by a desire to 'shake off a soiled legacy.'

'*Thankfully*,' millions of people ignored the new decree and went ahead with their traditional Thanksgiving celebrations. If anything, his proclamation seemed to strengthen the country's appreciation for the original name. Devlon's decree proved to be wildly unpopular.

AS CHRISTMAS APPROACHED, the battle over holiday names intensified. Following the unpopularity of his Thanksgiving decree, Devlon didn't publicize his decision to rename Christmas. However, it soon became apparent that the Federal Government's name for the holiday was now simply: "Sol." When questioned about it, the Administration's

Communications Director explained that the name was merely a clever play on "December Solstice." However, a few brave scholars pointed out that "Sol" had also been the name of the Roman holiday celebrated on December 25th in honor of *Sol Invictus*, the ancient Syrian sun god. The one who was later adopted as the chief god of the Roman Empire under Emperor Aurelian.

MEANWHILE, as the country veered further toward paganism, the Christian revival was growing explosively. Movements like the one in Center Springs had become widespread, bringing conversions and miraculous healing to thousands around the country and throughout the world. The churches had become a crucial support network for communities across the country, providing food and necessities for the growing number of people in need. This dynamic had now grown so apparent that news networks produced segments on how important these church-led ministries were becoming.

Athaliah bristled at this. Soon after the New Year, she announced the Administration's response in a press conference.

"I'm pleased to announce a new government program to provide food and necessities to needy families throughout our nation. New Distribution Network Centers will soon be established in cities and towns across America to provide for needy families that this calamitous climate terrorism has injured.

"I am also announcing a Justice Department investigation into alleged criminal conduct by numerous religious organizations claiming to help their communities. Charges have been filed in dozens of these cases, including illegal tax evasion, unauthorized commerce, and embezzlement of funds.

"Today, more than 200 arrests have been made among leaders of these organizations. We will take our responsibility seriously to protect vulnerable citizens from these unscrupulous predators."

· · ·

"...DID you hear about Reverend Wilkes and PJ?" Anna asked emotionally as I answered her call.

"Hear what?"

"They were both picked up by Federal agents this morning! Sheriff Flanagan was just here to let your uncle Mike know."

"Where did they take them?"

"Right now, they're being held at the local jail. The Sheriff said they might be sent to Stockslock pending trial."

"For what? What are they being charged with?"

"The same as all the other Pastors... they're accused of tax evasion and hate speech."

"Hate speech? That couldn't be further from the truth! And how could they be evading taxes? The tent services don't even take offerings!"

A thought immediately came to mind... "We have to do a podcast tonight — an appeal for people to pray... pray for a miracle!"

"Alright... I'll get Josh. I get off work at eight o'clock — is that too late?"

"No, that's perfect. I'll start praying about it and getting ready — tell Josh to meet me online, and we can work together on it. See you when you get here."

A GLOBAL PRAYER VIGIL...

THE INTRO MUSIC and graphics faded as a forest of pictures rained onto the screen, falling so thick that they overlapped and covered one another. They were pictures of men and women — rabbis, pastors, and Christian workers — who had been arrested. The last two images to fall at the front of the pile were PJ and Pastor Wilkes.

"All of the people seen here have been unjustly arrested in just the past few weeks, and there are hundreds more. The Sheen administration has declared war on faith-based ministries as part of their war against God.

"Tonight, we will lift them before God's throne, asking for His miraculous intervention. We're asking all of you who are seeing or hearing this message to join us in praying for that miracle — even if you're watching this after the podcast has ended. Believe me; God has a different view of time than you and I. Your prayers will make a difference tonight.

"Lord, we don't know what outcome You have ordained for these unjust arrests, but we know that all things truly do work together for good when we place ourselves in Your hands. These men and women are your servants who have dedicated their lives to Your work and the service of others. We join together as your people, from all around the world, in the unity of spirit, to ask You to intervene on their behalf.

"We humbly plead for all of them and give You all the glory. Please magnify Your name tonight and demonstrate the power of Your sovereign hand!"

THANKS TO ANNA, Word had gotten out earlier in the day that there would be a prayer vigil at the tent for Pastor Wilkes and PJ. The tent and surrounding field were packed — especially with hundreds of those who had been dramatically healed in the past year. The podcast was being broadcast through the PA system as the crowd prayed urgently along with us.

The AV crew was live-streaming from the tent, showing panoramic scenes of thousands of people standing or kneeling in urgent prayer. In fact, throughout the country, the congregations of arrested leaders were spontaneously coming together in prayer, joining together with us. This incredible move of the Spirit quickly spread worldwide as more and more tuned in to the live podcast and joined their hearts with us. My voice in the background was soon replaced by other voices who picked up the intercessory plea, as one person after another led the remarkable group of gathered hearts in an ad-hoc global prayer meeting. Soon it was more than a million strong!

"But an angel of the Lord by night opened the prison doors, and brought them out," Acts 5:19

As THE EVENING wore on and the intercession intensified, a series of individual occurrences began to take place across the country, none of them unusual enough to draw attention by themselves. Well-dressed men and women in business suits and carrying briefcases began to show up at police precincts, county jails, and prisons. In each case, they delivered signed and notarized court documents ordering the release of individual prisoners, all of whom happened to be rabbis, pastors, or church workers. In each case, the well-dressed messengers waited for the prisoners' release and escorted them outside, only to suddenly disappear from sight.

At roughly the same time, Obadiah was meeting privately, along with a few trusted Senators, before an emergency session of the Supreme Court. He presented evidence exonerating the prisoners on grounds that their arrests resulted from government abuse of power and without due process or merit.

In a remarkably speedy ruling, the court chastised the Administration for 'a clear abuse of Executive power' and ordered the immediate release of all affected prisoners. For his protection, Obadiah's name was withheld from the record of the proceeding, which referred only to a 'credible confidential source.'

IT WAS NEARLY midnight when a police car pulled into Carmine's parking lot with its lights flashing, drawing the nervous attention of the crowds. Members of the camera crew focused on the officer who climbed from the driver's seat — we could see that it was Sheriff Flanagan himself. The sheriff opened the car's rear door, and out stepped Pastor Wilkes, followed quickly by PJ.

Both pastors raised their hands in the air in gestures of triumphant praise as the crowd went wild. The pastors bounded to the tent's rugged pulpit, and everyone grew quiet, waiting for them to speak.

"We want to thank all of you sincerely for your prayers. Tonight God has performed a miracle!"

Cheers swept through the crowds.

"The reports are still coming in, but it appears that, like us, the people you've been praying for are being released all across the country." PJ looked to the Sheriff to confirm that it was okay to publicly read the paper in his hand. Sheriff Flanagan nodded yes with a smile.

"I have here a copy of the court order that was delivered less than an hour ago."

'By order of the Supreme Court of the United States.
In the matter of Defendants et al. v. The U.S. Justice Department.
Regarding Executive Order 98267-54544.

It has been determined by the court that numerous violations of the First, Fourth, and Fifth Amendments have been duly shown and that sufficient cause for arrest or imprisonment has not been demonstrated.

The motion for dismissal of said charges is hereby granted, and all prior convictions due to violations of said Order are reversed. The Court orders the defendants' immediate and unconditional release.'

Anna looked at me with tears of joy and took my hand.

"This is amazing... over a million people were praying with us. God heard us!"

"He always hears," I said with confidence, buoyed by what had just happened. "He heard us even before we started to ask."

Coverage of the night's events dominated News reports the entire next day. Sheen's press secretary, Ermine Pounder, canceled the day's press briefing, and calls to her office were met with responses of 'no comment.' It was late the following day when the President's Attorney General stood before microphones.

"In adherence with the Supreme Court's ruling on the President's Executive Order, we have suspended active investigations. The Order is being reviewed for changes to comply with the court's findings. At that point, we fully expect to re-institute our enforcement efforts. This is merely a procedural delay."

My caller-ID lit:

- Ward O'Malley -

...I muted the TV as I answered it.

"Hi, Jimmy. I have to say, last night was incredible! Barbara and I were online praying with all of you. The speed of the court's ruling was a true miracle."

"Thanks for being there," I said sincerely. I glanced back at the

TV where the AG was still speaking to reporters... "It looks like it's a temporary victory."

"They have to say that to save face," Mr. O' tried to reassure me. "We'll be ready with Legal Defense if the time comes when it's needed."

"There were thousands of cases," I noted. "How much would it cost to defend them all?"

"Millions, no doubt," he admitted. "We'll just have to trust the Lord. God is still on the throne."

AFTER WE HUNG UP, Mr. O's words kept repeating in my head...
...*God is still on the throne.*
Surprisingly, it triggered a sudden memory of a detail in Amos' epitaph that I hadn't thought much about in months:

...help from none but His own Throne.

I recalled running my fingers over the verse engraved on the rim of his crypt — I could practically feel the cool marble against my fingertips as I mulled it over:

...Thou sittest in the throne judging righteously.

There was some connection between all these references; I could sense it!
Just then, Uncle Jim happened to walk in the front door. A question started out of my mouth almost before I knew it....
"What do you think of when you hear the term: 'Throne of God?'"
"Well, mostly the Judgment Seat, I reckon," he answered without a second thought. "It reminds me of that window at the old church. It

sure made an impression on me as a young boy. I've had that scene on my mind fer my entire life."

"Window?" I asked. "Which window, exactly?"

"The Great Throne scene in the stained glass," he said, acting as though everyone living in Center Springs ought to know all about it. "It's the most memorable thing about the old church, without a doubt. Fills nearly the whole wall up behind the pulpit. A man couldn't miss it if he was half-blind.

"I guess you've never been inside the old church," he added, noticing my clueless expression.

"N-no, I haven't," I admitted. I'd love to see it, though."

"Well, I guess you could use the secret passage to head up there and check it out fer yerself."

He read the sudden surprise in my face — I'd never told him where the passageway led. Without my needing to ask, he explained....

"I cleaned up some o' your footprints in the mausoleum a while back; looked like you'd been walking in the graveyard. It didn't take much t' figure how they got there."

I held my head in my hands, realizing how stupid I'd been! I was so concerned about being seen in the dark that night that I hadn't wanted to use a light — I never thought to check for footprints!

"Wow," I said, clearly embarrassed. "I'm glad it was you and not anyone else."

Uncle Jim waved his hand dismissively. "No worries. I don't reckon there's anyone else but me wanderin' through our locked mausoleum lookin' fer footprints."

He might have been right, but I still felt like I should have been smarter. I wouldn't make that mistake again.

UNCLE JIM LOOKED at me curiously....

"What made ya ask yer question about the throne?"

⌘

7

THRONE OF GOD

"What makes ya think it's a clue?"
~ Uncle Jim

Every once in a while, Uncle Jim had a way of throwing me off balance with one of his questions. While sounding innocent enough, he had again managed to put a finger precisely on what I most tried to hide. I knew that he had already pieced together the connection between the secret passage and the church, but I wasn't sure if I ought to reveal the underground room or its hidden provisions. He waited calmly for my answer but didn't give any hint of dropping the question or letting me off the hook.

"The th-throne?" I stammered. "Oh... well, I guess... I was just thinking about it, that's all. I was talking to Mr. O'Malley, and he happened to mention that God is still on the throne. It made me think about how that's true...."

The look in his eye signaled clearly that he wasn't buying my explanation.

"No need t'be explainin' — I reckon it ain't none o' my business."

I stared back at him, no doubt looking like a deer in headlights. Then it dawned on me that, of all people, Uncle Jim was likely to be the one person I could confide in about this. He already knew about the secret passage and clearly knew more about the old church than I did. There was little doubt that he could keep a secret — he'd kept the one about feeling responsible for my great grandpa's death for over seventy years!

I gathered my thoughts and did my best to explain truthfully.

"You're right; that's not the reason I asked." I looked at him, slightly embarrassed, then continued.

"I think there's a clue in Amos' epitaph that has to do with God's throne. I'm not sure what it means yet, but it could have something to do with that scene you referred to in the stained glass."

He scratched his chin and thought for a minute.

"A clue, ya say? His epitaph... hmm." I never saw the connection b'fore... maybe yer right."

I recited Amos' epitaph; after churning it in my mind for a year it was committed to memory. Uncle Jim considered it carefully as he listened:

> *In the Journal of Time, thy deeds are known.*
> *With angels' wings, provision sown.*
> *Seek help from none but His own Throne*
> *Naught but Heaven is thy home*

"Help from none but His own Throne..." he repeated thoughtfully. "I suppose that could be pointin' to the window's image. What makes ya think it's a clue?"

I explained my discovery of the underground room and its mysterious locked chest.

"Amos said there were provisions inside it and that I would figure out the secret to opening it when the time came — when we needed it. I've been trying to figure out the throne clue for more than a year."

Uncle Jim scratched the top of his head, holding his cap in the other hand.

"Well, I'll be honest; I ain't been inside the church m'self fer a good many years. None o' the folks I used t' know there are livin' anymore. Gettin' inside is likely t'be a trick for you. It ain't like y' kin show up on a Sunday mornin' for a look 'round — you'd be recognized for sure."

I thought aloud... "Maybe I could ask Reverend Wilkes to talk to the pastor there."

"That's only gonna raise questions I don't think yer wantin' t' answer." He thought for a moment....

"I remember an ol' tunnel from the coal shed that ran under the churchyard. Lou an' I used t' play in it when we was kids. That was years ago — can't say if it's still there."

"The coal shed?" I wondered.

"Yer right... it's probably long gone by now," he conceded.

I thought silently to myself — it was dark the night I went there to meet Frank, but I was pretty sure I remembered seeing an old building behind the church in the moonlight. It wasn't much bigger than a shed.

"I think we should check it out," I suggested. "Do you think anyone is at the church today?"

"I reckon not on a weekday morning."

I thought for a second. "You could drive there and check if the coast is clear. I can take the secret passage and meet you at the mausoleum."

Uncle Jim seemed prepared to object at first but thought better of it. He shrugged his shoulders as a slight smile lit his face. "I reckon a little adventure could do us both some good."

WE MADE our preparations and compared notes as I lifted the hatch to the root cellar.

"It'll take me about 20 minutes or so to reach the mausoleum," I said, checking the time on my watch.

"Ok. I can drive there in about ten... that gives me ten minutes or so t' look 'round."

"Here, you take the mausoleum key," I said, handing it to him. "I've got enough to carry." I held up the gigantic key to the secret door and a lantern in one hand and a gallon of kerosene in the other.

He helped me down the ladder, handing me my supplies and a backpack with a packed lunch.

"That's fer later, in case yer search takes a while."

I CAME PREPARED this time with extra flashlight batteries along with the gallon of fresh fuel for the other kerosene lamps. The key to the secret door seemed even larger as I struggled to grip it with the same hand that held the fuel can. Convenience obviously wasn't a top consideration in Amos' design. Remembering the backpack, I slipped the large key into it and then closed the secret stone door behind me.

The tires on my bike had gotten a little soft from sitting for so long. I had to stop and use the bike's air pump to fill them back up, adding a few extra minutes to my trip. I started off through the cavern with the lit lantern hung in front and the kerosene riding in the basket.

The water level in the underground spring was still surprisingly deep, although it might not have been flowing as rapidly. Thoughts of the cavern soon faded, however, as my mind replayed this morning's conversation with Uncle Jim. I knew that having my extra mouth to feed for so many months hadn't been easy for him. There hadn't been much for him to sell from the farm's milk or eggs. He had whatever profit he made from the crops, but I knew he'd been generous with his pay to Pete and had other bills to pay. It was a sure bet that his resources must be running thin.

Aside from all that, the drought was starting to worsen, and we both knew that the upcoming year would get a lot harder. I just hoped that whatever Amos had left in the way of provisions was at least enough to help out Uncle Jim.

Five minutes later, I reached the base of the second staircase. After stashing the fuel can in the underground room, I checked my watch then quickly started up the long stairs. I was running about five minutes behind.

UNCLE JIM WAS WAITING for me in the mausoleum. I emerged slightly out of breath to find him sitting on the staircase, facing away from the mausoleum's secret door. He appeared startled when I walked up beside him and said hello.

"Wha... I'll be!" he exclaimed. "I didn't hear ya come in."

"Yeah, it took some work, but the old door runs pretty quiet now," I agreed, feeling admittedly proud of my work.

It was a cold January day, and the temperature inside the mausoleum was sub-freezing. I rubbed my hands together to warm them and nodded up the steps toward the vault's entry gate as I pulled on a pair of gloves. "Is anyone out there?"

"Don't appear t' be," he confirmed. "I did a quick walk 'round — looks like the ol' coal shed's still there, though it's a mite tumbledown. The church doors are locked; figured it'd be smart t'check 'em."

"Good idea," I said with a smile. It hadn't occurred to me to check something so obvious.

I raised the collar of my coat and pulled my hood up over my head against the cold — not to mention any unwanted observers. Uncle Jim locked the gate behind us.

The old shed was weathered and worn but stood solidly. It hadn't been used in years, as evidenced by the growth of hedges that blocked the door. That was probably the reason why it wasn't locked. I confirmed that I could squeeze inside, then spoke through the hedges to Uncle Jim.

"You should probably wait in your truck where it's warm and keep an eye out. If anyone comes, blow the horn."

He called back that he understood. "Watch yerself in that old coal shoot — there's no tellin' what condition it's in."

The hatch for the coal shoot wasn't hard to find... it covered most of the floor in the small shed. Its old hinges were rusted, making it more of a struggle to open than it should have been; they screeched loudly as it opened. Down inside, past the spiderwebs, I could see a few scraps of abandoned coal still sitting in the coal bin below. It looked like a good seven or eight-foot drop.

A chain hung down from the shed's ceiling and lay coiled beside the open hatch. I appreciated the winter gloves I was wearing as I dropped their rusty links down the shoot and used them to climb down. Once at the bottom, I squinted into the pitch-black tunnel in front of me.

Climbing from the coal bin, I stared into the pitch dark tunnel. Just then, a quick flash suddenly erupted in the darkness.

———————

THE NEXT THING I KNOW, I am standing with Chozeq at a construction site. At first, it appears to be a barn, with its high ceiling and wood plank floor, but I quickly notice the sight of polished wood and the smell of fresh varnish. Turning toward a commotion behind us, I realize that it's not a barn they are building; it's a church. A gleaming wooden altar rail has been recently installed along the edge of a raised platform. Behind it, a large group of men is working to raise a huge window using ropes and pulleys. I watch with interest as it is lifted into place behind the pulpit — anticipating the image that I expect it contains.

"Looks like a perfect fit, Clarence," one of the men congratulates another. "That's some fine framing work you've done... truly fine."

There is a flurry of activity as a small army of men raise ladders and gently push the window into place, securing it carefully. Others can be heard from outside as they add the trim to its exterior.

My attention is drawn to three men seated on one side of the room, speaking with a fourth, younger man, who is standing. One of them stands and looks back at the others, placing his hand on the young man's shoulder. As he turns his face toward us, I recognize Amos immediately. It's clear that he notices Chozeq and me — he acknowledges us with the slightest subtle nod as he looks directly at me, then quickly focuses his attention on the men seated in front of him.

"Jeremiah, you have truly outdone yourself with this fine work. It's a genuine masterpiece!"

Jeremiah nods his head gratefully. "It was a labor of love, I assure you."

"A labor of love! In that case, perhaps I can have my nine hundred dollars back," the man seated beside him jokes.

Jeremiah's face reddens as he begins to stammer, but the joking man puts an end to it with a slap on Jeremiah's knee. "I'm only joking, man! It's fine work — well earned and more than deserving of such a price."

Amos speaks warmly to the man: "How can we thank you, Oliver, for all you've provided to this work!" He pauses with a glance at the young man beside him... "My son Raymond here has expressed his great sense of debt for your charitableness. If not for your generous support, this church building would not be standing."

"I feel it a blessing to have been able to help. You were a good friend to my father; Dad often spoke of your days together in the war. He would have wanted this as much as I."

Amos addresses him gratefully. "It is certainly a blessing that we cannot repay. Not only this building but the fine mausoleum as well. We are truly humbled."

"May your parents rest there in peace. It's the least I can do — you saved my father's life. I wouldn't be here today had he not made it home from the war." He stands and shakes Amos' hand, taking up his hat to leave.

Jeremiah stands as well. "Thank you again, Mr. Jennings, Sir."

Oliver accepts his handshake warmly and looks again at the enormous stained glass window. "That's fine work, son... truly fine. I may call on you for a project I have in mind."

"Yes, Sir. Thank you, sir."

Raymond offers to walk Mr. Jennings to the door. As soon as they are out of earshot, Amos calls Jeremiah aside, deliberately walking with him in our direction. He stops a few paces away from us and speaks to him quietly.

"Have you arranged for the secret compartment that we discussed?"

"Yes," Jeremiah confirms. "It's directly beneath the gold engraved nameplate. Pressing downward on the frame just beneath the two kneeling angels will cause it to spring open — press in both places simultaneously."

"Beautifully done," Amos commends him.

Jeremiah nods gratefully as he turns his attention toward the window, anxious to ensure it is installed correctly. Amos, meanwhile, looks directly at me and winks.

I STAGGERED SLIGHTLY as the scene abruptly ended, returning me to the pitch dark coal tunnel. A glance at the display screen of my watch confirmed what I'd come to expect — no time had passed.

Now armed with new information, I was even more determined to explore the mysterious stained glass window. I pulled out my flashlight and started down the dark corridor, finding a closed door at the other end. I was honestly surprised to find it unlocked. Pushing it open carefully, I did my best to avoid disturbing whatever appeared to be leaning against it from the other side.

I found myself squeezing between the basement wall and some kind of tall panel. Once I reached the edge and slipped out from behind it, I could see that it was a large painted mural — likely used as a background in a recent Christmas play.

A harrowing few minutes of navigating through Sunday School supplies and furniture finally brought me to a staircase that led upstairs to the main sanctuary.

The scene inside the church looked surprisingly familiar, despite 100 years of intervening time since the visit I'd just experienced with Chozeq. The sight of the enormous stained glass window in the finished sanctuary took my breath away. I quickly saw why it had made such an impression on Uncle Jim as a boy. In the darkened room, its ethereal setting and bright golden hues seemed as vivid as when it was first installed. I wasted no time making my way onto the platform and up to the window frame.

The golden plaque at the center of the windowsill gleamed in the midday sun.

Dedicated in Loving Memory of
Oliver Burr Jennings (1825–1893)
By his son
Oliver Gould Jennings
"May thy soul be at God's right hand."

THE KNEELING ANGELS that Jeremiah referred to were easy to spot in the window's depiction. They knelt on either side of a humbly bowed soul who was being judged as the angels read his name from the Book of Life. The great Judge was welcoming him with open arms.

I felt along the window frame, unable to detect any kind of button or lever. Nonetheless, when I pressed on the frame in both places, the wood bowed slightly downward. A clicking sound signaled that the secret compartment had opened, and I saw the golden plaque spring forward ever so slightly.

With my fingertips, I carefully pulled it open. Inside was an unusual-looking key with four opposing bits at the end, wrapped in a handwritten note. It repeated one line of the epitaph:

With angels' wings, provision sown.

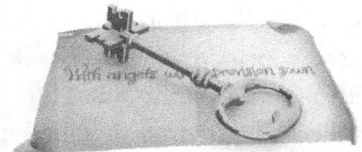

I LOOKED at the stained glass mural again, noticing how the tips of the two angels' wings touched one another at precisely the point where the key lay hidden. That had been what the clue pointed to all along.

NOW I JUST HAD TO FIND ITS matching keyhole.

⌘

8

PROVISION SOWN

With angels' wings...

Uncle Jim was leaning forward attentively in the driver's seat of his truck as I came around the bend from behind the church. He hopped out and waved with an all-clear sign for me to make my way through the graveyard. We reached the mausoleum's gate at the same time.

"I left everything just like I found it in the coal shed," I confirmed. He nodded as he pulled open the gate for me to enter, then quickly closed it behind me.

"Did ya find what y' were lookin' fer?"

"I think so," I said, pulling the strange key from my pocket to show it to him.

"Well, I'll be... how in heaven did ya find that so quick...?"

"Heaven had a lot to do with it, I guess," I said, cutting off his questioning. He understood my reluctance to explain further and nodded acceptingly.

"The sooner you're out o' sight, the better," he said, looking around at the road. He quickly locked the gate behind me then offered me a clean rag. "Fer yer footprints," he suggested helpfully.

"Thanks," I accepted with a grateful smile, then made my way down the stairs and toward the secret door, wiping up coal dust footprints as I went.

Once inside the secret passage, I paused to light the lantern and resealed the door behind me. Thoughts of the morning's events swirled in my mind, especially about the revelation that a wealthy friend of Amos had paid for the church and mausoleum. I guess that explained the enduring quality of the mausoleum's construction. It was still sturdy after a century and a half.

These thoughts were rumbling around in my mind when I reached the underground room. My excitement was quickly building as I set my lantern on the table, hardly able to wait to use the key I'd discovered. I impatiently filled the other two lanterns with fresh fuel and finally lit them.

The room glowed brightly with the light from all three lamps, making it easier than ever to carefully inspect the mysterious chest in the center of the room.

It was immovable — literally. The close inspection confirmed it to be embedded in the stone floor. As noted before, the chest's outer shell was as thick as a bronze cannon barrel. I suspected that a direct hit with a cannonball would have about as much effect on it as on the cannon that fired it.

The chest didn't seem to have a discernible front or back. There were no hinges or latches that might hint which way it opened. All the way around, just beneath its lid, was a locking mechanism consisting of thick appendages that clamped like teeth against the sides, disappearing into reinforced gaps with interlocking bolts. The whole thing reminded me of a bank's vault. I had to wonder whether Amos' wealthy friend, Mr. Jennings, had something to do with building this as well.

After studying it for several minutes, it seemed clear that the lock must be in the lid itself — that suggested that it had to be operated somehow from the top.

Sitting undisturbed for more than one hundred years had allowed a layer of dust to accumulate on top. It covered the surface nearly a quarter of an inch thick. Brushing it off with my hands removed most of it, except for a stubborn remnant of grime. I looked around for something else to brush with and finally used my gloves, which worked better than I expected.

I began to realize as I rubbed it that the dull metal plate directly on top was engraved. In its badly tarnished brass surface, I was eventually able to read what it said — the words were not entirely surprising.

With angels' wings, provision sown.

I COULDN'T HELP SMILING as I looked at the confirmation that this was the place the clues had all ultimately pointed to.

I settled back for a break, peeling off my dusty gloves and laying them aside. The exertion from all that scrubbing had tired me out, and I was suddenly aware of my thirst. My watch confirmed that it was past noon. I decided to take a seat on the floor and see what kind of lunch Uncle Jim had packed in the backpack.

I was rewarded with a jug of water and a chicken sandwich on homemade bread. He had even thrown in a bag of home-baked cookies. The delicious meal hit the spot.

Fully satisfied, I climbed to my feet again to see about unlocking that mysterious chest. With the top cleaned off, I began to see something I hadn't noticed before. One feature had already been obvious — the engraved brass plaque was mounted on a ridge that ran across the top of the chest from end to end. I hadn't noticed that the ridge itself had a strangely familiar shape to it. As I considered it, the realization finally dawned on me — I knew where I'd seen that exact shape before. It was the same as the molding on the windowsill at the church.

Looking at the ridge more carefully, I noticed what appeared, at first, to be scratches along the ridge a short distance from the center. I poured some of the water from my jug onto one of them and carefully washed it until the pattern in the metal became clear — it was an angel's wing.

With growing enthusiasm, I quickly washed the opposite side and confirmed that another wing was also carved there. The clues were obvious! I smiled as I looked at both wings and reread the engraving on the brass plaque. Placing a hand on each wing, I pressed down as hard as I could. The clicking sound gave me a thrill as the brass plate between them sprung open, revealing a shallow compartment underneath.

The brass plate was hinged, opening upward like a door. Beneath it, I was surprised to find not one keyhole but two. Yet as surprising as that was, I was thrilled because, from the look of them, I had both keys with me!

The first keyhole was X-shaped, exactly matching the four opposing bits on the key from the windowsill. The second keyhole was two inches across and shaped like a giant asterisk of twisting branches with openings for nubs in precise positions, matching the one for the secret door.

I eagerly retrieved the new key from my pocket and the secret door's key from the backpack. As expected, both of them fit the chest perfectly. At first, my attempts to turn them only showed how tight the gears had become. Eventually, the window key began to turn, ending with the satisfying click of several tumblers sliding into position. As I'd suspected, the larger door key would need to do most of the work. Using it as a crank, I began retracting the claw-like clamps until they disappeared inside the thick lid.

As soon as the crank stopped, the lid sprung loose and opened an inch or two on one side. I was able to easily lift it open the rest of the way, thanks to a sophisticated system of pulleys and counterweights that rendered the massive lid practically weightless.

I WASN'T sure what I expected to find inside the huge chest. Maybe I had visions of gleaming pirates' treasure. Instead, the outer chest contained a smaller metal box inside it. That one was about two feet long and a foot wide, with handles on each end. Although smaller, it was not light; I decided to open it in place.

Thankfully, that was not difficult. It opened lengthwise, with no lock of its own. As I lifted its lid, the first thing I saw was a small stack of envelopes sitting in a metal tray that covered the top of the box, hiding whatever lay beneath. I lifted the first envelope and saw that it had been addressed to me; it was in Amos' handwriting. Opening it, I pulled out a letter and carefully unfolded it.

Dear Jimmy,

If you're reading this, you've opened the chest. Congratulations.

The provisions stored here have been scraped together over a good portion of my lifetime. I'll admit I had some help in acquiring them; my good friend Oliver Jennings provided the investment guidance that proved most beneficial.

I have desired to provide something more than words to assist you in the challenge with which God has entrusted you. Here enclosed you'll find several certificates of ownership for company shares that Oliver has assured me are likely to be of some value to you in the future. In addition to those several pieces of paper, I have deposited what I could in the way of real gold and silver.

I trust that you will honorably and prayerfully put it to use for God's glory and purposes.

Godspeed, dear friend.

In His eternal love,

Amos

My hands were shaking as I opened the other envelopes, finding stock certificates:

- Ten shares of General Electric,
- Twenty-five shares of Coca Cola,

- Two thousand shares of Standard Oil of New Jersey.

Lifting the metal tray, my heart skipped as I looked down at sleeves of gold and silver coins standing on end and filling the box's entire length and width. Opening the top of one of the wrappers, I pulled out a single coin. It was a 1910 Ten Dollar Gold Indian Head — there were five stacks of them. Each unopened sleeve said it contained 100 coins. Each was wrapped in its original paper sleeve, in uncirculated condition.

When I had taken an inventory of the well-organized coins, I found that the box contained:

- Five stacks of Ten Dollar Gold Indian Head coins,
- Fifty stacks of One Dollar 'D' Indian Head Gold Eagle coins, and
- One hundred stacks of Silver Half-Dollars.

I carefully withdrew three coins, one of each type, and put them in my pocket. Hopefully, Uncle Jim would know how to tell what they were worth.

I carefully placed the three envelopes of stock certificates in the backpack and replaced the tray, closing the metal box. Finally, I closed the lid on the outer chest and locked it tight.

———————

My MIND WAS RACING through a million thoughts about what to do. *Could you even spend one of those coins anymore?* As soon as that thought crossed my mind, another rushed in… *it's worth a lot more than the face value! But how does someone exchange something like that — especially so many of them? What about the stock? How does that work?*

While wrestling with all these distracting thoughts, I somehow managed to collect the keys, slide the backpack onto my shoulders, douse the lanterns and make my way down to the bicycle while barely realizing that I'd done it. By the time I finished peddling to the other staircase, I'd made up my mind that I would give Mr. O'Malley a call. He would know what to do.

STILL DISTRACTED as I reached the root cellar, I pressed the lever to open the secret door and blew out the lantern in the same motion. At that point, while standing in pitch darkness, it occurred to me that I probably should have switched on a light first.

A SPLIT SECOND LATER, another flash erupted in the darkness.

THE NEXT THING I KNOW, I am standing with Chozeq in the Cabinet Room at the White House. Sixteen cabinet officials are seated around the large oval table. Golden nameplates in front of each member identify their cabinet positions. I'm surprised to see how young some of them appear to be, especially the Welfare and Internal Revenue secretaries who barely look old enough to be out of college. Athaliah is seated to the president's right, behind a nameplate entitled 'Unity Enforcement Agency.' She is speaking in flowery words that do nothing to mask the venom in her voice.

"It is time to strengthen our emergency measures; the country is in crisis! As the Secretary of Unity, I must urge the strongest possible action to quell public unrest."

The Homeland Security Director leaned forward in his seat. "We are taking the strongest measures possible to reign in the violent protests. One hundred percent of our National Guard Reserves have been mobilized."

"I'm not talking about protests!" Athaliah snapped indignantly. "With all that the country is suffering, it is understandable that those who are underprivileged and oppressed will make their voices heard. I'm talking about the unrestrained religious zealots who continue to undermine the public's confidence in our government institutions. They are the ones dividing this country."

"What would you propose we do this time?" Jarvis Gordon, the Attorney General, asked with visible annoyance. "We can't just arrest everyone who gives a Sunday sermon!"

Athaliah glared at him with a look that could curdle milk. The AG tugged on his shirt collar to relieve the heat building up under his necktie.

"That's enough!" Devlon broke in. He leaned back in his seat and calmly looked at Athaliah. "What do you propose?"

"In light of these dire conditions, we must suspend certain Constitutional protections for the greater good. In particular, the First through Fifth Amendments."

"You're talking about suspending the Bill of Rights!" the AG exclaimed in shocked disbelief.

Devlon's eyes scanned the room, measuring the reactions of each cabinet officer before speaking. His gaze settled on his Chief of Staff. "Obadiah. You've been around this town longer than anyone else here. What do you make of the Secretary's proposal?"

Obadiah cleared his throat nervously as a sudden bead of sweat appeared on his forehead. He glanced at Athaliah; she seemed tensed like a cat poised to pounce.

"Well... it is certainly within your powers as president to declare a state of emergency."

Obadiah measured his words carefully as he continued. "As a former Senator myself, I would, of course, take into account the likely reaction of the Congress to any such measure. Perhaps, it would be ill-advised to enact something that could be construed as treasonous or otherwise difficult to justify. The Congress retains the power to impeach, after all."

Devlon leaned back and stroked his chin as he considered Obadiah's answer. "I see..." he said thoughtfully. "Perhaps he makes a good point," he says to Athaliah. Her eyes narrow into angry-looking fissures.

Devlon turns toward his Attorney General. "Jarvis, what has your department come up with to get around the Supreme Court's ruling?"

"First of all, there needs to be sufficient cause for these arrests — a law has to have been broken. It can take time to build a case that will hold up in court."

Devlon ponders the answer for a moment then turns back to Athaliah. "Propose a few laws... some innocuous regulations that they are sure to violate. We'll slip them into upcoming budget measures."

"Something like, 'dispensing counsel without a license,'" Vice President Strident suggested. "Or 'Lifestyle discrimination,'" the Welfare secretary added. Others began offering more ideas as the meeting suddenly became more collegial, albeit darker.

Obadiah remained silent as he did his best to hide his appalled reaction.

THE ECHO of their spirited exchange was still ringing in my ears as the scene around me suddenly changed again, leaving me standing in the root cellar's pitch darkness.

⌘

9

SHOCKED

"How in blazes is that possible?"
~ Jim Van Clief

U ncle Jim was seated at the kitchen table as I lifted the hatch from the root cellar and climbed up. He had been waiting there for me since he arrived home.

He didn't speak right away, waiting to see if I'd discovered what I was searching for. Perhaps he mistook the distracted concern in my face for disappointment. However, the concern I was feeling had nothing to do with Amos' treasure.

"From the look o' you, I'd say the search ain't gone so well," he guessed as I closed the hatchway door and turned toward him.

I looked up, momentarily confused, as I shook off the memory of Devlon's Cabinet meeting.

"Oh... n-no, it went great, actually. I found it. I found what Amos left there — the provisions."

I retrieved Amos' letter from my backpack and offered it to him, letting him read it. He handed it back to me after reading — there was an uncertain expression on his face.

"What is it he left ya'? Looks as though it's caused ya' some worry."

"Oh — no, I'm not worried about that. I guess I'm just a little tired, is all. The provisions are pretty incredible, actually. To be honest, I don't even know what they're worth."

I remembered the coins in my pocket and placed them on the table. "I found these... there are hundreds more of them; they all look brand new like that."

His eyebrows lifted in surprise as he studied the coins. "Well, I'll be... hundreds o' these, ya say?"

"Do you know how we can see what they're worth?" I asked hopefully.

"Well, sure," he said, finally placing the coins back on the table. "A friend o' mine has a coin shop over-town. I used t' collect 'em myself before I sold-off my collection. I never had any as good as these here, though. They look t' be uncirculated... mint condition."

He pointed toward the counter beside the cupboard. "Fetch me the phone an' my address book." I handed him his cordless house phone and the little black address book beside it. He quickly looked up a number and put the phone on speaker as he dialed it.

Someone answered on the first ring... *"Gladwell Stamp & Coin."*

"Joe, it's Jim Van Clief here."

"Mr. Van Clief, it's been a while. Good to hear from you — what can I do for you?"

"Hoping ya' might answer a question 'bout a few coins, t' see what they're worth."

"Well, sure. I'll have to look at them to be sure, but I could give a ballpark. What kind are they?"

"This first one is a Ten Dollar Gold Indian Head, 1910. Mint condition.

"Mint, you say?"

Uncle Jim looked at me for assurance. I nodded my head in confirmation... "They're still in their wrappers," I whispered.

"Still in the sleeve," he confirmed into the phone.

We heard Joe whistle in reaction. *"Book value on a mint coin like that is a thousand dollars. If you had an unopened sleeve from the mint, then a collector might bid double the book value for it."*

I could feel the blood leaving my face. Uncle Jim saw my reaction and quietly asked: "How many are there?"

"Five sleeves," I said, hardly believing the value I was calculating in my head. That was five hundred coins.

"What about an Indian Head Gold Eagle Dollar? It's also 1910, mint."

"Are you kidding me?" Joe answered in an amazed voice. "What'd you do, find an old bank vault in a time capsule? Here's the thing... FDR took all the gold out of circulation during the Second World War and melted it down. It was illegal even to own them. That's why those coins are so rare."

"It's got a letter 'D' beside the year. What's this one worth?" Uncle Jim asked.

"Oh my gosh, I can't believe it! That's another thousand easy."

My elbow slipped off the table, and I nearly bumped my chin. Amos' box has fifty sleeves of those! That was over five million dollars worth.

If Uncle Jim had known how many there were, he might have been as choked up as I was. He motioned for me to stay calm and picked up the last coin, describing it.

"There's one more I need yer help with... It's a 1910 silver half-dollar, looks like a Liberty Head."

"I suppose you're gonna tell me that's uncirculated too."

Uncle Jim saw me nod yes. "Yup," he answered aloud.

"Those were called Barber half dollars, named after Charles Barber who designed them. If it's mint, it could be worth seven hundred."

I was holding my head at this point. I didn't even want to mention that there were 100 sleeves of those — 10,000 coins!

"If you're interested in selling, bring 'em in. I'd love to have a look at them."

"Much obliged, Joe. I'll check first to be sure you're there when I bring 'em down."

· · ·

HE HUNG up the phone and looked at my white face with a confused expression. I spun around the paper I'd been scratching my notes on — pointing to where I'd circled the total value of what was in the chest... $12,500,000.

He picked the paper up and checked the numbers, whistling as he slid his hand over the top of his head in disbelief.

After doing our best to take in what we'd just learned, I remembered the stock certificates. I laid them on the table.

"THESE WERE THERE TOO.... I don't think they're worth as much as the coins, but we should probably check. I thought maybe Mr. O' could help us figure it out."

Uncle Jim thought about that idea for a second. "I suppose he'd understand since he already knows about Amos' Journal. But ya might need ta' tell him 'bout the secret passage," he cautioned.

I thought it over for a second... "I think we should. We can trust him."

He nodded, accepting my decision. I put my cell phone on the table and hit speed dial, switching on the speaker.

"Hi Uncle Ward," I said as he answered. "I need your help with something...."

For the next ten minutes, I did my best to explain the secret passage's discovery and Amos' secret storehouse of provisions. I finally came to the shares of stock and described them to him.

"The first one is for ten shares of Edison General Electric. The date? ...It's April 5th, 1889.

"The next one is for twenty-five shares of Coca-Cola, purchased on September 5th, 1919.

"The last one looks bigger. It's for two thousand shares of Standard Oil of New Jersey. The date was August 15, 1901."

"Alright, Jim, I'll research these to see what they're worth today. Keep them in a safe place; I think they could be worth a great deal."

I was surprised by his comment. In case he was right, Uncle Jim offered to put the certificates in his old safe. He led the way down the stairs to the house cellar, where the old cast iron safe lay tucked away, and placed the envelopes inside.

THURSDAY MORNING...

UNCLE JIM WAS SERVING Thursday morning breakfast: pancakes and crispy bacon. Anna arrived right on time to join us for our Thursday tradition.

"How are things at the sub shop?" I asked Anna as she took a seat at the table.

"Your Uncle had to raise prices, it's getting harder and harder to find supplies, and they're way more expensive. The number of customers has thinned out too, especially with the tent meetings being stopped for winter."

I silently wondered whether helping out Uncle Mike would be a legitimate way to use some of Amos' provisions. Uncle Jim seemed to read my thoughts as he interjected:

"I reckon there's gonna be lots worse troubles up ahead if this drought don't let up."

After breakfast, we ran through the morning chores, and Anna spent time with Elroy and Rosie. She had quit calling them 'Little' Elroy and Rosie a while ago — by now, they were actually pretty huge.

When eleven o'clock rolled around, Anna excused herself to leave for work. "Have to get ready for the lunch crowd," she said. It brought to mind all the times I'd said the same thing to other people. I missed those times.

"Wish I could go to work with you," I said honestly. She just wrapped her arms around my neck and smiled.

"Me too," she teased, then sealed it with a goodbye kiss that elevated my blood pressure three or four points.

IT WAS JUST before noon when Mr. O' called. I placed my phone on the table and answered.

"Hi, Uncle Ward. I have you on speaker… it's just me and Uncle Jim."

"I tracked down those stock shares," he began, getting right down to business. *"You probably should be sitting down for this."*

Uncle Jim and I shared a glance, and I slid into a chair at the kitchen table. "Bad news, eh?" I guessed.

"Not exactly, unless you're referring to the taxes you'll owe," he said mysteriously.

Uncle Jim sat down across from me. "OK, We're sitting," I confirmed.

"I'll start with Edison General Electric. As you probably guessed, the company changed its name in 1919 to 'GE' and founded both RCA and NBC. So, accounting for stock splits and reinvested dividends, your ten shares have grown to more than 612,000 shares. They're currently worth about seven million dollars."

I gulped. "You're kidding… 10 shares did all that?"

"That's right," he confirmed.

"The next one I looked into was Standard Oil of New Jersey. That was the corporate name for Standard Oil, owned by John D. Rockefeller and a few partners. After the company was split up in an antitrust ruling, those shares became Esso, which took its name from the 'S' and 'O' in Standard Oil. Later, Esso became Exxon Mobile. The stock has split several times and has paid a dividend for forty years in a row."

I held my breath and waited for him to tell us what it was worth. He finally got to the bottom line.

"So, after all is said and done, those 2,000 shares have grown into 1.7 million shares, worth about ninety-five million dollars."

"Did you say ninety-five million?"

"You heard right," he said with a chuckle.

I did the math quickly in my head…. "So, just those two alone are worth over one hundred million dollars!"

"That's right. But you haven't heard what's left.

"That stock certificate for 25 shares of Coca-Cola was purchased for $1,000 in the company's initial public stock offering on September 5th, 1919.

After accounting for reinvested dividends and splits, those shares have grown to 6,747,707 shares. At yesterday's closing price, they're worth $372,596,354. They're earning annual dividends of over $11 million per year."

I was utterly speechless. Uncle Jim calmly took off his cap and scratched his head, then narrowed his eyes as he tried to comprehend what Mr. O' was saying.

"How in blazes is that possible?" he questioned.

"Well, mostly because of the dividends," Mr. O' explained. "Since they were never paid out in cash, they converted to additional shares. The stock has split 11 times over the years, and the company has paid a dividend every quarter since 1920. The dividend has increased each year for all these years. Over time as the number of shares kept growing, so did the dividends, which created even more shares."

"What do you think we should do with them?" I asked him.

"I've been giving that a lot of thought," Mr. O' said seriously. "Based on what you read to us from Amos' journal, it looks like the markets are going to crash hard. It could be at any time now. I believe God led you to these now to give you time to redeem them before that happens."

"Redeem… you mean to sell them?" I clarified.

"That's right. Of course, it complicates matters that they think you're a wanted fugitive."

"I *am* a wanted fugitive," I confirmed with a sigh.

"Right. Well, in any event, you're not in a legal position to complete a stock sale, especially one of this size. But I think we can get around it with a private trust. The trust will be held in your name until you are free to access it. In the meantime, you can have the final say over how it is invested and managed."

I looked at Uncle Jim, and he nodded that it made sense to him. I agreed and asked Mr. O' to go ahead and set it up.

"I'll start the paperwork right away. Once it's set up, we can add the stock and then make the sales."

"Thanks, Uncle Ward. While you're at it, please make the first trust investment a charitable contribution… to the legal defense fund."

"That's very generous, Jimmy. Are you sure?"

"Amos may have left it in my name, but it's not my money — none of it is mine. God has plans for it, and right now, it can do the most good defending those who have been called to serve Him. Believe me, they're going to need it soon."

"How much did you want to contribute?"

"ALL OF IT."

⌘

10

PRESSED

"We are hard-pressed on every side, yet not crushed; perplexed, yet not unto despair; pursued, yet not forsaken; smitten down, yet not destroyed."
~ II Corinthians 4:8-9

Athaliah grins with a satisfied smile as she delivers news to her father.

"The new laws slipped through Congress without a hitch." She looks at Devlon admiringly. "How did you know that no one would read what was in those budget bills?"

"It's Congress' best-kept secret," Devlon enlightens. "No one has the time to read a 20,000-page bill. If it's not described in the index, they'll never see it."

"Excellent news," Bahal agrees. "Perhaps now we can deal with those meddlesome believers once and for all. What is the next step?"

"The Attorney General is mobilizing new enforcement efforts as we speak," Devlon explains. "Those pastors and Christian workers who are found to be violating the new laws will be rounded-up."

"It's not enough to just arrest them this time," Athaliah urges. "We have to be sure their church websites are shut down. Their computers must be confiscated and their email accounts seized." She taps a finger against her lips as she thinks... obviously relishing her newfound power. "We must crush them... disgrace their people." An idea fills her mind, revealed by the sinister grin on her face as she ponders it... "Dig up dirt on as many as we can — plant it if we have to. Undermine their people's trust by forcing Pastors to turn over notes from their counseling sessions. We'll make them available as 'public records.'"

Bahal nods approvingly. "A good start. There must be many others who oppose these groups' religious beliefs," he adds, drawing on his long experience in pitting groups against one another. "We may be able to use them to our advantage."

"There are many who oppose them," Devlon readily agrees. "Many see them as intolerant of the new enlightened lifestyles. It would be a simple matter to assist them in filing suits against faith-based schools, businesses, and even families with these accusations. I know many judges who are sympathetic to their progressive causes — with the proper government backing, they would be pleased to terminate those parents' parental rights and place their children in 'appropriate' homes."

THE SCENE ENDED ABRUPTLY. It had awakened me from a sound sleep, and I lay in bed considering it soberly. A glance at the clock revealed that it was almost 5:00 AM, nearly time to be getting up anyway. I made my way to the desk and switched on the lamp, opening my journal to a blank page to record this latest troubling scene.

After writing all that I could recall, I sat rereading the account, trying to remember seeing any clue as to when it takes place. They were in Bahal's office at the Four Seasons Hotel — I recognized his suite. Devlon and Athaliah were dressed in warm clothes, and the sight of their coats lying nearby hinted that it was still winter.

It had only been a few days since I was shown the cabinet meeting where these new laws were cooked-up, but that didn't mean the two events were as close together as that. On a hunch, I quickly checked the news feed on my phone for any mention of budget measures. Sure enough, a bill was being prepared for a vote in the House next week.

It finally occurred to me that there was someone who could tell me for sure. He had been in that cabinet meeting himself.

I TYPED a quick text to Silas...

— Need your help —

UNCLE JIM STOOD at the griddle as I entered the kitchen carrying the morning's milk can. He welcomed me with an approving nod — I was getting pretty good at the barn chores if I did say so myself.

"Lily was feeling a little rambunctious this morning," I informed him as I washed my hands — referring to Lily, the cow.

"She gets restless from bein' cooped-up in winter," Uncle Jim observed. "I'll take her out later t' roam a spell. Looks like it's fixin' t'be another sunny day."

His mention of sunshine must have triggered the same thought in his mind as mine... *every day is sunny — it's a drought.* Neither of us mentioned it.

"The French Toast smells terrific," I complemented — hungry for breakfast after already finishing an hour of work.

Just as I was speaking, the front door opened, and Anna let herself in, making her way toward the kitchen. "That smells awesome!" she said, sounding like an echo of what I'd just said.

I met her for a quick good morning kiss as she entered the room, continuing on my way to the cupboard to set the table. She followed me as I grabbed the plates while she gathered silverware, helping arrange the place settings.

"Hi Uncle Jim," she said to Mr. V., adopting my way of addressing him. He smiled back at her, obviously delighted by her company. He would have smiled in the same way no matter what she called him.

We were just sitting down to eat when my phone chimed with a new text message. It was from Silas:

— *call me* —

"WOULD it be alright if I make a quick call?" I asked apologetically. "It's kind of important." They both looked at me with concerned expressions. "It's nothing too serious," I quickly explained, "— nothing to worry about. Please go ahead and start without me while it's hot."

"Suit yerself," Uncle Jim accepted. "Anna and I'll try t' save ya some, but I ain't makin' any promises." He winked at her as he said it, and she agreed.

"That's right... no promises," she repeated with a smile.

I scrunched my eyebrows at them as I slid a few slices onto my plate... just to be on the safe side. That accomplished, I made my way into the living room and dialed Obadiah's number. He picked up on the second ring, obviously waiting for my call.

"What is it, Jim - are you in any danger?"

I was tempted to say, *yes - the entire US government is chasing me*, but decided it wasn't a good time for a joke.

"I'm ok... everything's fine. I just need to ask you about the new laws being voted on next week. The ones hidden in the budget bills."

He was quiet for a moment, and then I heard him sigh. "I suppose I'm not surprised that you know about them," he conceded. "What do you need to know?"

"What's in them? Where are they in the bills, exactly? I know that they're going to become law; we can't stop that; I want to prepare people for what's coming."

He considered my request quietly before answering. "To be honest, I've been in a terrible turmoil over it all week asking God what to do. I believe your call is an answer to prayer. You just need to be sure not to share these details with anyone, not anyone at all. If it gets out, then folks here will know it was me who told you."

"You have my word," I promised.

"The bills are posted on the House Finance Committee website; they're required to be public record. Look for the markup copy of bill HR 665-1. Search for the reference: 19629. That's a reference number for the acronym 'SFBI' — that's what they're calling it, the SFBI Act. It stands for 'Stop Faith-Based Indoctrination.' All the relevant sections will be tagged with that reference number, but you won't find any mention of them in the index or main synopsis."

"Thanks," I said, scribbling *sfbi* and 19629 on the nearest piece of paper. "Don't worry, no one will know." After the call ended, I stared at the scribbled note, considering what needed to be done. I'd have to search the Bill alone, collect all the related sections, and then ask for help from Anna and the others.

"This bacon sure is delicious...." Anna's voice echoed from the kitchen with an exaggerated hint for me to return to breakfast. I folded the note and shoved it into my pocket, rejoining the others.

THE FOLLOWING DAY...

AFTER COPYING all of the sections related to SFBI into one file, I shared it with Anna and Josh, who posted it on our site. We planned a special podcast for later that evening to get the word out.

"Uncle Ward, we're going to need the Defense Fund's help," I said anxiously as he answered my call. "The new budget Bill contains laws targeting believers. A copy is posted on our site."

He logged in and scanned the new measures as we talked.

"These are incredibly broad and deceptively worded," he commented in amazement as he read them. "The Devil himself could have written them."

"That's not far from the truth," I accepted.

"Do you think these will really pass?" he asked in a worried voice.

"I know they will," I said sadly. He didn't question my remark, quickly deciding on a course of action instead.

"I'll gather a legal team to begin preparing challenges," he said reassuringly. "Another prayer vigil wouldn't be a bad idea either."

SURE ENOUGH, despite our efforts to sound the alarm about the hidden measures, the budget bill passed quickly. The Administration did a masterful job of orchestrating a crisis that threatened to shut down the government unless it was enacted immediately. Nothing seems to motivate politicians as effectively as the threat of a government shutdown.

BY EARLY MARCH...

DOZENS OF PASTORS and Rabbis had been charged with violations of the new laws, and lawsuits had begun to emerge from scores of activist groups against any businesses or schools that honored traditional values.

This rising tide of oppression emboldened other radical groups. With behind-the-scenes encouragement from the Administration, they organized mass protests in which violent mobs burned churches and terrorized communities. After weeks of such attacks, not a single arrest had been made. The protests were hailed as freedom rallies whose participants were heroically fighting against outdated prejudices and intolerance.

For Devlon's administration, all of this mayhem served as a convenient distraction from the widespread suffering caused by the worsening drought. It helped to have new villains to blame for the country's unrest. Especially since the government's inept drought response now amounted to little more than food rationing and troops in the streets.

To ratchet-up tensions even further, Social Service bureaucrats and activist judges were empowered to challenge parents' rights to teach traditional values in their homes. With Athaliah's encouragement, they removed children and placed them in more 'compliant' foster homes.

The Legal Defense Fund was inundated with pleas for help and made the difficult decision to shift focus to help a growing number of those families as its first priority.

On the nightly news, the scenes of chaos were sobering.

"A dozen more churches were burned today in cities across the country," the anchor reported on TV as Uncle Jim and I sat together to watch. The scenes showed angry mobs setting fire to churches and smashing the offices of small businesses as riot police stood passively looking on.

The newscast went on to report new government statistics on the state of the economy.

"The government reported today that employment tax revenues have hit a new low this week as employment figures reached the lowest level in recorded history. To fill the growing budget gap, Congress announced 'The Fairness Act,' an emergency measure authorizing the IRS to seize private assets from large corporations and high-net-worth individuals. President Sheen has been pushing for the measure."

MARKET CRASH...

MR. O'MALLEY HAD BEEN RIGHT about the impending market crash. Congress followed through on its Fairness Act within weeks of its announcement, and President Sheen signed it into law immediately. Once empowered, the IRS wasted no time seizing more than a trillion dollars in private assets.

As those invested assets were liquidated, the stock markets were thrown into a free-fall, triggering the largest global financial crash in history. Millions of people's savings and retirement accounts were wiped out. Thanks to Mr. O's foresight, Amos' stock shares had already been sold weeks earlier.

BY EARLY JUNE, the conditions in many cities had triggered a mass exodus. Everyone with the ability to leave them fled. Those left behind faced rampant crime, violence, and gang rule in neighborhoods that had become war zones.

Despite all of that suffering, the Administration ignored the growing crisis, focusing all of its energy on its anti-faith campaign.

⌘

11

DAILY BREAD

"Give us for today...."
~ Jesus, Matthew 6:11

While Center Springs was spared the worst of the violence sweeping the country, it was not exempt from food shortages and business closures. Many of the families we knew were struggling to meet basic needs.

"THE CAVERN SPRINGS are still flowing; they've just slowed a little," I reported to Uncle Jim as I returned from my latest visit to the underground room. I placed the ten Gold Indian Head coins I'd just retrieved on the table.

"It's God's providence; there's no doubtin' it," he said gratefully. He sat down and stared across the room at nothing in particular, drawing a hand to his chin deep in thought. "I ran into Grace O'Brian when I was Overtown today. She says there are a heap o' families hurtin' bad.

Lots of em don't know where their next meal's gonna come from. Sure wish there was enough here at the farm t' feed em all."

I sat next to him, thinking about it for a moment, then a thought hit me. "There is," I said, lifting one of the coins. "We have plenty of water to share... and we can buy the food we need. I'm sure Amos would agree... I mean, I'm sure he would *have* agreed," I quickly corrected myself.

Uncle Jim gave it a moment of thought and looked at me. "I reckon you're right about that," he agreed. "The supermarket ain't gonna be much help though; it's near as empty as one o' my dusty fields. But I know where we can get us some more dairy cows and chickens. We'll be needin' some help t' care for em all."

"I'll call Anna and Pete. I'll bet we can get some of the FCS kids to help too," I offered.

WITH THAT HELP and volunteers from the churches in town, we soon arranged a food and water delivery service for families who needed help. The Pastors' families were on the list, as well as Anna and her mom, who had now both lost their jobs to the drought. Anna and Lena volunteered to help on the farm — they welcomed it, both being farm kids themselves. Uncle Mike was soon helping too, having been forced to close the sub shop.

Never to be underestimated, Anna tracked down a group of suppliers where we could still get canned goods, rice, and other essentials. Most of the suppliers were in Canada. Pete's dad organized a group of his fellow longshoremen to make weekly supply runs for us.

Meanwhile, Uncle Mike turned the main barn into an efficiently organized warehouse that would have made a major distributor envious. The dairy barn and chicken coops were soon filled with noisy livestock. Uncle Jim was in his glory. He hadn't seen the farm this busy in decades.

"Good morning Jimmy," Anna's mom said with a smile as she climbed from her car. I stood in the barnyard with a milk can in each hand, just coming from morning chores. Anna climbed from the passenger side and smiled at my immobilized arms holding the heavy cans. Then she surprised me with a hug around my neck, planting a soul-stirring kiss on me. Her mom laughed at the surprise in my eyes as I stood defenseless against the bold attack.

"Just making sure you know I'm here..." Anna said playfully as she backed away. She messed up my hair and then ran off to check on Elroy and Rosie.

Her mother shook her head — partly in amusement, not wholly approving of her daughter's actions. "You'd better get those inside and stay out of sight," she suggested, glancing at her watch. "The other volunteers will be getting here soon."

She was right. I had to keep a low profile when the volunteers were around, limiting my outdoor work mainly to the early morning barn duty. Despite the early hour, it felt good to be occupied with something else besides terrible news reports.

Uncle Mike pulled in close behind them. He greeted Lena warmly and then took one of the large milk cans from my hand, holding the porch door for me to enter.

I lifted the heavy cans into the refrigerator in Uncle Jim's kitchen. As refrigerators go, his was pretty huge — it was built into the wall, really more of a refrigerated closet. But it was already filled with a half-dozen cans of fresh milk and several shelves of eggs.

"We're gonna need more space," I noted.

Uncle Mike agreed with me. "I know a guy," he said as he handed me the can he was carrying. "It's Joey's restaurant... he's bein' evicted. I bet he'd sell us his old walk-in in a heartbeat. If it's awright with Mr. Van Clief, we could set it up in th' barn."

"...Th' name's Jim," Uncle Jim reminded him in a friendly prod as he entered the kitchen behind us. "Sounds t' be a good idea."

"What's our distribution list lookin' like?" Uncle Jim asked Lena as she followed him in.

She checked the clipboard in her hand, flipping a few pages.

"About fifty deliveries for today. Looks like we're up to just over three hundred families altogether."

Uncle Jim turned back to Mike; "I reckon we oughta pick it up today if we can."

"I'll give Joey a call," Uncle Mike agreed as he pulled out his phone.

———————

TWO DAYS LATER — *mid-June...*

PETE WAS HELPING with the finishing touches on the walk-in refrigerator assembly when a text message drew his attention.

— talk? —
...Radison

Pete stopped what he was doing in surprise. Lately, his calls and texts to Radison had gone unanswered; it had been almost two months since they last spoke.

"Hey guys, I need to make a call..." he said to Nyle and Uncle Mike.

"No sweat, we got this," Mike nodded. He was busy holding a ladder for Nyle, who was wiring the lights.

Pete stepped outside the barn and dialed Radison's number. "Hey! What's up?" he said when it was answered.

"Shirley don't want me here no more," Radison blurted as if he was reporting a crime.

"Shirley..." Pete repeated, piecing it together quickly in his mind. "Shirley Oram — your foster mom?"

"Yeah. She don't want me."

"What happened?" Pete could hear the emotion in Radison's voice. He couldn't tell if the boy was angry or crying — maybe both.

"She don't like my friends." Radison cursed a streak of obscenities that Pete couldn't believe, giving the clearest clue yet about what was going on. "Jay-Jay, Juice an' Scamp, they're like my bloods! They're my family! They're all th' family I got!"

"You've got your dad too," Pete reminded him. There was silence on the line for a moment, and Pete heard a sniffle. Radison's reply was cynical.

"What's he gonna do - set me up a bunk in his prison cell?"

Pete could tell the toughness was an act — underneath, he could sense the boy's hurting. He remembered his grandmother's pastor, Pastor Jerome.

"What about Pastor Jerome? Maybe he can help you find a place to stay until you get a new foster family."

"That dude's in jail too. The Feds arrested 'im with all the other preachers."

Pete sighed. "How about the counselors at school?"

"School's out. Besides, I wasn't goin' much anyway."

Pete held his head as he listened, feeling more concerned and powerless by the minute. The line was silent for a moment while he gathered his thoughts.

"Where are you staying?" Pete asked.

"I don't know... I guess I'll find someplace."

"Look," Pete said seriously, "she can't just throw you out with no place to go. She'll take you back until a new family is found; she has to. Just go back and apologize. Stay there until this blows over.

"In the meantime, I think you need to visit your dad again. I'll talk to PJ about that."

Radison seemed calmer. The reality of having nowhere to go had begun to sink in.

"OK," he answered, sounding more like an eleven-year-old boy again.

"Call me later and let me know what's going on," Pete insisted. Radison promised to give text updates.

As soon as they hung up, Pete dialed PJ and shared what had happened.

"I'll call the Warden and set up a visit," PJ promised. "Chase will be happy to see him again; he talks about it every time we meet."

While they were on the phone, the two of them prayed together for Radison, then Pete found me in the root cellar, and we prayed for him too.

NEWS OF PASTOR JEROME'S arrest hit me pretty hard — especially the way Radison said he was arrested "with all the other preachers." I thought I was in touch with everything that was happening but quickly realized that there was a tremendous amount I didn't know about.

The city had joined forces with the Administration in its anti-faith campaign. It stood to reason that cities all over the country were doing the same thing. It gave me a new appreciation for all the efforts that Sheriff Flanagan must be expending to protect Center Springs from their demands.

I immediately contacted Uncle Ward, who promised to send them help.

SHIRLEY ORAM, Radison's foster mom, agreed to let him stay until Social Services found him another foster home. Pete and PJ left early the following day to pick him up for a visit to Stockslock.

When they pulled up to her address this time, there were no smells of fresh-baked bread or cakes. The bakery downstairs was closed and dark. Every store in the endless row of small storefront shops along Steinway Street was closed and gated. The neighborhood seemed eerily vacant. The two of them climbed the staircase to the narrow upstairs landing and knocked.

Radison answered the door anxiously while PJ was still knocking. He had been impatiently waiting there for some time.

His foster mom yelled from the other room as he prepared to leave: "You be sure and get back home before dark, ya hear?"

PJ answered on Radison's behalf, "We'll be sure and bring him home before dark, Mrs. Oram. Thank you for allowing him to come with us."

"Makes no difference t' me," she replied dismissively. "I just don't mean t' go searching the neighborhood for him after dark. The streets here are dangerous enough even when we're locked inside."

"Yes, ma'am," PJ added as he said goodbye and closed the door. They heard the door's latches locking behind them as they started down the stairs. Radison had already run ahead and was waiting outside next to the car.

The trip to Stockslock took nearly two hours, leaving an hour for them to have lunch before the start of visiting hours at 2:00. Pete pulled out the packed lunch that Mr. V. had prepared for them — chicken salad on homemade bread and fresh-baked cookies. Radison gulped down his sandwich as though it was the first meal he'd seen all day. After watching him eat it, PJ offered him half of his own sandwich, which Radison swallowed just as hungrily. They let him have all the cookies.

As a surprise, PJ had arranged for them to meet in person in the Chapel. Chase had a broad smile on his face as he greeted his son. Radison nervously held out a hand to shake, and Chase used it to pull him closer, wrapping him in a tender embrace. There was a tear in Chase's eye as he finished and stepped back.

"It's good to see you, son," Chase said, looking Radison in the eye closely. Radison looked away, still unsure what to think of the father he was meeting for only the second time in his life.

"They told me about the trouble with your foster mom," Chase said sympathetically. "I'm really sorry— I'm sorry about everything."

Radison didn't answer. He shoved his hands into his pockets and stared at the floor.

PJ nudged Pete as he spoke up; "We'll wait in the back. You guys can talk."

Chase invited Radison to sit down on the front pew, then took a seat beside him. It took time, but Radison eventually began to open up and was soon regaling his father with stories of his best skateboard moves, friends, and personal triumphs. They talked for an hour.

. . .

RADISON WOULDN'T ADMIT IT — maybe he didn't fully appreciate it at the time, but that hour had formed one of the best memories of his life. It fed a part of him that he never knew existed before that moment, a part of him that had been starving.

⌘

DELIVERED

"but deliver us from the evil one...."
~ Jesus, Matthew 6:13

A few days later...
Pastor Jerome was shocked when lawyers from the Legal Defense Fund showed up to pay his bail. When the clerk returned his meager belongings, he powered up his phone to find a message waiting from PJ.

> *If you're hearing this, you've been released; congratulations. Call me when you're able. Radison needs a new foster home — he may need a place to stay in the interim.*

Jerome quickly dialed PJ's number.

"WHAT A SURPRISE... I don't know how to thank you! Somehow I'll pay you back for the bail money."

"It wasn't me," PJ clarified. "We have a mutual friend... Jimmy Moretti."

"The boy who's on all the news reports? H-how...?"

"He's the one who helped us find Radison. He led us to you too."

"Well, praise the Dear Lord! How he ever found me is a true miracle."

"Miracles are pretty common around Jimmy, as you've probably noticed," PJ joked.

"Well, I'll surely do all I can for young Radison. Is he still there on Steinway Street?"

"For the time being, yes. Mrs. Orem has asked him to leave."

"So many good families have left the city... they'll likely have a hard time finding another decent foster home," Jerome worried. "Do you still have Bea's number at Social Services — the woman who helped us last time?"

"Bea Goodall? I still have her number but haven't spoken to her since then. That's a good idea; I'll give her a call."

LATER THAT AFTERNOON...

"BEA SAID the same thing you did," PJ shared as Jerome answered his call. "Many of their foster families have moved away from the city. She's inundated with requests for foster homes."

"That's not all," Jerome answered, sounding stressed. "When I returned to the church, I found it full of families who've lost their homes. The riots here have burned down half their neighborhood."

"Tell us what you need," PJ vowed.

"The church has set up sleeping quarters in the Sunday School rooms, but we're in desperate need of everything — bedding, blankets, clothing, and food. Some have barely eaten in days."

PJ's MESSAGE blast to the churches in Center Springs received an immediate response. It was picked up and forwarded in a widening cascade to friends in the thousands. By that evening, donations of blankets, clothing, and other essentials began to pour in, collecting in large piles on the tent's platform. Uncle Jim and the team added a donation of food — enough for at least a week.

"How will we get all this up there to the city?" Anna's mom asked. The group debated forming a caravan of cars when Pete's dad pulled up in a tractor-trailer carrying an empty forty-foot shipping container.

"Fill 'er up!" he shouted as everyone applauded.

IT WAS early morning when the truck pulled up to Calvary Hill Church — the sun was just peeking over the horizon. Pastor Jerome held his head with both hands in astonishment as he saw the truck's size full of relief supplies. He met the truck in the street.

"I'm Jay," Pete's dad introduced himself from the truck's driver's seat. "This here is my son Pete. Where should I pull in?"

"God bless you! God bless you! I can't believe it!" Pastor Jerome stared at the huge shipping container in disbelief. "How much of that is full?"

"All of it," Jay assured him.

Jerome was dumbfounded. "I-I don't know if we have room inside to put it all," he said awkwardly.

"Not a problem. We'll leave the container; you can use it as storage as long as you need it. Before I drop it, though, there are a bunch of eggs and milk we'd better unload first."

Pastor Jerome just kept shaking his head in disbelief as he watched Pete and a group from the church unload enough food to feed the church full of families for a week. Once the food was safely unloaded, they agreed on a place at the rear of the church parking lot, and Jay expertly dropped the container into position.

The church's front lawn was filled with grateful waving families as they finally drove away.

Word quickly spread throughout the neighborhood that the church had become a refuge for displaced families. By the time the next delivery arrived a week later, the number of refugees had grown. Next door, the parsonage welcomed the women and girls while Pastor Jerome stayed with all the men and boys.

PROTESTERS ATTACK...

WORD of the makeshift refuge soon reached the local news networks, who sent camera crews to herald the Church's efforts. Not everyone was in favor of those efforts, however. It didn't take long for the same opposition groups responsible for the riots that burned the neighborhood's homes to show up, protesting that it was a church being used. They surrounded the church grounds, threatening anyone who tried to enter or leave. After several days of their protests, the news media moved on, turning their short attention span to the next popular focus. The protests didn't fade away, however. It soon became clear that the groups were being directed from elsewhere. Not only that, the more that the news coverage faded, the more violent the protesters became.

PASTOR JEROME SOUNDED TERRIFIED when PJ answered his call two days later. "I'm afraid they're going to break the doors down or set the building on fire!" he worried. "We've called the police repeatedly, but they don't seem able to help."

PJ kept him on the line as he called my phone and conferenced me in. Hearing what was happening, I took a chance and sent a text to Silas. He agreed to quietly join the conferenced call and listened as Pastor Jerome described the increasingly dire conditions.

"We're running low on food and water — the supply trucks haven't been able to get through. The people here are in fear for their lives!"

Obadiah encouraged me via text to keep them on the line as he urgently worked behind the scenes. Within the hour, we heard a sudden wild commotion coming from outside the church.

"SOMETHING'S HAPPENING!" Jerome exclaimed. "It-it's the army... National Guard — they're driving the protesters back!"

He described the scene outside in stunned disbelief as the troops pushed the protesters further and further away until they had cordoned off the entire block. A water tanker truck arrived in the church parking lot as the violent groups were cleared away. The church property had become a guarded water supply checkpoint!

Obadiah assured me that the troops would remain for as long as needed. I thanked him, deeply grateful for his help while never revealing it to the others. His involvement had to remain a secret.

When we finally said goodbye to Pastor Jerome, what had previously been the sounds of terrified prayers in the background had turned to joyous shouts of praise.

———

LATER THAT EVENING, I sat on the front porch admiring the peaceful night as the distant sound of worship at the tent carried over the summer breeze. The farm had fallen quiet for the night, and Uncle Jim had gone on to bed. I sat awake for a little longer despite the early morning chores that I knew would wake me before sunrise. The day's events replayed in my mind, and I couldn't help breathing a grateful prayer for the way things turned out.

Amos' voice interrupted the porch's quiet, drawing my attention to where he stood, leaning against a porch rail.

"Today was one of my favorite examples of God's deliverance. A truly fine day."

I welcomed him with a smile. "You never wrote about today in your journal."

"Well, I couldn't give away Obadiah's cover, now could I. There's no tellin' where a journal might wind-up once it's written."

It didn't surprise me that he knew about Obadiah's help.

"I guess you also know that I found your key in the church window frame. Did you know how much those provisions would be worth when you left them?"

"I reckon not. I hope it was enough to cover some of the work you're called to do."

"Yeah, I think it will be. We're using some of it to buy food for families; I figured you'd be ok with that."

"That seems like a fine use for it. You just let the Lord lead you, son. He's the one who put it in your hands. Whatever it is that He asks you to do, you just do it and don't give a second thought to whether I'd approve of it or not." He looked over his shoulder into the night and drew a deep breath. "I reckon I'll be long gone to my rest by this time. I won't be worryin' about those old certificates where I'm aimin' t'be."

I thought about the date on his resting place in the mausoleum but kept it to myself. "You were right about what would happen after the temple dedication. You said that's when all Hell would break loose. It sure has. Did you know that I'd be visible the way I was outside the temple?'

He looked at me for a moment as if replaying a few more extraordinary scenes that I was yet to learn of. "These are days for feats of faith and valiant exploits. Don't worry, that isn't the last of what God's got in store, and it sure-enough isn't the most amazin' of 'em."

I was surprised by his comment. That night's events had seemed pretty extraordinary to me. What could be more extraordinary than materializing out of thin air and decreeing a drought over half the continent?

Amos continued encouragingly. "Just remember what I told you about God glorifying Himself in your weakness. It's in your own weakness that God will show the world His undeniable power. You just keep focused on Him, and He'll work out all the rest when the time comes."

His mention of time brought to mind my travels to the future. I thought again of Chase's execution and Radison's sorry condition. "How much time is left? For the world, I mean."

"Well now, that's a right-honest question," Amos answered thoughtfully. "I, sure enough, haven't been shown the answer to it. You can rest assured that His coming won't be a clock's tick late, and it won't be a tick early either. When the last soul to enter the kingdom has found safe refuge in Christ, that's when time will be up for the church."

He looked over the barnyard in the moonlight and listened approvingly to the sound of a cow or two lowing from the dairy barn, then studied the height of the moon in the night sky. "Speakin' of time, you'd best be gettin' off to bed. Those morning chores come awful early."

I stood up at the porch rail and followed his gaze, nodding in agreement. When I turned to say goodnight, he was already gone.

IN BAHAL'S HOTEL SUITE, Athaliah is pacing the room angrily. "That Legal Defense Fund of theirs is starting to make my blood boil! They've thwarted our efforts at every turn."

Bahal's eyes narrowed. "How are they funding such a large caseload?"

"Most of their attorneys are donating their time," Devlon explains, revealing intelligence gained by his Security Agencies. "Yet, somehow, they have managed to post bail for over a thousand of those arrested. What's more, they are winning a majority of their cases, providing them with returned bail for use on still more cases!"

"Where are the sympathetic judges you spoke so confidently of?" Bahal challenged.

"Their rulings are being overturned on appeal," Athaliah exclaims in disgust.

"Our own appeals are faring no better," Devlon complains. "If we're not careful, they will be back to the Supreme Court in no time. We know too well how that court is likely to rule."

"I see..." Bahal says as he leans back in his chair and presses his fingers together in deep thought. "It seems we must tilt the Court more in our favor."

"How would you propose that we do that?" Devlon questions.

"Leave that to me...." Bahal says with a sinister gleam in his eyes. "Have some more-friendly judges standing by — in case there were to be any unexpected openings."

———

THE FLASH of light in my darkened room left me staring at my bedroom ceiling, pondering what I'd just heard. A plan quickly formed in my mind as I breathed a prayer. It would start with calls to Frank DeMassi and Silas first thing in the morning.

⌘

UPHOLDING JUSTICE(S)

"It seems we must tilt the Court more in our favor."
~ Bahal

T he sun was beginning to rise as I took a break from the milking and removed my gloves, pulling my phone out of my pocket. I hadn't wanted to wake Obadiah and Frank any earlier — their minds needed to be sharp for this.

I TYPED separate text messages to each of them — being sure not to leave a trail that connected them to each other. We'd begun to use 'B3' to identify Bahal, Athaliah, and Devlon (Frank and Silas were really into code names):

— B3 threat to SCOTUS —
— Have to move fast —

They both responded in under a minute.

...Frank
— Go ahead... —

...Silas
— Details... —

I DIALED FRANK'S NUMBER, and he picked up immediately.

"Talk to me..." he answered, already in full mission mode.

"Hang on; I'll conference-in Silas," I answered.

Obadiah picked up just as quickly.

"Yes?" he said carefully.

"I have your friend on the line," I alerted him, using his own way of referring to Frank.

"You're getting good at this kid," Frank commended. His comment was a way of letting Obadiah recognize his voice on the line.

"I'm listening...." Obadiah said, keeping his words to a minimum.

"Bahal is going to target the Supreme Court Justices. Devlon is preparing new nominations that will stack the court in their favor."

Obadiah was taken aback. "Target... do you mean *murder?*"

"He's done it before; remember Governor Taylor's assassination?" I reminded him.

"Well, what proof do we have that he is after the Justices? That's a grave accusation, even for him."

"I can only say that I'm certain of it. I heard them planning it myself."

Obadiah fell silent, no doubt remembering how I'd foreseen other things with remarkable accuracy. Frank was used to hearing me divulge things inexplicably — his silence was because the wheels were turning in his head. He was making a plan.

"I'll arrange a special protection detail — guys I trust," Frank said. "We'll need the Justices to go along with it, but we have to keep it quiet. If the AG finds out, he can pull the plug."

"I'll handle the Justices," Obadiah volunteered. "I agree; we must use the utmost discretion."

"We're on this kid," Frank said reassuringly. "Let us know right away if you get anything else."

AFTER THEY HUNG UP, I put my phone back in my pocket and pulled my gloves back on. There were still another dozen cows to milk.

IT WAS EARLY in the afternoon when Frank called back.

"Your intel was good, as usual, kid. My guys just found a bomb planted in the Chief Justice's car. They're searching all the others. We have agents posted at their homes as well."

"Thanks, that's great news... that they found it, I mean."

"It's thanks to you. No one would have caught it if you hadn't tipped us off. The Justices are pretty outraged — B3 didn't do themselves any favors, that's for sure."

"Do you know how it got there, exactly? Can you catch whoever planted it?"

"It was a professional job, that's for sure. The surveillance cameras at the garage were electronically jammed; whoever did it was in and out in under five minutes. Don't worry, though; my team is all over it. They won't get through us with anything short of a full-scale invasion force."

"Thanks. I'll be praying for you.... All of you."

"Appreciate it, kid. That's the best defense we could ever have."

"WHO WAS THAT?" Anna asked as I hung up the phone. She was just climbing down the ladder to join me in the root cellar.

"Just a friend," I answered, quickly shifting the topic. "How are the food supplies holding up? The deliveries to Calvary Hill church must have taken a bite out of our stocks."

"A bite... clever," she jabbed, making fun of my choice of words.

"Yeah, it has. I had to double our orders with our suppliers, but the good news is that they can give us what we need. Are you sure there's enough money?"

"Yeah, God has us covered," I assured her.

She smiled and came close, offering me a quick hug and kiss. "I just came down to tell you lunch is ready."

"Thanks," I said gratefully, motioning for her to go first. I checked my phone one more time as she turned around, making sure there were no more updates from Frank or Silas.

As it turned out, the day's unusual adventures were just beginning. I placed my hand on the ladder to climb when a flash changed my surroundings once more.

I find myself at the prison. I'm outside... standing in the prison courtyard. Quickly looking around, I recognize a few of the guys I'd met in the prison chapel. They're throwing a ball around and laughing at each other's jokes. Billy and Jack are there with them — clearly changed men from the days when they were called Lobo (the wolf) and Jackal.

A sense of something dark draws my attention. It's coming from an area where a guard is standing a few feet away, off by himself. Most of the other guards are gathered nearer to the guard station on the other side of the courtyard. He seems familiar — I search my memory for where I've seen him before.

He is staring at the inmates — mostly at one or two of them. Following his eyes, it looks like he's watching Jack and Billy. There's a grimace on his face as he watches them; he's obviously not their greatest fan.

While I'm watching, he lifts his phone, answering it. I can hear his conversation clearly.

"Yeah, Mr. E. I got my eye on 'em right now. You wanna watch? No problem."

He carefully turns until the phone at his ear is positioned with its camera facing the two inmates. A second later, shots ring out, and Jack and Billy are both thrown violently to the ground. There is chaos as the other inmates are urgently rushed back inside. Guards run frantically, aiming their weapons through the prison fence toward the perimeter outside where the shots originated. I instinctively run toward Jack and Billy as several guards kneel to check on the fallen men. Other guards in helmets and flak vests scramble outside the prison grounds, aiming their rifles toward the distant woods.

I've just reached the fallen pair as I see Jack rising from the ground. Not Jack's body — it's his soul. He looks down at the scene below, but not with a look of terror or sadness; it's a curious look that is infused with joy. He holds his hands out and stares at them — glowing with light, then notices that he's in the air... floating. I stand and catch his eye, nodding to him as he recognizes me. A huge smile fills his face, and then he looks up, hearing a call that I can't hear. In a streak, he is suddenly gone.

I hear one of the kneeling guards speaking below me and look down.

"This one's gone," he says with his fingers on Jack's neck, seeking a pulse.

The sergeant is checking on Billy: "He's alive, barely. His pulse is weak." He looks up at one of the other guards, "Call in a Medevac! We need a chopper! For god's sake, find that shooter!"

Looking back at the guard on the phone, I see his eyes suddenly grow dark and then flash red as they are transformed into snakes' eyes. He has a satisfied smirk on his face as he watches the scene. It suddenly occurs to me where I've seen him before — he was the guard with Billy on the day he met with Ed Corvo — the day that Corvo shot mom. He was also there with Jack the day that he was delivered from the demon legion. He's Bahal's inside man.

WHILE I STAND FOCUSED on him, another flash transforms my surroundings. I'm in a house. The sun has set, obscuring any view of the outside, but the room is well lit and handsomely appointed, with expensive furnishings and an elaborate entertainment system. Pictures on the wall catch my eye, and I recognize the face of the same man — Bahal's man. Hanging on the wall beside the photographs are a college diploma and a military award; across each of them is boldly printed the name, *Tate Hammer.*

While I'm taking this in, Tate himself enters the room. He's in casual clothes, with an open bottle of beer in one hand and his phone in the other. I watch as he lays the phone on the coffee table and sits down beside it. The phone is on speaker.

"You have proven yourself very useful to me, Mr. Hammer...." I recognize Bahal's voice. "Your marksmen have demonstrated their skills very effectively indeed. They may be of great use to me. In fact, there is another matter in which I can use their assistance."

"I'm sure there is," Tate answers with a smirk. "They don't come cheap."

"Naturally," Bahal answers smoothly. "Such skills are valuable indeed. I'm prepared to offer one million dollars per target."

"A million each, eh? How many targets are there?"

"Nine to choose from. Any five of them will do."

THIS TIME the shift in scene brings me to a cavernous building made of granite and marble. As I get my bearings, I notice golden lettering above a large marble arch that identifies the ornate structure as the Library of Congress. The harsh daylight and long shadows outside hint that it is late in the day. Crowds are milling around everywhere. Looking up from the huge main reading room, I see the building's dome rising high above; its windows are lit with the golden light of an approaching sunset.

From the corner of my eye, I notice a group of workmen in blue coveralls. They seem out of place in the plush surroundings. A closer look reveals an unsurprising detail... the man in the center is Tate Hammer. While I'm watching them, two more workers join the group

— five men in all. The last two are pushing a tool cart that looks to me like the perfect place to conceal a small arsenal.

As they make their way through a set of double doors, I begin to follow, realizing as I do how strange it is that I've never often explored very far in my travels before (except when flying). The door they've gone through has closed by the time I reach it. My first instinct is to grab the door handle, but it passes through my fingers. Taking that as a clue, I decide to push forward and find myself inside the hallway on the opposite side of the door. The group is entering a freight elevator at the far end of the hall — too far away to catch before it closes.

I start toward it anxiously, and the next instant, I'm suddenly standing inside the elevator with them, having moved there without walking at all.

The men are strangely quiet as they stand together in the elevator, making me realize they are carefully staying in character for the camera in the corner of the elevator's ceiling. When it opens on the fourth floor, they quickly exit and make their way to a room at the end of the hall. As I enter with them, I see that it's a large supply closet.

It's at this point, once safely inside, that they begin making their final preparations. An access door is opened in the ceiling, reached with a ladder already in the supply room. A hatchway is unlocked and pushed open, revealing an exit onto the building's roof. A hidden compartment in the tool cart is opened, and each of the men retrieves a high-powered rifle from inside, then begins checking his gun's scope and ammunition. Long cylinders are attached to the gun barrels that I guess must be silencers, then they compare their watches and sit down to wait.

It's not until Tate raises his phone that I finally learn the most crucial piece of information.

"In position, ready to play," he reports.

GLANCING down from over his shoulder, I can see the date and time on the screen of his phone...

...August 8th, 8:22 PM

ANOTHER FLASH QUICKLY SWALLOWED ME.

ONCE AGAIN, I was holding onto the ladder in the root cellar. Anna had just climbed out of the hatch above me. I stopped to catch my bearings, immediately grabbing a piece of paper to write down the key details.

Aug 8th
Library of Congress
Rooftop
8:22 PM

⌘

14

ON GUARD

"How well do you trust the Warden?"
~ Jimmy

I
t was evening when PJ called to report what I already knew; that Jack Shaw had been killed in a shooting at the prison and Billy Mansell was in the hospital.

"How is Billy?" I asked.

"I'm with him now. He's still unconscious, but the doctors think he'll live."

"I guess the bed rest will do him good," I offered.

I struggled internally with whether to tell PJ what I knew about Tate's involvement and the coming attack on the Supreme Court. Something told me that, for now, the fewer who knew about that, the better. I'd already shared the key details from my notes with Frank.

"Did you talk to Chase? How are the other guys handling it?" I asked.

"Chase wasn't there when it happened, but some of the guys from the group were with Jack and Billy at the time. Chase got permission for them to pray together in the chapel afterward. They were shaken up but otherwise are doing alright. I've been asked to hold a memorial service for Jack there on Friday."

"Do the inmates have any theories about who was responsible?" I asked.

"The inmates?" PJ repeated, considering the question. "I guess they probably have ideas about who their enemies are, that's for sure."

I felt like I had to tell PJ something about the danger. It wouldn't be right to let Tate finish the job on Billy. "They should probably keep Billy away from the prison for a while longer — until they catch whoever tried to kill him," I suggested.

"The Warden agrees with you. There are guards posted at his hospital room around the clock."

"How well do you trust the Warden?"

"Warden Grey? Pretty well, I guess. He's a friend."

"You have to keep this to yourself, don't tell anyone except the Warden — if you trust him. Tell him to keep an eye on the guard named Tate Hammer; don't let Tate get near Billy. He has to keep him away. Make sure the Warden knows he can't tell anyone else about this, especially Tate! There's more going on than I can share. It's bigger than what's happening at the prison."

PJ was quiet for a moment as he took in what I was saying. "O-OK," he stammered.

"I mean it, PJ, don't tell anyone else — don't even say his name out loud!"

"Y-You mean, I should write it down for the Warden and hand it to him?"

"I'm just saying we can't risk anyone hearing it — the word could get back to Tate, and there's more at stake than just what's happening there at the prison."

PJ released a deep breath. "Wow, this sounds heavy... a-alright — you have my word."

AMONG THE INMATES, Jack's death stirred a boiling pot. There had already been others jockeying to take over the role that Jackal previously held as the unofficial prison boss. Now that he was gone, the competition got serious. The spiritual revival that led to so many inmate conversions had grown the number of believers remarkably, but they were still outnumbered in the general population.

Tate was all too happy to turn up the heat on that boiling pot even further. With techniques and connections he'd cultivated for years, he spread the word that Jackal's powerful 'benefactor' was looking for a new Inside Man. The one chosen would have to prove their loyalty. Tate expertly spread rumors to inflame tensions between rival groups, creating even wider divisions and greater hatred between them. His goal was to create chaos and see who clawed their way to the top. In the meantime, the chaos served his own purposes, keeping the other guards and the Warden occupied to hide his own nefarious dealings.

Tate's well-practiced act wasn't fooling the Warden any longer. PJ shared my information with him, explaining only that he'd heard it from a confidential source. The Warden respected PJ's pastoral role and naturally assumed an inmate had told him. It was enough for him to begin a careful investigation into Tate.

He soon learned about Tate's stately home and the new Ferrari in its five-car garage. It was a lifestyle that didn't match a correctional officer's meager salary. The Warden's growing suspicions were confirmed further when Agent DeMassi informed him of the FBI's investigation into Tate as well.

Working together, Frank and Warden Grey carefully coordinated surveillance efforts. They learned about Tate's conversations with Bahal and a network of other crime dealings. Before long, they also uncovered Tate's 'team' of mercenary assassins, most of whom had served together in Tate's military unit. It became clear that the team was busy planning something — Frank had a pretty good idea of what it was.

OVER THE NEXT TWO MONTHS, several more bombing attempts were foiled, thanks to Frank's careful tracking, along with extra help from Amos' journal and a few travels of my own. In the process, Frank was able to piece together more of Bahal's operations, following a web of connections that ran through crime syndicates in countries around the world.

"HOW ARE THEY DISCOVERING OUR PLANS?" Athaliah complains angrily. "It's as though they hear what we say in private!"

"We've scanned everywhere for surveillance devices but have detected nothing," Devlon explains in frustration.

"It is the boy," Bahal answers. "Our enemy has given him knowledge beyond mortal ability." Bahal sits pondering the problem quietly. "We must find the boy."

"Good luck with that," Devlon dismisses in frustration. "We've been searching for him for two years with no success."

"The enemy hides him from us. Perhaps we should not seek *him* at all," Bahal hints.

Athaliah's face darkens with a sinister expression as she understands her father's remark. "His friends... yes, of course. Those minister friends of his."

"We tried arresting them already," Devlon reminds the others."

"Who said anything about arresting them?" Bahal asks with an evil smirk. "We simply need to follow them until they lead us to the boy."

"Don't you think we thought of that?" We've been watching them since the beginning," Devlon objects.

"That is the problem," Bahal observes. "Merely watching is not enough. "We must increase our surveillance. Track their every movement and listen to every conversation. Learn who they speak to and all that they say and hear."

"We can tap their phones," Devlon notes, thinking aloud. "There are tools that can turn their phones into surveillance devices, even when they are not being used. But we would need access to their phones to modify them."

"That shouldn't be hard," Athaliah grins. "Just bring them in for questioning and *'secure'* their personal effects." She runs her fingers over Devlon's shoulders as she considers it. "Would, say, eight or twelve hours be enough time for your people to fix their phones?"

"More than enough," Devlon smiles.

THE FLASH of light that ended the scene returned me to the farmhouse bedroom, where I was kneeling beside the bed. It was not surprising that Bahal and the others had finally noticed that we had inside information on their plans. It was more surprising that it had taken them this long to piece that together.

I thought about the best way to warn PJ and Pastor Wilkes about their impending arrest and the modifications to their phones. It seemed like there wasn't much point in hiding where the information came from; I was pretty sure they'd believe me regardless. After a few more minutes of praying about it, I yawned and looked at the bedside clock. Those dairy cows would be waiting for me awfully early.

"IT COULD WORK TO OUR ADVANTAGE."

Frank's words surprised me as I told him about Devlon's plan. PJ and Pastor Wilkes were on the line with us, seeking advice.

"They'll never suspect that we know," Frank explained. "That means anything the Pastors say will be taken at face value. We can use it to lead them away."

Pastor Wilkes wanted to see if he understood what Frank was suggesting... "You want us to lie to them and deliberately lead them astray?"

Frank sounded slightly embarrassed. "Well, it's not really a lie — it's more like acting — following a script. It's to save Jimmy...."

Pastor Wilkes chuckled and cut him off. "I understand, Agent DeMassi. I'll do whatever it takes, of course."

"That makes two of us," PJ chimed in. "The idea is brilliant."

"I can't claim credit for it," Frank confessed. "It's 'Spy-School-101.' The most important thing is to act like you have no idea they're listening. Don't forget that the phone's mic could be hot even when not being used. Assume they can listen even when you think the phone is powered-off. They'll likely have control of the cameras, too, so be careful where you aim them."

"Will they really be listening all the time?" Pastor Wilkes wondered. "That must be an incredibly boring and tedious job."

Frank answered confidently, "As a matter of fact, if it's coming at the direction of the President, there will probably be a small army listening."

"It sounds like a mission opportunity," PJ joked. "We'll have a captive audience to practice our sermons on."

"That's not a bad idea," Frank agreed with a laugh. Turning serious once again, he buckled down to business. "Let's work on the script...."

AN HOUR LATER, an elaborate yarn had been spun, placing me somewhere in Canada, ...or so they would claim to believe ...being sure to add that no one knew for sure. Frank reemphasized that the phones would be listening even when they appeared to be shut off. He gave tips on ways to temporarily interfere with the surveillance by placing the phone beside a loud radio or against a vibrating fan.

All that was left to do was to wait for their arrests.

THERE WASN'T long to wait. It was early the following day when a team of UEA agents surrounded each of them as they were leaving their homes. However, rather than taking them to jail, they brought them to a government office building, where they were detained and interrogated for hours. Finally, after more than eight hours in which no charges had been raised, they were released, and their personal items were returned to them.

That evening, and for the next several weeks of evenings, the agents who monitored their phones received a ringside seat to the tent meetings, including a chance to witness hundreds of tearful conversions and dozens of people being miraculously healed.

AUGUST 8TH...

THE JUSTICES WERE ESCORTED by their security detail to the side door of the Supreme Court building. It was not the door they usually used. They were exiting through the cafeteria on the north side of the building, away from their normal exit on the south side that faces the Library of Congress. It was 8:15 PM, fifteen minutes earlier than their expected departure time.

Armor-plated limousines pulled up to the building as the nine Justices were surrounded by security agents and rushed down the stairs one by one. By 8:20, they had all been safely spirited away.

Meanwhile, on the fourth floor of the Library of Congress, Tate and his men patiently waited to make the next move in their carefully planned mission. They rose to their feet at exactly 8:28 PM and moved swiftly onto the roof, spreading out into their positions along the building's north ridge. With rifles loaded and ready, they took aim at the South exit of the Supreme Court and waited for their targets to emerge.

At exactly 8:31 PM, the court's south door opened, causing the five men to focus with hyper-vigilance on the image in their scopes' viewfinders. They were so focused that they were completely unaware of the agents moving silently around the dome behind them. Five seconds later, the popping sound of 5 rifles firing simultaneously delivered a powerful tranquilizer dart to the neck of each of Tate's men, including, of course, Tate himself.

I could practically hear the smile on Frank's face as he described it.

⌘

15

A YARD FROM HELL

"I've never seen it this bad...."

Late August...

Frank DeMassi stood behind a line of police cars and armored vehicles outside the State Street First National Bank. He led a SWAT team that had taken up positions around the building. Inside of it, an unknown number of masked gunmen had taken at least two hundred hostages.

That would be bad enough, but the situation was made even worse when one of the hostages was dumped outside the door. The woman appeared to be paralyzed with fear, unable to speak or move, and with a look of abject terror on her face. Her heart rate was beating out of control. It was as if she was locked in a terrifying nightmare from which she could not awaken. The gunmen said that she was an example of what would happen to the others if their demands were not met.

The invaders wanted the bank to turn over a priceless ancient artifact from its safe deposit boxes. As far as Frank could learn, it was a golden amulet from Mesopotamia.

Frank's phone rang — it was his partner calling from FBI Head-quarters....

"Talk to me," he said abruptly as he answered it.

"The amulet belonged to Xerxes McSheffrey. He was a Scottish national who lived in the U.S. for the past thirty years."

Frank picked up on the past tense in her description: "...Was?"

"He was found dead this morning at his estate in South Hampton. It looks like a heart attack."

Frank glanced over at the released hostage; paramedics were working frantically, trying to get her heart rate under control.

"What did you find out about the amulet?"

"Not much. McSheffrey bought it from an unidentified art dealer in 2004. It's believed to have been part of a collection that went missing from a Bagdad museum during the Iraq war. It was never recovered."

"If the Iraqis wanted it back, why would they resort to hostage-taking?" Frank wondered.

"They deny any involvement, of course," His partner explained.

"So, what's so special about it?" Frank asked. "I guess it must be priceless?"

"That's the thing that doesn't add up," she said thoughtfully. "McSheffrey bought it for just $100,000; not exactly priceless. There are other artifacts from the same period that are worth millions."

Frank felt an odd tug in his spirit. Something told him that there was more to the amulet's importance than just its monetary value.

"What kind of amulet is it, exactly?"

"I'll send a picture to your phone that I downloaded from the museum archives. The description says it was believed to have been part of the treasures looted from Samaria by an ancient king of Assyria called Sargon the Second. This particular pendant was espe-cially revered for having belonged to a pagan high priest who served under Jezebel, the Queen of King Ahab, of Israel."

Frank studied the picture on his phone's screen but couldn't make sense of it. "What's it supposed to be?"

"The description says it's a representation of something called a Goetia demon summoning Baal Grimoire... whoever that is."

Frank fell silent as a sudden realization dawned on him. It was more than an extraordinary coincidence that he had been reading about that very name just last night. It would have sent a chill up his spine if it weren't for the rise of a different feeling within his spirit - a sudden swelling of brave confidence. The words that he'd heard spoken to him in the churchyard came flooding back — *'the weapons of your warfare are not of the flesh, but mighty before God to the casting down of strongholds.'*

"I know what that means," he revealed to his partner on the phone. "Goetia means sorcery. Baal Grimoire was the name for the king of Hell — in fact, he was called the king of the kings of Hell."

Frank looked again at the paralyzed hostage as an unusual unction came over him.

"I have to go..." he said, hanging up his phone in mid-sentence. He stood for a moment at the open door of the ambulance where they were just loading the woman, then climbed in beside her. The EMTs looked at him in surprise. Before they could question him, he placed his hand on the woman's forehead and closed his eyes in a silent prayer.

Suddenly the woman gasped and sat up straight. Her eyes caught sight of Frank kneeling beside her, and she lunged toward him, wrapping her arms around his neck as she broke down in grateful sobs, thanking him over and over again.

When she finally settled down enough to regain her composure, she started to explain....

"I saw... a creature... he was coming toward me... he was terrible, like a horrible monster! I was his prisoner — I couldn't move; I felt like I was dying of fright." She broke down again and wept for several minutes, then she looked up at Frank and took his hand anxiously. "You saved me! I saw you in my dream; you were covered with light — as soon as you appeared, I felt myself being pulled to safety. I don't know how to thank you!"

Frank looked at her, feeling awkward. "I don't know how to say this, ma'am, but I'm not the one who saved you. I just prayed for you, that's all. It was the Lord who saved you."

He could see that his words had hit her like a flood; she was washed away in their wake. Frank felt moved to share his own experience in finding Christ himself. "It's by grace that we're saved," he explained as if reading her thoughts. "It's not by anything righteous that we've ever done. There's nothing we can do to deserve it or earn it... it's a free gift. I know *I* didn't deserve it — I didn't see how God could ever forgive me, but He did. He changed my life!"

The woman's eyes had clouded again with tears. The flood of emotion that swept over her intensified as she began to realize what it was that she was feeling. All the pain and emptiness in her life were suddenly illuminated by his words. It brought a sense of deep guilt and remorse, but it wasn't full of hurt and insecurity. It was deeper than that — it stirred something in her spirit... in the deepest part of her soul. There was another presence there... full of love and acceptance... a forgiving presence. It overwhelmed her shattered resistance and she began to weep.

This time the tears were of repentance. Soon Frank was leading her in a prayer to seek forgiveness, and before long, the two of them were sharing tears of joy as they rejoiced together over her newfound life.

A SHORT WHILE later they looked up and Frank offered her a wadd of tissues from the ambulance shelf, noticing the astonished look on the EMTs' faces.

"I'm Frank, by the way... Frank DeMassi."

"I'm Susan," she said as she wiped the tears from her cheeks. "Susan Fincrest."

The EMTs insisted on rechecking her heart; Frank waited outside. When she finally made her way out of the ambulance and caught sight of the bank in the distance, Susan stopped and took hold of Frank's arm. It wasn't fear that gripped her this time, but rather a memory.

"They plan to kill them — I overheard what they said. They're planning an assassination."

"Kill who? The hostages?" Frank asked in concern.

"No, not them. The presidents... the heads of state — world leaders."

"Which ones?"

"All of them!" she answered, alarmed at her recollection.

FRANK WAS STILL TRYING to comprehend what Susan was saying to him about assassination plans when shots rang out. They came from inside the bank!

Immediately, all of the bank's doors burst open at once, and a mob of panic-stricken hostages began fleeing into the street. The police did their best to escort the emerging crowds to safety as their numbers overwhelmed the surprised officers. It was clear that the gunmen had driven them all out of the building to create a diversion, preventing the SWAT team from entering the bank.

By the time Frank and his agents made it inside, the gunmen were nowhere to be found. Worse still, the bank's vault had been success-fully opened, and McSheffrey's safe deposit box was lying empty — the pendant was gone.

EARLY FALL ~ A MONTH LATER...

SHERIFF FLANAGAN SPOKE on the phone with his good friend, Walt Fernandez, the Chief of Police in nearby Harbor City. They'd been close friends since the earliest days of their careers — when they were rookie cops together.

"I've never seen it this bad, Connor," Walt said. The sheriff could hear the worry in his friend's voice. "The gangs are out of control. They seem to be growing bigger every day; the schools are in chaos — half the kids are out on the streets."

"Can you put on more officers to enforce the truancy laws?" Connor asked.

"The schools don't want them. They end up being expelled — or they just turn around and leave again. As it is, rival gang members are fighting in the schools' hallways. I don't know what's gotten into the kids; they have no respect for anything — it's like they have no conscience."

"How's the drug problem?" Connor asked insightfully.

"It's worse than ever," Walt conceded. "That's feeding the gangs' growth for sure."

"Do you know where the drugs are coming from?"

Connor could hear the sigh in Walt's voice as he answered. "They flood over the border like they have a written invitation."

After thinking quietly for a minute, a sudden inspiration arose in the Sheriff's mind. "I know somebody who might be able to help. He used to be a Gangbanger himself — now he's a Reverend. He's done some amazing things with the kids here."

"I'll take any help I can get," Walt said, admitting his desperation. "If he can do anything at all, he'll have all the support my department can give him."

PJ WALKED UP to the black SUV parked outside his house and said good morning to the men inside. "I have some information for you," he said quietly as he showed them a thumb drive. He looked in both directions before handing it over. "It's a recording," PJ said as he dropped it into the agent's hand.

"What was that?" his wife, Baibina, asked as he came back in the front door.

"A gift. A few hours of my favorite music," he said with a sly smile. He looked back at the SUV to see the men listening to it intently — no doubt searching for hidden messages.

HE WAS JUST LEAVING his house to make his usual round of hospital visits at County General when his phone rang. He caught sight of the guys in the black SUV adjusting their earpieces as he answered it.

"Hi, Sheriff. Are you on a speakerphone? You never know who might be listening." PJ watched in amusement as the agents in the SUV looked at each other and then pretended to be checking their email.

Connor paused, unaware of the Pastors' phone taps. "Look, I have a pretty big favor to ask," he continued, letting PJ's comment drop. "I'll understand if you think it's a bad idea."

"Sure, what is it?" PJ said curiously.

"They're having a serious problem with gang violence up in Harbor City; it's gotten pretty dangerous."

"It's like that everywhere," PJ noted. "I've been seeing it on the news — seems like it's happening all over the country."

"Yeah, I'm afraid you're right. The Chief of Police in Harbor City is a good friend of mine. He and I were just talking when a sudden thought hit me...."

"YES," PJ blurted out, interrupting him.

"What...?" Connor said, surprised.

"Yes, I'll go. I feel it too — as soon as you started talking, I could feel an affirmation that God wants me there."

"G-great..." the Sheriff acknowledged, slightly amazed. "Let me know when you're ready, and I'll introduce you to Walt... Chief Fernandez."

"How about today?" PJ suggested with no hesitation.

A CALL to Pastor Wilkes for his help with the hospital rounds cleared PJ's schedule. Ninety minutes later, he and Sheriff Flanagan were pulling up to the police headquarters in Harbor City.

"This is the man I told you about... Reverend Rodriguez," Sheriff Flanagan said as he introduced PJ.

"Call me Juan," PJ said as he extended his hand.

"Walt Fernandez," the chief said as he introduced himself with a firm handshake.

The chief waved for his lieutenants and beckoned for Connor and

Juan to follow him as he headed for the city war room. Inside the room, a panel of screens covered an entire wall showing a live map of the city with the current location of every patrol car and beat cop. Large sections of the city were highlighted in orange, with hundreds of red dots scattered throughout.

Waving toward the maps, the chief explained. "I honestly don't know what you think you can do, Reverend, but I want to show you what we're up against. The orange areas are updated throughout the day; they show where there's active gang warfare. The red dots are the locations of murders in the past six months."

PJ studied the map quietly for a moment. "How many different gangs are there?"

One of the chief's lieutenants spoke up. "There are four major rival gangs, as far as we can tell, but we've also picked up splinter groups that operate under the major gangs' radar. They started out dealing drugs — narcotics mostly. Now they've branched out into protection rackets and extortion. Fire insurance, they call it."

"What are these blue areas?" PJ asked.

"Those are the water stations — the tanker trucks. The stations themselves are protected by National Guard. We do our best to protect the residents in the surrounding areas, but our officers face steep odds — we've lost six of our own so far this year."

Connor shook his head sadly. "I know you said it was bad, Walt, but I never imagined...." He turned to PJ, "I'm sorry to drag you into this, Juan; I'm not sure what I was thinking. I can't ask you to risk your life like this."

"You're not the one who's asking," PJ replied with a smile. "To be honest with you, this is exactly what I've been praying about for the past few months — it's been a call that's kept me awake for nights on end. I just didn't know where to start."

"What is it that you want to start, exactly?" the chief asked.

"Call it a mission, I guess."

The chief's second lieutenant shook his head. "I'll be honest with you, Reverend, this is no place for a Gospel Mission — those neighborhoods are a living hell!"

Juan just turned again to look at the map of raging war zones and nodded his head in agreement. "I'm a big fan of a man named Charlie Studd," he explained as he continued to study the map. "He was a missionary to China, India, and the Congo in the early part of the last century. Someone once asked him why he chose to serve in such dangerous places.

"'SOME STRIVE to live beneath a Chapel Bell...' he answered the man, '...I'd rather run a rescue camp a yard from Hell.'"

⌘

16

DARKNESS AND LIGHT

"...he who believes on me... greater works than these shall he do...."
~ Jesus, John 14:12

J uan parked his car inside the blue zone, where the Chief had suggested. He insisted on going alone, knowing that any involvement by the police would just make it harder for him to connect with the gangs. He breathed a heartfelt prayer as he ventured from the protected zone on foot.

He walked a half-dozen blocks when a large group of teenage boys rounded the corner in front of him. PJ knew immediately from their tattoos and dreadlocks that he'd met his first gang.

"Yo. Wait up!" One of them shouted to the others in a command that they instantly obeyed. The one who shouted it stared at PJ. "Whatcha stupid or sumthin? This-here is Posse's concrete jungle mon... seen?[1]"

PJ was unfazed by the boy's question — asking one of his own: "What's your name?"

The boy seemed irate that anyone would ask that question; he pointed at himself with both thumbs. "I be rankin these Rudeboys.[2] You're talkin to Badrick the Don. Everybody knows me 'round the Bario. You a Five-O[3]? Put me deep or you better jet.[4]

"Good to meet you, Badrick. I'm not with the cops. I'm like a preacher — my friends call me PJ."

"Picture that![5]" The other boys laughed. "You be frontin us, mon. What are you speakin' on? Seriously, mon — you a druggler?"

"I'm serious," PJ said calmly. "I used to be a gangbanger like you until God saved me from it."

Badrick whistled in disbelief. "Now I know you're smokin us. You must be down with the Five-O." He pointed at PJ with both hands, "Serve him up, boys!" PJ heard the clicking sounds of fifteen switch-blades opening.

A GUNSHOT RANG OUT before PJ had time to react, and Badrick dropped to his knees. PJ saw blood oozing from the young man's chest. The rest of the gang turned on their heels and ran for cover. Seconds later, PJ found himself in the middle of a gunfight as rival gangs opened fire from opposite sides of the street.

PJ could not see the troop of powerful angelic guardians that had suddenly surrounded him. He told me later that he felt a boldness that was clearly irrational under the circumstances. His only instinct was to grab Badrick and drag him to safety behind a nearby stoop.

Badrick lay gasping for breath as PJ pulled off his own shirt and wadded it into a ball, pressing it against the boy's wound. As he was doing that, he prayed — hard! Bullets were flying overhead as he worked to save the boy's life.

"Listen to me, Badrick! God sent me here for a reason — it was for you. It's not too late to make things right with God."

"The look of terror in the boy's eyes expressed more than words ever could. He managed to whisper through weakening coughs... "I don't want to die…. Please don't let me die…!"

"Don't try to talk," PJ cautioned him. "Save your strength."

"Y-you a preacher?" he stammered. PJ nodded his head. "P-pray for me… p-please d-don't let me die!"

PJ nodded OK and began to pray aloud, keeping his eyes fixed on the boy's. "Lord, you care about Badrick more than he knows — so much that you sent me here for this very moment. Bring him now to a saving knowledge of your grace - take him into your arms and make him your child."

PJ sensed a sudden compulsion to pray for healing despite the boy's hopeless odds. Overwhelmed with this irresistible unction, his eyes squeezed closed, and he pressed both hands against the boy's chest.

Just at that moment, Badrick began to feel himself lift from the ground but quickly realized that his body wasn't moving. Instead, he was rising above it. He looked at PJ kneeling beside him with his hands on the lifeless body — PJ glowed with an aura so bright that Badrick found himself shielding his eyes.

It was then that Badrick noticed the messenger hovering above him. The angel's presence radiated warm light — it felt so good against his frigid soul! She didn't speak a word but touched his forehead, and Badrick understood all she was sent to tell him. She communicated that she was sent in answer to his grandmother's prayers for him. More than that, he understood that he needed to help PJ. He didn't know what that meant but had little time to consider it before he found himself instantly back in his own body.

PJ felt a rush of power flow through his hands but couldn't tell whether it had come *from* the boy's body or *into* it. The next thing he knew, Badrick was weeping. When the boy lifted his hands to his face, PJ knew for certain what he'd already expected — a miracle had happened.

Late October...

THE DROUGHT soon reached a critical state, just as Amos had written. Much of the country was descending into chaos as businesses failed, throwing thousands out of work. By God's providence, the old Spring was running freely in the secret cavern, and any houses in town that were old enough to have wells still had crystal clear water flowing from them. The food delivery service was going strong; in fact, it had never been bigger.

We learned that PJ was using the food we sent to his family to help families in Harbor City.

"Why in tar-nation didn't ya say so?" Uncle Jim exclaimed when he heard about it. He insisted that we expand our help to the new mission in Harbor City.

The value of Amos' coins had appreciated more due to the stock market crash. With many banks being routinely robbed, there was no more secure place for them than the secret vault where Amos had left them. I had just retrieved another ten coins for Uncle Jim to sell and made my way back to the Root cellar when a sudden flash interrupted me.

MY EYES ARE STILL ADJUSTING to the sudden daylight as I take in the scene around me.

A guy who I'm guessing is about my age is greeting PJ with a broad smile. I can guess that it's Badrick, based on PJ's description of him. Badrick is standing with a dozen former members of his gang at the mission's rented storefront entrance. A few dozen others are already inside, including an older woman that Badrick refers to as GramMa.

"God is makin' wonders!" Badrick's voice practically thunders with enthusiasm. "Me boys an' me swept the streets fer lost ones... ya know? These-here are wantin' what we found..." he points to the three young women and a younger boy who are standing beside him. They look at PJ and around at the others nervously. Tears are visible on their faces, and the boy is holding his arm, which is blackened and swollen.

"They said you can help our little brother — he needs help! We were sleeping in the alley, and something bit him," one of the girls explains tearfully.

"We pray! God be a healer — right Pastor Juan?" Badrick says confidently.

The boy winces painfully when PJ touches him. The atmosphere in the room is electric as everyone there begins to pray together. The surge of anointing is evident to PJ, just as he has felt so many times before. A corner of the small storefront holds a fresh pile of crutches and braces — even GramMa's walker has been discarded there.

He prays silently, without any fanfare. When he opens his eyes, the boy's arm is fully restored, and tears are streaming down their faces. PJ explains the salvation message to the four of them, and soon they have all dropped to their knees, anxiously following as he leads them to the Lord. The room echoes with the others' shouts of joy and worship!

SUDDENLY A ROCK SMASHES one of the front windows. Outside, the street has begun to fill with gang members — there seem to be hundreds. PJ motions for everyone with him to move inside, away from the door, asking them to be calm. He gestures for them to pray.

"Ese Vato! Yo - Bad-Rick!" someone shouts from outside. "There's word in the jungle that you is all débil.[6] We hear you got religion or some s***. Guess you don't care no more 'bout your barrio, so we come to burn it down. You wanna stop us, you better Baile![7] Right here - right now!"

Badrick starts toward the door, but PJ stops him with a hand on his chest. He pats the place where the young man still bears a scar from the bullet that almost killed him. I see Badrick nod back at PJ acceptingly, but the fire in his eyes reveals his growing indignation.

PJ stands in the doorway facing the menacing crowd and quickly assesses the scene. Gang members fill the street in front of him and extend more than a block in each direction. It seems like more than one of the city's gangs is present — it appears to be all of them. If PJ had been able, he would have seen that a dark hoard is responsible for bringing them together. The leather-winged creatures are mixed in among and hovering above the angry mob.

"Lay Raza…[8] Where You From?[9]" The same spokesman shouts out. He seems to be the clear leader. "You a marrano?[10]"

"He's that preacher!" someone else shouts.

"Out o' the way preach," the leader demands. "Nuestra awetado 'y vatos," he says in Spanish *(Our anger is with the guys inside.)*

"Not today," PJ answers back calmly.

"I ain't askin' Preach! You startin' t'get on my nerves! Them boys is droppin the flag[11] — that ain't allowed. It's Rafa (the rule)!" He turns to all of the gang members around him and shouts... "Rifan... Rifamos![12]" A loud cheer echoes through the canyon of buildings as the raucous crowd waves their machetes and pistols in the air.

PJ spreads his arms in a welcoming gesture as he shouts loud enough for all of them to hear. "We're not here to start trouble. This is God's house — we're here to meet with Him. Anyone who wants to join us is welcome."

"We ain't joinin' you freak!" The leader pulls his gun and aims it at PJ. "I'm givin' ya ten seconds to get your sorry self out o' the way, or you'll be meetin' God face to face!" As he is saying that everyone with a gun around him does the same. The sound of a hundred guns being cocked runs through the crowd as the leader shouts out the count-down: "...nine ...eight ...seven..."

Inside the small storefront church, everyone has bowed anxiously in prayer, begging God for deliverance. Badrick moves to his Gram-Ma's side and shields her as he kneels with her to pray. Inwardly PJ is praying too — like he's never prayed before in his life! He is bravely keeping his eyes on the gang leader who is counting down his death sentence, trying his best to hide the nervous terror inside him.

PJ is still standing alone in the street with his arms spread in a protective gesture as the countdown reaches zero, then I see him squeeze his eyes closed as the first gunshot rings out.

EVEN IF HIS eyes had been open, he would not have seen Ardent's sudden appearance standing directly in front of him with his enormous wings spread wide. Other huge angelic warriors have appeared as well and are standing on both sides of Ardent — three powerful hosts on each side. They shield the storefront behind them with an impenetrable wall that stops every bullet in mid-air, sending them dropping harmlessly to the ground in a shower of hot lead.

PJ can hear the guns and opens his eyes in wonder, realizing that he feels no bullets. A sudden boldness fills his spirit with such force that it erupts from deep within him in a tremendous shout….

"…STOP…!"

His command emerges like a thunderbolt echoing through the air to his utter amazement and surprise. When its sound strikes the vicious gang members, they are thrown backward with its force. He watches them tumble like dominoes in an expanding wave until all of them have been knocked to the ground or against cars and buildings. Even more astonishing, when they finally lift themselves, all of their weapons are gone.

The group huddled inside the storefront church looks on the scene in shocked amazement and then breaks into spontaneous shouts of praise.

Meanwhile, Ardent and his powerful troops make short work of the demon hoards, which flee the scene like terrified prey.

PJ watches the gang leader who had fired on him moments before as he stumbles toward him, shaking noticeably, and then drops to his knees in the street. The young man's eyes have begun to well with tears, and when PJ places a hand on his shoulder, he is suddenly slain in his spirit under the powerful anointing that surges through him, dropping to the ground unconscious.

When the other gang members see what has happened, some turn to run, while many of them begin to rush forward and kneel in the street as well, feeling their dead consciences pricked with the Spirit's overwhelming drawing.

Moved with a burning message, PJ opens his mouth and begins to preach to them the words of life.

⌘

17

DUE SEASON

"The eyes of all wait for You; And You give them their food in due season."
~ Psalm 145:15

T hanksgiving had a distinctly different feeling this year. It was not a better feeling. For the first time in my life, I knew that the nation truly had little to be thankful for. After a year and a half of drought, the entire country was embroiled in conflicts amid widespread hunger and poverty. I knew that the burned-out cities destroyed businesses, and mayhem were outward evidence of an even more devastating problem — that God had withdrawn His blessing from the nation. It now lived under a curse.

Of course, that was not to say that **we** had nothing to be thankful for. The blessing of revival had not dimmed. If anything, the curse around us had only drawn even more souls toward the kingdom. The tent meetings in Center Springs were as vibrant and overflowing as ever, and the same was true in other cities throughout the country and around the world.

Our podcast shared amazing stories of what God was doing, showing some of the hundreds of videos received each week from around the world. It was thrilling to watch massive crowds worshiping under the ministering care of vast hosts of angels! Chozeq and I visited many of those crowds; I wished that I could show that reality to others. They *will* catch a glimpse of those angelic hosts one day — *everyone will.*

ANNA and her mom arrived at the farm early on Thanksgiving morning to pick up food supplies. They were so early that I was just making my way to the dairy barn to start my morning chores; sunrise wouldn't arrive for another two hours. They were bringing the food to Uncle Mike's Sub Shop, where Thanksgiving meals would be prepared and distributed for free throughout the day. Pete and a bunch of other FCS kids would be there to help too.

"Is this when you get up every day?" Anna asked in partial disbelief. "How do you even stay awake?" She sipped from her thermos cup of hot coffee, brushing hair away from her puffy, half-asleep eyes.

I pointed at the long dairy barn with my thumb. "Rustling with angry cows tends to keep me awake."

She stared at the barn in concern. "They're angry? Really?"

"Well, maybe irritable would be a better word," I admitted. "I suppose it's understandable. Waking up connected to a milking machine probably makes for a rude awakening."

She shoved me with one hand, shaking her head as she hid a smile. I followed her to the main barn to help load her mom's car.

"I wish I could come with you to the shop," I said honestly as they prepared to leave.

"I know..." she offered, letting me steal a quick kiss before she got into the car. "We'll be back around 4:00 to help with dinner. Watch out for those angry cows." She flashed a smile as she pulled her door shut, and her mom backed away to turn the car around. I watched as they drove off.

———————

UNCLE JIM STARTED on Thanksgiving dinner preparations early. By the time I brought in the milk, he already had a large pot of potatoes scrubbed and peeled and a bowl of stuffing ready for the oven. Vegetables were a little hard to come by this year, but he had managed to keep a small garden behind the house that yielded enough for a healthy meal. He was busy cutting green beans, peas, and carrots as I entered the kitchen.

"They'll be here around 4:00 unless they run out of meals before then," I informed him.

"God bless 'em," Uncle Jim said approvingly. "We'll aim fer 5:00 an' adjust accordingly. Go on and grab an apron; you can start-in pluckin' turkey feathers."

———————

JUST AFTER NOONTIME, my phone rang — it was Pete.

"Hey, how's it going over there?" I asked as I answered.

"It's great; it's a blessing, man. The lines have just started getting long. Your Uncle Mike and Mrs. Mirabella are amazing cooks; the meals are excellent."

"It sounds awesome," I agreed, a little wistfully.

"The reason I called is 'cause I got a text from Radison. Ya know, it'll be two years ago this week when his grandmother died."

"Oh yeah, that's right. How did he sound?"

"That's the thing, I couldn't really tell, and he didn't pick up when I tried to call him."

"What did his text say?"

"It was short…."

> — *Nothanks Giving* —
> — *bet u miss yur mom... I get it* —

"Oh man, the poor kid."

"Yeah. Anyway, I was thinking maybe we should pray for him or something."

"Good idea," I agreed. "Is PJ there? We should ask him to join too."

As soon as Pete told him what we wanted, PJ lifted his voice, announcing it to the whole group around him.

"A boy we know needs God's help. His mom died when he was a baby, and his father is in prison for life. He's been in foster care since his grandmother died two years ago — it was two years ago this week when she died. His name is Radison. Let's bring him before the Lord in prayer."

I listened over the phone as everyone in the Sub Shop began to pray together while PJ led them.

> "Lord, you love Radison more than we can comprehend.
> We know that you see him in his hurting, and you
> desire to wrap your arms around him — to shelter
> him beneath your wings.
> At this difficult time for him, please give him comfort.
> Send your protecting angels to keep watch over him
> and preserve his feet from falling — we ask you to
> spare his life! Bring him to a saving knowledge of
> your love. However long it takes, don't let him ever
> be away from your pursuit!"

THE SCENE that instantly surrounds me is jarring but not wholly unexpected. Radison is sitting alone outside the Calvary Hill Church. Sounds coming from inside suggest that the church is hosting dinner for a large number of people. The wet streaks on Radison's face are clear evidence that he's been crying. A stuffed duffel bag looks like it's been tossed haphazardly on the step beside him.

While I'm watching, Pastor Jerome steps outside through the church doors. He seems surprised to see Radison sitting there.

"Hello, Radison. Why aren't you at home having Thanksgiving dinner?"

"Mrs. Oram threw me out. She don't want me there no more."

"On Thanksgiving Day?" Jerome said sadly. "How did you get here?"

"I took a bus to 85th... walked from there."

"Are you hungry? We're having Thanksgiving dinner inside; come on in and join us."

It's evident from the way Radison licks his lips that he is hungry, but he looks toward the door reluctantly. "Could I just eat out here? I don't know nobody in there."

Pastor Jerome could have made the case that he knew lots of the people inside — Radison had grown up in this church. Instead, he insightfully understands the boy's awkward embarrassment.

"Wait here," he offers, "I'll fix you up a plate."

Jerome emerges a few minutes later carrying two plates and sits down on the step beside Radison, joining him for dinner. He watches as the boy inhales his food, looking as if he hasn't had a meal in days. When he's done, the Pastor looks at his own untouched plate and then offers it to the boy. Radison accepts it without hesitation, quickly finishing that one as well.

"You want to talk about what happened with Mrs. Oram?"

Radison looks at the ground as he speaks, avoiding eye contact. "I guess she just hates me, is all."

Jerome sits silently, waiting for him to continue. Radison eventually begins to open up.

"She don't like my friends or any of the stuff I like. She was always yellin' at me; I couldn't do nothin right. She never really wanted me there anyway. It was just for the money and food stamps and stuff. I never even got much to eat or nothin' — she ate it all."

"Did she ask you to leave, or did you run away?"

"It was her! She made me leave, I swear! She packed all my stuff in that bag and everything."

"What are you going to do?"

"I don't know," he replies quietly. "Can I stay here... at least for a while?"

Jerome is quiet for a long minute. Radison draws his gaze away from the ground and looks up at him hopefully.

"Your grandmother was a great woman and a good friend. I owe it to her to see that you're cared for. We have some ground rules here. There are other families here with kids of their own — young kids; we won't stand for anything that leads them astray. You'll need to share a room with the other boys... we don't have much room, but we'll find you a bed. We can keep you until a new foster home is found. Are you willing to go along with all that?"

Radison looks at him with a surprisingly contrite expression as he accepts the Pastor's terms. "Yes, sir."

Pastor Jerome nods and places his hand on the boy's shoulder approvingly. "I saw some fine-looking pumpkin pie inside. What do you say we go check it out?" Radison's face lights with a smile as he nods his head yes.

THE SCENE outside the church faded, returning me to the farmhouse living room. PJ's voice over the phone revealed that he was still praying. Once everyone said amen, Pete lifted the phone to his ear.

"You still there?" he asked.

"Radison will be OK for now," I told him. "I think the crisis has been averted. He's staying with Pastor Jerome for a while."

"He's what? ...h-how?" Pete started to ask. Then he stopped himself and quietly accepted what I was saying. "...wow ...alright."

"You should give him a call again," I suggested. " I think he'll talk to you now."

CHRISTMAS SEEMED TO ARRIVE OVERNIGHT. When it came time to decorate this year, there weren't many trees to choose from — it had now been about twenty months since the last rainfall. The trees that did survive were so dry that they looked like they'd ignite into flame at the slightest excuse. Uncle Mike went scavenging around and found an old artificial Christmas tree that had been used by one of the

closed restaurants in town. He insisted on setting it up at the farmhouse, and we all decorated it together.

The Christmas Eve service at the tent was held earlier in the
evening this year. The Pastors were encouraging everyone to spend
time together with family and friends. Carmine opened his diner to
offer free meals to anyone who needed them on Christmas Eve. He
said he'd been inspired by what Uncle Mike had done on
Thanksgiving.

By eight o'clock, we were all gathered around the dining room
table at the farmhouse — Uncle Mike, Anna, and her mom, with
Uncle Jim and me. After all we'd been through together in the past
two years, it felt like we really were one family.

Once again, Lena and Mike managed to prepare a fantastic meal
despite the shortages of practically everything. One thing that we did
have plenty of was milk and cream. Uncle Jim and I made sure there
was an ample supply of homemade ice cream, and Lena made the best
cheesecake I'd ever tasted.

After dessert, we retired to the living room to open the few meager
presents under the tree. Mike and Lena slipped out onto the porch to
admire the clear night sky. I stood trying on the scarf that Anna knit
me. It was as tall as I was — long enough to wrap around my neck
about twenty times.

ANNA and I had just settled onto the couch together when her mom
burst through the door from outside. Tears were streaking her face —
but they were obviously tears of joy, as her face was lit with a radiant
smile. Mike followed her inside and grinned as Lena held out her
hand, proudly showing off the diamond ring on her finger!

Anna jumped from the couch and screamed as she hugged her
mom, suddenly wiping tears from her own cheeks. I walked to Uncle
Mike as he opened his arms wide and then wrapped them around my
back.

"Congratulations, old man! You finally did it!"

"It's thanks t' you kid. None o' this would be happenin' if it weren't for you an' Anna there." He leaned closer and whispered, "Anna's a great catch, by the way... jus' sayin'."

I definitely agreed with him. However, there was a nagging feeling that my marriage prospects would be better if I at least had a job and an actual place to live. Of course, there was also that small detail about being an internationally wanted criminal.

⌘

FULLNESS OF TIME

"There are no arbitrary times for God's interventions...."
~ Amos

News of Mike and Lena's engagement spread quickly, drawing the same universal reaction from everyone who knew them — what took them so long?

On the morning after Christmas Day, the two of them stood together loading cars for food distribution as Nyle and Caden entered the farmhouse driveway. They found a place to park along the driveway — out of the way of the distribution team and then walked to the barn together. Nyle greeted Mike with a handshake and a slap on the shoulder as Caden kissed Lena's cheek.

"Congratulations, guys!" Nyle said, beaming with a broad smile. Lena accepted his kiss on the cheek as she thanked him and smiled back, hugging Mike's arm. The two of them were beaming with the thrill of their engagement.

"We were so happy to hear it!" Caden said excitedly. "We just had to come and congratulate you as soon as we heard." Caden looked over at her husband with a smile as she placed a hand on her belly. "We have some exciting news too," she revealed with a wide grin.

Lena's eyes grew wide, and her mouth opened in a joyous surprise. "Ohhh! You're expecting?"

Caden nodded yes in confirmation, unable to hide her excitement.

Lena screamed an incoherent exclamation that did a better job of expressing her joy than any actual words. The two of them hugged again, suddenly chattering like schoolgirls.

Mike gave Nyle a congratulatory hug as well.

As the ladies became quickly absorbed in their own conversation, Nyle leaned closer to Mike. "Can we talk inside?"

The way he pointed to the farmhouse let Mike know that Nyle had something secret to discuss. Caden was still in the dark about my actual whereabouts — the couple had agreed together that it was safer that way because of her work at the TV station.

NYLE WAVED into the hidden camera in the pantry before knocking on the root cellar's hatch. He was the one who had installed the small camera that I was using to watch him as he knocked. He'd also installed the one above the barn door on which I'd just seen and heard the two couples greeting each other.

He didn't bother waiting for an answer before lifting the hatch door and poking his head in. After confirming that I was inside, he quickly climbed down. Uncle Mike followed close behind.

I stood up to welcome him. "Congratulations!"

"Thanks, man," he replied happily. "God is good!"

After a quick greeting, Nyle sat at the keyboard and examined the camera feeds approvingly, checking the two I just mentioned, plus another at the driveway entrance and two others — behind the house and on the front porch. He appeared satisfied that they were all working as expected. After that, he typed a string of commands, opening an encrypted link to his bank of servers. He opened a folder and scattered documents across the screen, drawing our attention to a complex chart of interconnecting lines.

"I've been monitoring the IP traffic to keep track of the government's search for the source of our podcast signal," he explained. "Lately, there's been a clear pattern emerging in the focus of their probes." He pointed to several places in the chart where lines converged. "I know our podcast traffic isn't leading them here because that's completely randomized. They must be focusing here for another reason— some other surveillance."

"Sorry," Uncle Mike said, trying not to sound as confused as he was. "What are we lookin' at?"

Nyle looked back at the screen as he answered, pointing to several points where most of the lines converged: "Those are the data hubs all around Center Springs."

The cause of the new traffic patterns dawned on me. I held up my hand, asking Nyle to wait, then jumped up the ladder and pulled the hatch shut. Dropping back to the ground, I kept my voice low.

"I think I might know what that traffic is." Nyle and Uncle Mike both looked at me expectantly.

"Devlon's agents bugged the pastors' phones. Frank knows about it, and so do the pastors. We don't want the agents to know that we know."

Nyle's face lit with a smile. "I should ask how you learned that but already have a pretty good idea. That's classic counter-intelligence; that's incredible!"

Uncle Mike looked confused again. "Wait... having their phones bugged is a *good* thing?"

Nyle explained. "If the agents think they're undetected, then they'll believe anything they hear. We can feed them any information we want, and they'll follow it."

"But it has to stay secret!" I emphasized. "If Frank knew I told you, he'd string me up."

Uncle Mike nodded that he understood, pulling his fingers across his lips as if he was zipping them shut.

Nyle studied his traffic chart again. "We can trace the traffic back to the surveillance origin — to the people who are listening."

"Ya mean it'll tell ya who they are?" Mike asked in surprise.

"Not their names… not necessarily, anyway. But we can trace to a MAC address and then cross-reference that with cell tower logs to see where they are."

In Uncle Mike's eye, I could see that he and I were both wondering the same thing — *how are we going to get cell tower logs?* But we didn't bother asking; Nyle just seemed to have that kind of information in his hip pocket.

PJ CONTINUED to spend most days at the mission in Harbor City. After the spectacular events at the storefront mission in October, several area churches began offering their support. The expanding crowd of converted gang members quickly outgrew the mission's storefront space, and they were welcomed by the city's churches. Their meetings were moved to a grand old church in the heart of the city, and its huge auditorium was soon packed three nights per week.

Badrick spent his days leading mission teams into the neighborhoods to round up hold-outs from the smaller gangs and any others that they could compel to come in.

The dramatic drop in the city's crime rate was so astounding to Chief Fernandez that he visited the mission himself to view it first-hand. He looked around in disbelief as he stood in the church foyer watching former gang members from rival gangs talking and laughing together. PJ welcomed the Chief with a handshake.

"I've got to admit; I would never have believed it," Walt said humbly. "You really are a miracle worker!"

"I'm not the miracle worker, but you're right — it is a miracle."

The Chief watched the friendly crowd as he accepted PJ's comment, unable to deny it. "There's no doubt about that. The Principal over at Harbor City High says their classrooms are full for the first time in years. He thought at first that he'd need police backup, but it turned out the returning kids are better behaved than the ones who never left. He's struggling now to recruit more teachers."

"I'll spread the word," PJ offered. Chief Fernandez nodded thanks, looking at PJ as if expecting him to walk on water next. PJ picked up on the Chief's vibe uncomfortably and looked around at the surrounding crowd. "The credit for all of this belongs to God."

I FELT COMPELLED to pray for PJ and the mission — I'd been having an uneasy feeling all day and couldn't shake it. It was a sense that even amid that city's revival, the enemy was not standing still.

As soon as I reached my knees, images began to fill my mind. They weren't actually visions, and I wasn't traveling. I suppose they could be described as daydreams, yet were so vivid that I noticed the smallest details— the dirt on the table, the devious expressions on faces as they plotted.

They were older kids, about my age. I recognized a few of them, recalling some of their faces in the angry crowd of gang members outside the storefront. They were among the ones who ran away.

It was clear as I watched that they were plotting a resurgence, but it would be hidden this time. Their methods would be subtle, pushing drugs and instilling hatred behind the scenes. They were targeting younger kids. Not recruiting them into gangs, but just befriending them and indoctrinating them. The smoky shadows that hovered in the room with them were familiar. I'd felt the presence of their kind at the glass temple and in Athaliah's meeting room. These sinister powers had a great deal of patience; they worked insidiously behind the scenes, quietly poisoning a younger generation.

As I watched the scenes developing, this new cancer began to spread through the city's neighborhoods. Attempts to stamp it out drove it to other cities where it found its way into elementary and Middle Schools like a gray sickness. I felt my heart beat faster as I saw images from Bushwick and recognized three boys being approached as they rode their skateboards —my heart sank as I recognized the boy in the middle. It was Radison.

· · ·

AFTER PRAYING over the scenes for a long time, I finally sat back, eventually making my way to my bedroom's small desk. I couldn't help feeling discouraged as I recorded what I'd witnessed in my journal.

Words that Amos once shared seemed to roll through my mind... *"Funny thing about time... it can't be changed, even when you try."*

I pondered the memory, struggling with it. Surely there must be some reason why God was showing me these events in Radison's life. There was still time for us to intercede — why couldn't we save him from the future that was coming? More of Amos' words that night came to mind as I pondered it.

"The gift is not about doing. The sooner you come to terms with that, the better off you'll be. God has His reasons for revealing what He reveals and hiding what He hides. His reasons are bigger than you and me."

These words seemed to rise and wash over me like a huge wave, leaving me tumbling in their wake.

I leaned my elbows on the desk and dropped my head into my hands, breathing the prayer that welled up from deep in my troubled soul... "What is the reason, Lord?"

AMOS' voice broke the silence in my quiet room. I was startled to hear him and lifted my head quickly to look. I looked him in the eye, finally registering the words he'd just spoken to me aloud.....

"...The things He reveals to us can surely be hard to
    grapple with."

I wasn't able to answer, unsure of the connection he was making.

"GOD NEVER DOES anything important at random times," he began to explain. "He always has a perfect time for those things. For the really important things, there's the *fullness of time.*

He paused for a moment as he thought about it. "What was it that

Paul wrote? *'...when the fullness of the time was come, God sent forth his Son.*[1]*'* What do you suppose that meant, exactly? It could not mean simply that God had waited long enough. It was not as if any time would do. There are no arbitrary times for God's interventions in history.

"Think of it, son. It was at the moment when earth most needed a savior that Christ was born in Bethlehem. But I'd dare say that it was also the moment when God most felt the need for men to be saved. The religious leaders of the day — those who were entrusted with ushering men to God — had instead become gatekeepers, blocking men's path. It was at the point in history when the greatest barriers had been erected to keep men from God — *that* was the *fullness of time.* God felt the pangs of separation from his beloved creation. When humanity sought for God but could not reach Him, God came to man."

His words struck me powerfully, and I felt tears well up in my eyes. The thought of it sank in for a moment or two as we sat in silence.

"Is that what He's waiting for in Radison's life... for the fullness of time?" I asked.

Amos sat down on the foot of the bed as he considered my question. "From what you've told me of the boy, God is surely doing something in his life already. It could be that there's great work still to be done. But the boy will need to seek God for it; it's not something you can do for him. Whatever path he is destined to travel before that day is the path that is needed. It is the journey that will lead him to where God needs him to be."

I thought of Uncle Jim and how it had taken him 90 years to come to Christ. "You must have worried about Uncle Jim for all those years it took him," I said, drawing the connection.

"For a number of 'em, most surely," he answered. "You'll recall, however, that I wasn't an old man when you and I first met, and God had already let me see James' turning. I reckon He may bless you with foresight into Radison's future choice as well. You'll just have to wait and see.

Amos contemplated that thought for a moment and added.

"Waiting for God's time can be difficult, but it's necessary. I know a young preacher who likes to say:

> *'He who goes ahead of the cloud of God's providence goes on a fool's errand... if providence tarries, then we must also tarry till providence comes.*[2]*'*

"I'll bet that preacher's name is Raymond," I said with a smile, suggesting it was Amos' son. He smiled and tipped his head, leaning it forward and slightly to one side as he acknowledged that I was right.

"It's good to see you again," I added, realizing that we hadn't said hello.

He nodded hello. "You'll have to forgive me for confusing the times we've been together. I reckon I was a mite younger when you met me last."

I just nodded, accepting that I've already seen him at many different ages in his travels. It must surely be confusing for him to keep track of the timeline.

"We met last about seven months ago, back in the Spring," I explained. "It was when Obadiah saved that church in Bushwick with the National Guard troops."

"That was a wondrous deliverance, most surely," Amos acknowledged as he recalled it. "Yet, as fine as that day was, days are coming that will make it pale in comparison. What God will soon do will shake all the world greater than anything that's been done yet."

He took stock of his surroundings, noticing the frost on the windows. "If it's the winter after those events, then things will soon be coming to a head." He looked at me with the kind expression of a grandfather advising his prodigy.

"When those days come, you'll know they've arrived; there won't be any doubting it. When you find yourself facing them, remember that God Himself is your strength. Remember that it's in your weakness that He'll show His greatest power. Trust Him alone and rely on His great strength; you'll need nothing more than that."

. . .

WITH THAT, he stood and placed his hand on my shoulder reassuringly. "Godspeed, lad." The look in his eye reminded me of a superior officer dispatching a soldier with special orders. I nodded thankfully and watched his gaze as he faded from sight.

⌘

19

A LION ROARING

"Be watchful: your adversary, the devil, as a roaring lion, walks about, seeking whom he may devour."
~ 1 Peter 5:8

The final words that Amos had spoken to me seemed to replay constantly over the next few days.

"When those days come, you'll know they've arrived; there won't be any doubting it."

I wondered what kind of events could rise to the level of importance that he described. I also seemed to sense that when they did, I'd somehow find myself right in the middle of them.

I DID my best to push those thoughts out of my head for now and focus on what I was doing. Right at the moment, the challenge was a failed pump on the milking machine. With a small pile of dismantled machine parts already lying nearby, I laid down the pump's impeller section and removed the old motor, confirming that it was seized. I chided myself for neglecting to oil it; I should have known better, especially knowing how old it was and how much use it'd been getting lately.

Thankfully, Uncle Jim had a spare motor, proving once again how much experience he had with the farming business. He'd obviously been doing it a while.

By the time the pump was running again, I was an hour behind in my chores, and the cows were getting restless. I soon realized how difficult it can be to persuade a bunch of 2,000-pound cows to move into places they don't want to go. Uncle Jim eventually arrived to save the day, easily showing me a thing or two about leading livestock.

DUE TO THE DELAYS, the sun had already risen by the time I deposited the milk cans in the walk-in refrigerator and emerged from the barn. The sight of a car pulling up the drive from the road stopped me, forcing me to duck back inside. Uncle Jim realized my predicament and walked out to the car to meet it.

The car's driver spoke through his open window:

"Mister Van Clief, it's è good t' see you, my friend."

I'd recognize that voice anywhere — it was Carmine... Mr. Giovani. I heard the car door close as he stepped out.

"I'm è sorry for not comin' è sooner. I jus want t' tell you how è grateful I am. All that you're è doing for people... an' for my è family. We'd be è starved if not for you."

"That's awful kind of ya', but I don't reckon I'm the one deservin' thanks," Uncle Jim replied. "It's God who's doin' the providin' an' folks from the church are doin' all the work."

"You're è humble man, my friend. All of this... the cows... the chickens... it's a big è job, that's for sure. I wanna help you. I admit I'm è no farmer, but I can è do work. I owe you. Let me work for you on è the farm."

Through the crack in the barn door, I could see Uncle Jim scratching his head as he debated what to say. His reply was unexpected, obviously surprising Mr. Giovani as much as it did me.

"I'll tell ya what. I'd be more'n pleased if you'd take some o' these eggs an' milk an' reopen your diner for needy families 'round here. I know there are plenty of old folks who could use a cooked meal. You kin charge what you like, I know you've got expenses, same as anyone. But maybe you kin afford t' give 'em some kinda break if the eggs an' whatnot are free."

Mr. Giovani was speechless. He looked confused for a moment, unable to believe what Uncle Jim was saying. I saw him wipe a tear off his cheek as he struggled for words.

Uncle Jim held out his hand to shake. "Have we got a deal?"

Mr. Giovani ignored his hand and wrapped his arms around him in a hug. I saw Uncle Jim smile at the gesture as he patted him on the back. "I reckon that's as good as a handshake," he said as he looked over at me and gave me a wink.

New Year's Eve...

A New Years' Eve service was planned again at the tent. It was hard to believe that two years had passed already since the night I 'appeared' at that first New Year's Service. It would soon be two years since the dedication of the glass temple — and two years of the drought. A restless expectation pervaded my spirit and ran through me like pulsing electricity. It was growing stronger each day.

All week long, I'd been mulling over Amos' words about how *'things will soon be coming to a head.'* The look in his eye as he wished me *Godspeed* had conveyed more than just good wishes — it had the feeling of an earnest prayer.

I sat at the laptop in the root cellar and watched a Livestream from the tent as crowds gathered to pray. It was still mid-afternoon, but the tent had already filled. The ringing on my phone drew my attention to the caller-ID... it was Nyle.

· · ·

"ARE YOU KEEPING OUT OF SIGHT?" He asked me mysteriously as soon as I answered.

"What else would I be doing?" I said wistfully.

"Stay there. I'm watching the phones that are monitoring PJ & Rev. Wilkes — there are at least twenty of them right there at the tent grounds; they have it surrounded. My guess is that they're half-expecting you to show up again — you don't have any plans like that, do you?"

"Plans? When does God ever follow plans? Not that I know about anyway." I said honestly.

"Alright, I see your point. I'm just saying — if they see a clear shot this time, they're likely to take it first and announce it later."

"I don't expect to be there tonight, don't worry. Besides, it wouldn't be the first time I've been shot at."

"Yeah, you've got a point," he conceded. "I don't know about light-ning this time, though. There hasn't been a storm cloud in a while."

"In about twenty months, as a matter of fact," I added, quickly doing the math in my head.

"Okay, I get it — you've got this under control," he accepted. "Just don't take any unnecessary risks."

He didn't have to remind me that the risk wasn't just to me — someone else could get hurt in my place. Mom's sacrifice was still fresh in my mind, even after more than two years.

"Thankfully, I'm not the one who has it under control," I noted, breathing a grateful prayer.

WHILE I WAS STILL SPEAKING with Nyle, my phone ran with another incoming call — this time, it was Frank.

"Hang on," I said to Nyle, "I have another call."

"Listen," Frank said immediately as I answered. "Bahal's men are on the move. They're planning something tonight, and it looks like it's in Center Springs."

"What do you think it is?" I asked, already assuming a connection to Nyle's surveillance.

"If I had to bet, I'd say they're targeting the tent meeting — they might be expecting you to make another appearance. You're not planning to, by the way, are you? Cause that would be a disastrously bad idea."

"I'm not, don't worry. But I think you should hear what Nyle just told me. He's been tracking their surveillance. Can I conference you in?"

"Hey Nyle, I have Frank on the line; can you tell him what you told me?"

Nyle described his tracking, finally adding: "There are at least twenty of them already there at the tent grounds; they have it surrounded. More are arriving as we speak."

Frank sounded more concerned the longer he listened. "These guys aren't Federal Agents — they have no rules. This is more dangerous than I realized." He paused as he thought for a moment. "Do the local police still have those checkpoints setup — are they still checking for weapons?"

"I think so... I'm not sure," I had to admit it'd been a long time since I'd been to one of the tent meetings myself.

"They still have a checkpoint," Nyle confirmed, "but I don't know how closely they're really checking. It's been pretty quiet for the past two years. We have to alert them."

"If Bahal's men are already on the grounds like you say, then it may be too late," Frank warned. "We'd better warn the sheriff — he has to know the full extent of the threat. It can't come through official channels, though; they'll be monitoring those."

"I'll call Uncle Mike," I offered. "He can get a message to Sheriff Flanagan. The Sheriff will trust him."

"Do it," Frank agreed. "I'm coming up there." He paused as he checked the time. "It's still early, I can have a team there in two hours, but we'll need a landing site away from the tent grounds to avoid attracting attention."

"Use the field behind the Old Hill Church," I suggested.

"I can send you the coordinates," Nyle added in agreement.

"We'll need transport from there for a dozen men and their gear."

"My van will hold at least half of them," Nyle volunteered.

"Uncle Mike's van can hold that many too," I quickly added.

WHILE FRANK FINISHED DESCRIBING his plans, my thoughts turned to the real security force that watched over the tent grounds — their angelic presence had been vigilantly guarding it since the first day.

I interrupted the conversation...

"...We should pray."

Frank stopped what he was saying, and there was a short silence — I could sense the Spirit's moving in each of our hearts; they felt it too.

"The enemy may be planning an attack, but God is still the one in control," I reminded them both. "This is God's ground-zero — it's sacred ground. They must be desperate if they're bringing the battle here." Nyle and Frank readily agreed, realizing that nothing we planned ourselves could possibly match God's protection. We spent the rest of the call praying together — arming ourselves with the ultimate weapon.

SHERIFF FLANAGAN TOOK action immediately after getting the alert from Uncle Mike. He quickly mobilized his entire force and called in extra reinforcements from the State Troopers. They doubled the number of checkpoints while officers fanned out across the tent grounds, checking bags and vehicles.

The first confirmation of the threat came shortly after the search began when a State Police chopper spotted a sniper on the roof of Carmine's Diner. The sniper surrendered quickly — probably a little too easily, in fact.

FRANK'S CHOPPER landed near the old church just after sundown. Nyle and Mike were waiting for him at the edge of the field, along with Sheriff Flanagan.

"Good to see you again, Sheriff," Frank said as they shook hands.

"The name's Connor," the Sheriff responded with a friendly nod. He quickly briefed Frank and the others, describing the security in place at the tent grounds, as well as the arrest they'd already made.

"He surrendered without a fight?" Frank asked, making sure he heard correctly. "That doesn't smell right. Sounds like he was a plant to make us think that the threat is over."

"That was our take on it, too," Connor agreed. "He's being interrogated down at the station."

"May as well lock him up," Frank advised. "He isn't likely to talk, and if he does, I doubt we can believe anything he says.

"Show me telemetry," Frank requested as he waved to a man on his team. The man placed a tablet in front of him, showing a satellite view of Center Springs. The tent grounds were brightly lit, revealing that it was a real-time image. Frank leaned close to Nyle and hid what he was saying from the others with one hand.

"Do we have locations on those phones?" Frank quietly asked.

Nyle responded by pointing at the tablet screen and tracing a pair of circles around the tent grounds with his finger, one inside the other, forming a donut-shaped ring around the tent.

Frank pointed at the area as he turned to his telemetry officer. "Get me the elevation for this area."

The man typed a few commands, causing the elevation lines of a relief map to appear over the places that Nyle had pointed out. Frank scanned for the highest points and then zoomed in on the high-resolution satellite image.

"These are our targets," he finally said, tapping his finger on a large camper and several buses that were parked in the area.

"I can send my deputies to question them," Connor offered.

"Too dangerous," Frank warned him. "These guys are pros; there's no telling what they might do. They won't think twice about shooting first." He thought for a moment as he studied the screen... "We'll have to wait for them to make their move. We'll need to get in range."

⌘

20

STAND

"Stand still and see the salvation of the Lord who fights for you."
~ 2 Chronicles 20:17

"We need to keep the crowds at a safe distance," Frank said with genuine concern in his voice.

Connor answered thoughtfully, "We can have the deputies move people, but won't that arouse suspicion?"

"How about drawing them away? Maybe something could draw them forward toward the tent," Nyle offered.

"One of the Pastors might have an idea how to do that," Connor began to suggest. "We can call them...."

"No!" Nyle interrupted, realizing that Connor didn't know about the surveillance of the pastors' phones. "...I mean, I have a better idea. I'll go there and talk to PJ directly."

"That's good," Frank quickly agreed with Nyle. "Let's move out." He looked at his watch... "If they're going to make a move, I'm guessing it will be around midnight. That gives us a few hours to gather intel and get in position."

Nyle offered a final suggestion. "Mike could take a team to the farmhouse. I'll take the rest up to the target area and park in the back?"

"Roger that," Frank accepted. He pointed to his team as he split them up:

"Dwain, Fitz, Cliff, Bree, Dara, and Leo — you're with Mike. The rest of you are with Nyle and me. When you get to the farm, use the cover of darkness to make your way to positions — here;" he pointed at several places on the satellite map, and they added the coordinates to their wrist devices. "Radio check," Frank finally requested.

Each member of the team sounded off, testing their comm-links.

MIKE'S VAN exited the church lot first and headed for the farmhouse. A minute later, Nyle pulled out, following the Sheriff's patrol car for the ten-minute drive to the tent grounds. The Sheriff ensured that Nyle's van was waved-through when they arrived at the checkpoint. A few minutes later, he was backing into a space in a remote section of the parking area. Frank's team slipped out the back door and quickly disappeared into the dark night.

It only took two or three minutes for their reports.

"Confirming — there's an armed sentry outside the target camper," the first agent reported over the radio. *"Infrared shows heat signatures for five more inside."*

"Roger that," Frank responded.

"Bus 1 is empty," the second agent reported. *"Looks like it belongs to a church group."*

"Bus 2 has action," the third reported. *"I count a dozen heat signatures. The two in the back are holding weapons... they appear to be sniper rifles — military issue."*

"Bus 3 is the same," the fourth agent added. *"I count six inside and two outside."*

"Roger. The Camper, plus Bus 2, and Bus 3 are considered hostile," Frank acknowledged.

"Why so much firepower for a sniper operation?" Nyle wondered aloud to Frank.

"Only 3 or 4 of them are snipers," Frank explained. "The rest are for fighting their way out. If this goes down, the scene will be a bloodbath."

"Lord, help us," Nyle prayed. He checked his watch, "I guess I'd better go and warn PJ."

"What are you going to tell him?"

"The truth, I guess. I think it's best if he understands the urgency."

Frank nodded, accepting Nyle's reasoning.

THE WALK from the parking area to the front of the tent took about ten minutes. Rev. Wilkes was at the pulpit, and PJ was seated behind him. Nyle made his way around behind the main platform and tapped PJ on the shoulder.

"Those Bibles you asked for are here," he said, using their agreed code phrase to get PJ's attention. PJ immediately understood — he left his phone behind and followed Nyle a short distance away to talk.

"What's up?" PJ asked. Nyle looked at him uncomfortably, trying to decide where to start.

"There's a threat. We think some snipers are here tonight looking for Jimmy."

"For Jimmy? He's not here," PJ said with a confused look.

"I know... but it's New Year's Eve, and, well, you know."

PJ nodded that he understood. "Who else knows about the threat?"

"The Sheriff - and the FBI."

"Are they getting ready to arrest them?" PJ asked, looking back over the crowd.

"It's a little more complicated than that...." Nyle did his best to bring PJ up to speed.

PJ stood silently for a minute as he took in all he'd just heard. "How many are there?"

"Twenty-Six, that we know of."

PJ's eyes widened, "Are you sure it's safe — should we just end the service now?"

"That's your call, of course. We're not sure what they'll do, though, if everyone starts to leave. They might try to create a scene to draw Jimmy out," Nyle explained.

PJ closed his eyes and breathed a prayer for wisdom. Just as his head bowed someone touched him on the arm, getting his attention. He was surprised to see one of the girls from the youth group standing beside him — tears were streaking her face.

"I'm sorry to bother you, Pastor, but I've had this feeling that I need to tell you something. It's been weighing on me so heavily... I just have to say it. It's a message from the Lord, I'm sure of it."

PJ felt a chill as he heard what she said. He just nodded to her, asking her to continue. She looked him in the eyes as she spoke, and a sudden anointing seemed to come over her, infusing her spirit with boldness and strength. She gripped his wrist as she spoke, and her words poured over PJ like a spring of water from Heaven.

> "This is what God says to you.
> "Don't fear, I am with you; don't be dismayed, for I am your
> God; I will strengthen you; yes, I will help you. I will
> uphold you with the right hand of my righteousness.[1] You
> will not need to fight in this battle: Stand with my people,
> set yourselves, stand still and see the salvation of the Lord
> who fights for you.[2]
> For just as a mighty lion with fierceness defends his cubs, so
> will the Lord of Hosts come down and fight for you in this
> place tonight. Stand and see — stand fast!"

As soon as she finished speaking, a flood of tears suddenly filled her eyes, and she fell against PJ as he hugged her with a thankful embrace, patting her on the back reassuringly.

"Thank you!" He said to her, holding her by her shoulders. "Your message was from the Lord... it was an answer to prayer!"

She smiled through her tears and nodded gratefully. Her friends embraced her as they turned and walked away together.

PJ looked at Nyle with new confidence.

"I'll invite everyone to the front for a watch-night dedication — a prayer vigil."

Nyle was speechless for a moment as he took in what had just occurred. He could tell that tonight was shaping up to be something more than even he had expected. "Oh- OK, right. That's a good idea," he agreed. "We think the biggest threat will be shortly before midnight."

ONCE UNCLE MIKE had safely delivered his passengers at the farmhouse, he joined me in the root cellar. He was carrying one of Frank's radios to keep in touch with the assault team. We listened as Frank instructed the arriving agents to take positions in the darkened fields, telling them to fix their rifle scopes on the camper and the hostile buses.

"The snipers will most likely be on the roof when the time comes," he explained.

While we listened to the radio conversation, a knock at the farmhouse's front door interrupted us. We listened as Uncle Jim answered it, hearing the sound of Lena's voice as she entered the living room.

"Is Mike here? I see his van outside...."

We heard Anna's voice as she entered right behind her mom: "Where's Jimmy?"

Uncle Mike and I looked at each other in realization. In all of the day's excitement, we'd completely forgotten about our plans for New Year's Eve.

Mike headed up the ladder first, and I quickly followed, emerging together with uncomfortable looks on our faces. We were dressed in the day's work clothes and hadn't even washed up for dinner yet.

"What's going on?" Lena asked with a surprising degree of intuition.

"Is something wrong?" Anna immediately added.

Uncle Mike and I gulped and looked at each other.

"No... well, I guess... maybe. ...Yes," we both stammered.

With awkward timing, the crackle of Frank's radio sounded from the root cellar, and one of the agents could be heard reporting....

"HOSTILES ARE IN SIGHT. *I'm locked onto the sentry that's standing outside the camper.*"

Lena's face fell nervously. "Who's that?" she asked uncertainly. "Why are they telling you that?"

Mike grabbed a kitchen chair, offering it to her. "Maybe you'd better sit down."

I did the same for Anna and then joined Uncle Mike at the table. Uncle Jim stood at the counter — he was all ears, like the others.

Mike slowly recounted what had transpired, explaining how Nyle and Frank had reported a threat from Bahal's men. He described the meeting at the old church with Frank's team and the Sheriff and explained how he and Nyle had transported them to the tent grounds. In all of his descriptions, he carefully avoided mentioning the part about a sniper threat.

"Why are they here — what do they plan to do?" Lena asked with the precision of an expert interrogator.

Uncle Mike swallowed and glanced at me as he attempted to answer. "We're not sure, exactly, but think it's a possible... sniper threat."

"A sniper threat?" Lena said in a slightly higher octave. "Who's the target?"

"Me. At least, we think it's probably... most likely ...me." I said, feeling more than a little awkward about it.

Both women responded with simultaneous bursts of advice and insistence that I'd be crazy to go to the tent tonight... there was no way they'd allow it... it was absolutely out of the question!

I held my head in my hands, waiting for them to finish and settle down. "Don't worry," I insisted. "I don't plan to go *anywhere*."

The sound of another short status update from the radio cut the air like a punctuation mark.

Everyone grew quiet. Anna took my hand and looked at me; "What are we going to do?"

"The only thing we *can* do — we have to pray."

I slipped from my chair and knelt beside it while Uncle Mike, Anna, and her mom did the same. Uncle Jim took a seat and leaned his elbows on the table, clasping his hands together as he joined us.

MEANWHILE, Nyle made his way back to his van, where Frank monitored the situation. A new feeling seemed to emanate from all around him as if the tent grounds glowed with God's anointing. He had a sense that even the ground he walked across was holy, as words from the girl's message reverberated in his mind:

> The Lord of Hosts will come down and fight for you in
> this place tonight.

A chill ran up his spine as he considered it.

As soon as he reached the van, he told Frank everything that had happened and shared PJ's plan.

Frank had honestly been feeling something too. Ever since his arrival at the old church grounds earlier in the evening, he hadn't been able to shake his powerful memories of the night that he and Jimmy prayed there together. The night he found the Lord. The words that he'd heard spoken aloud to him in the churchyard that night came flooding back as Nyle was describing the girl's message — *'the weapons of your warfare are not of the flesh, but mighty before God to the casting down of strongholds.'*

He checked his watch and scanned the scene around him for the hundredth time, this time with a feeling that everything had suddenly changed.

BACK IN THE FARMHOUSE KITCHEN, each of us had been taking turns leading in prayer for the past hour. We'd honestly lost track of time. There was a growing sense of God's presence among us, and as time

went on, we became more and more convinced that something miraculous was about to happen — a mighty deliverance was about to be
seen.

Uncle Jim's words resonated in our hearts as he pleaded for God's
protection. I echoed his plea for God to intervene: "Yes… move with
Your presence among us tonight."

"Oh yes… move, Lord!" Anna's mom repeated.

"Yes, Lord… Our defender!" Anna added with tremendous
unction.

It was Uncle Mike's words that seemed to shake the room as he
suddenly called out: "Oh God, You are our strong tower! Lord of
Hosts, come and fight for us tonight!"

———————

IN AN INSTANT, I suddenly find myself high in the air, with Chozeq at
my side. The sight around me makes me gasp in astonishment; the sky
is filled with powerful warriors — an enormous army. I am
surrounded by angels!

⌘

21

DRAGON'S FOE

*"Jehovah opened the eyes of the young man, and he saw: and, behold, the
mountain was full of horses and chariots of fire round about...."*
~ *2 Kings 6:17*

L ooking down, I can see the tent grounds stretching wide
below me, with their powerful angelic sentries standing
guard at the four corners.

Crowds are moving forward like a streaming flood; it looks like PJ
has called everyone to gather together around the altar. I can see
ministering spirits moving among them, glowing like translucent
lights.

Standing in stark contrast to those, there are shadowy powers as
well — groups of them occupy dark places toward the back of the
field, among the parked cars. My eyes are especially drawn to a pair of
dark forms who are moving through the crowd — they are making
their way toward the front.

Focusing my attention on them, I instantly find myself standing
directly in their path. They are perfectly still, as if frozen in time.

That's when I notice that everyone is frozen — the entire scene around me has stopped. I'm able to see every detail about the troubling pair. They are women in their late twenties, wearing long flowing coats with hoods pulled over their heads. The most striking thing about them is the expression on their faces — cruel and sinister. They seem amused by the scene of worshipers around them as they push their way forward. I'm suddenly reminded of where I've seen their faces before. It was at the temple of Anath — they were two of Athaliah's priestesses.

As I'm LOOKING at them, the scene around me quickly changes, and I find myself standing across a darkened room from the same two priestesses. The room is lit only with candlelight, and its air is filled with thick smoke and the smell of incense. My eyes are drawn to a stone table in the center of the room and the presence of another woman wearing a horned headdress who stands beside it. Without seeing her face, I recognize her immediately — it's Athaliah.

On the stone table is a large book that appears extremely old. Its ornate pages contain hand-drawn lettering and images. Athaliah is reciting some incantation and takes a drop of blood from the hand of each of the women and then from her own hand, collecting it in a small golden cup. Into the cup, she pours a smoking mixture — created from a prescript in the strange book.

Holding the potion aloft, she repeats the incantation in a louder voice. While she is speaking, her voice deepens and echoes god-like from the room's stone walls. When her eyes open, they are glowing yellow — the eyes of a large predatory cat.

"COME CLOSER..." she thunders.

The priestesses obey eagerly, holding their hands pressed together in front of them in a praying gesture. As Athaliah repeats the chant once again, the women open their mouths wide and tilt their heads back, and then Athaliah spills the smoking concoction from the cup into their mouths.

Immediately, the priestesses' eyes begin to glow a fiery red, and the sound of fierce snarling begins to emerge from their throats. Suddenly, from each of their open mouths, there emerges the head of a snarling wolf with dripping, razor-sharp fangs and fire-red eyes. The demon-hounds snap at the air fiercely, growling in bloodthirsty rage. Smoke from their nostrils reeks of sulfur and brimstone.

"OBEY ME, BEARERS OF DEATH..." Athaliah commands them.

The fierce beasts are immediately silenced, except for their continuous low growling.

> "THESE HOSTS YOU WILL OBEY.
> WHEN THEY CALL, YOU WILL ARISE.
> CONCEALED WITHIN THEM, YOU WILL STAY.
> THEIR SHAPE AS YOUR DISGUISE."

> "TONIGHT, YOU WILL FEAST UPON OUR ENEMIES."

Athaliah shouts another command in a language I don't recognize, and the beasts are suddenly drawn back inside the women's throats. The priestesses' eyes flare more brightly red before fading and transforming back into those of their human hosts.

"YOU KNOW WHAT YOU MUST DO... GO!" Athaliah commands. The priestesses bow and look to each other with evil grins, pulling the hoods of their coats up over their heads.

THE NEXT FLASH that engulfs me returns me to Chozeq's side in the air above. As I catch his eye, I see him nod to me, and then he grips my shoulder with a smile.

"To the fray... my friend!"

In a streak, we are immediately descending toward the ground at a blinding speed — an instant later, we land with a brilliant flash of light at the rear of the crowd.

FROM THE REACTIONS of those around me, I could tell that I was now clearly visible. People staggered, shielding their eyes as they moved away in surprise. I spotted the cloaked priestesses a short distance ahead of me among the crowds and shouted to them, surprised at how powerfully my voice carried over the open field.....

"HOUNDS OF HELL — The Lord rebukes you!"

THE TWO OF them turned toward me with gleeful expressions and threw back their hoods. Their eyes glowed fiery red as they opened their mouths and the loud, hideous snarls of demon beasts emerged.

People around them began to run, clearing a wide space between us. I fixed my eyes on them, knowing what to expect next.

The grotesque sight of the priestesses' mouths opening unnaturally wide brought screams from onlookers. The screams grew even louder as the demon-hounds' fierce heads emerged, followed by their huge wolf-sized bodies as they leaped to the ground. They howled and snarled as they barred their razor teeth, dripping with a foul stench that burned the ground like acid as it fell from their mouths. Streams of smoke from their nostrils made people cover their faces at the overpowering smell of sulfur and brimstone.

I shouted at them again, determined to keep them focused on me and no one else.

"BEARERS OF DEATH — you have no business here. This ground on which you stand is holy ground!"

THEY STOOD GROWLING and snarling at me in a standoff. Neither fleeing nor attacking. It suddenly occurred to me that they were doing exactly what Athaliah intended. They had gotten me here — out in the open, with my back to the snipers' guns.

As soon as I thought of it, a set of loud blasts rang out.

MOMENTS EARLIER, Frank and Nyle had seen the bright flash of my arrival as it lit the night. They jumped from the van, and Frank was immediately on the radio barking orders to his team.…

"E.M.P.-1, GO!"

"E.M.P.-2, GO!"

The blasts of both pulses going off in quick succession sent a shock wave through the air, lifting the rear of both buses momentarily off the ground.

"Team 2-GO!" he shouted.

The muffled sound of silenced rifle shots delivered a spattering of thuds that flattened all four of the camper's tires.

Bahal's men aimed the barrels of their high-tech automatic weapons through the windows of both buses and prepared to return fire, only to find that their guns had become inoperable. Frank's team, along with a small army of Rangers and Troopers, quickly surrounded their vehicles, shielded behind the nearby cars.

SUDDENLY, a loud commotion erupted from inside the buses, mixed with terrified screams. Soon two dozen hideous leather-winged creatures emerged, flying into the air, some with fresh blood on their talons. They swooped toward the agents and troopers with terrifying shrieks, impervious to the bullets that struck them from all sides.

"Can you get a clear shot at the snipers?" Frank asked the team in the fields.

"Negative, we're too low. Too much interference."

The fearsome beasts were swooping lower and lower over the heads of the Rangers and Troopers, who were powerless to fight them. Frank breathed an urgent prayer and immediately heard the words of the Lord's promise echo through his mind:

'...The weapons of your warfare are not of the flesh.'

"Lord, save us! Fight for us!" He cried out.

ALL AT ONCE, with blinding streaks of light, the demon creatures were sent tumbling skyward. Frank and the others stood in shocked awe as they saw the brilliantly glowing angelic warriors who struck them. The demons battled back defiantly, screeching and shrieking as the angels fought them with flaming swords, leaving fiery wounds in the dark creatures. The creatures hissed and railed against the bright warriors and bared their sharp jagged teeth but were soon pulled higher into the air and surrounded by the overwhelming angelic army.

Amid this commotion, snipers on the roofs of all three vehicles took determined aim with their long guns and squeezed the triggers.

A split second later, the blinding flashes of three enormous lightning bolts shattered the night sky! Pieces of the snipers' guns, along with sections of the camper and bus roofs, were sent flying through the air.

THE PRIESTESSES BECAME enraged as they saw the snipers destroyed. They shouted at their demon hounds with orders to attack!

The two huge fiends bounded across the field toward me with eyes flaming bright red and fangs bared. They leaped into the air from a dozen feet away, flying at me with their mouths open wide in a blood-thirsty assault.

They had no sooner left the ground when two more lightning flashes caught them in mid-air, consuming them instantly in a burst of flame.

Still raging with hatred, the priestesses threw back their shoulders and were suddenly tossed backward to the ground as their demon masters emerged defiantly, flying into the air with talons bared and shrieking in a hideous wail.

The creatures immediately found themselves surrounded by the tent grounds' powerful sentries and an army of angelic warriors with flaming swords. Powerless to resist, the creatures hissed and clawed the air like captured animals. Beside them, a legion of bright warriors forced the rest of their defeated demon hoard to the ground.

I pronounced on them all the sentence that God's Spirit decreed....

"DEMON BEASTS — YOUR CHAINS AWAIT YOU. TONIGHT YOU ARE
BANISHED TO HELL IN JESUS' MIGHTY NAME!"

The angels' swords bathed the creatures in brilliant light, piercing their wings like fire. Then the ground suddenly liquefied underneath them, swallowing them up, and they disappeared beneath the earth.

THE PRIESTESSES SAT COWERING on the ground nearby, alone in the cleared field. They covered their heads with their arms in terror at the sight of the angel army. They were still shaking from the terrible ordeal they'd just experienced. Chozeq and the angelic sentries stepped aside as I made my way over to the frightened women.

"God has freed you tonight," I said reassuringly as I knelt beside them. "Those demons won't hurt you anymore." There was still fear in their eyes as they looked at me, and they drew back as I offered them my hand. I did my best to reassure them that I meant them no harm.

"You feel guilty, I know. I know what it's like to feel the guilt of sin. But you can be free of guilt tonight — you can be forgiven. Jesus paid for your forgiveness; He died for you, in your place."

The women's eyes welled with tears as they clung to each other.

I looked up and saw PJ and Pastor Wilkes breaking through the edge of the crowd a short distance away. PJ's eyes kept jumping from me to the extraordinary sight of angelic hosts around us. Most of those in the crowd had fallen to their knees in awe at the astonishing sight of skies filled with bright hosts, in addition to those standing behind me on the ground.

PJ looked at the frightened women and motioned to several other women from the ministry team, who gently approached them. The former priestesses welcomed their embrace as tears began to flow steadily, soon breaking into heartfelt sobs.

THE PASTORS tentatively approached the place where I stood. I could see their eyes watching the glowing warriors with awestruck wonder.

"This is Chozeq," I said in introduction. Chozeq bowed his head in greeting and smiled. PJ's legs wobbled unsteadily, and I caught him — he hugged me with the hug of a dear friend. He could hardly contain his emotion as he stepped back and looked me in the eye.

"God said He was going to fight for us tonight," he said breathlessly. "I should have known that you...."

"This was all God," I interrupted. "Believe me, I'm just as amazed and surprised as you — I've just had a little longer to get used to it."

MEMBERS of the Livestream team began to gather around us, staying a safe distance away. A camera crew from the TV station appeared as well. They had captured the incredible events live, streaming them to millions of viewers. One of the crew held out a wireless microphone, offering it to me. PJ gripped my shoulder and motioned toward them with his open hand in encouragement.

My first instinct was to decline the invitation, but then I felt the Spirit's voice bringing to mind His powerful charge:

You are my witness to this defiant generation. Speak the words I give you boldly and without fear.

As I reached for the mic, a message flooded my mind, startling me with its clarity and power. PJ could see the change in my eyes and stepped back, watching with the others. Chozeq and the four Guardians spread their wings, flooding the scene with light.

I looked out over the crowd as the message surged within me.

"The Lord of Hosts fought for us tonight!" I yelled. The crowd exploded in cheers of praise, continuing briefly before finally growing silent once again.

"We know that God has called us to live in peace with all men. We honor His command by loving and caring for one another. This is our first and greatest mission." I glanced at the former priestesses, who continued to sob, comforted by a large group consoling and praying for them.

"What we have seen demonstrated here tonight is equally true — evil is at war with us. We can never live in peace with evil. Peace between good and evil is an impossibility." I glanced over my shoulder at the glowing troops behind me and up at the army of hosts that filled the sky. I felt my face set with determination as the message burned within me.

"War will always rage between those two great forces until one of them is crushed. Peace between good and evil cannot exist; the very pretense of it would be a triumph for the powers of darkness. Jesus will always be the dragon's foe; that is not a figure of speech. He opposes him actively and vigorously, with every power in His mighty arsenal — with relentless determination to exterminate evil once and for all.

"All those who serve Christ, whether angels in heaven or believers on earth, must fight. We are born into the Kingdom to be warriors. We entered into a covenant at the cross never to make a truce with evil. Against the darkness, we are to be firm in defense and fierce in attack. The duty of every soldier in the army of the Lord is to fight against the dragon — daily, with all our heart, soul, and strength!

"We know that the dragon and his fallen legions will not decline the fight. They are incessant in their attacks. They spare no weapon, fair or foul. We would be foolish to expect to serve Christ without their opposition: the more zealous we are, the more certain it is that the cohorts of hell will attack us.

"It may be that the Church has become lazy and fallen asleep over time, but not her great enemy. He still pursues her destruction violently, with a restless spirit. He hates the 'woman's seed,' as John described the Church in Revelation, and would devour it if he could. That old dragon's servants hate it as much as he does and are just as active in their attacks. Friends, war rages all around us, and to dream of peace in that spiritual conflict is dangerous and misguided.

"The best news of all is that Jesus said that He'd build His church and the gates of Hell would not prevail against it. *Gates* have never attacked anyone. We are meant to be the ones who attack and lay siege to evil; we are the Lord's army — the army of the victorious King!

"Glory be to God, we know the end of the war! That terrible dragon will be cast into the lake of fire. Jesus will receive the glorious crown and the Kingdom, and He will reign forever and ever! Your crown of righteousness awaits you as well!

"So let us sharpen our swords tonight and pray for the Holy Spirit to give us nerve and strength for the conflict. Never has a battle been so important! Never a crown so glorious! Every man and woman to your post, you warriors of the cross. May the Lord soon tread Satan under your feet![1]"

CHEERS ERUPTED, filling the field and sky with praises as unnumbered angels raised their fists in triumph and shouted to the Lord. The crowds below joined them, leaping to their feet and shouting glory to God, many with tears streaming down their faces.

I looked to PJ and embraced him again, then turned to take one last look at the stunning Heavenly army arrayed around us. With my fist held to my chest, I saluted Chozeq and the others, then a flash of light engulfed me, and I was gone. The mic I was holding thumped as it dropped to the ground where I'd been standing.

⌘

GATHERING FORCES

"I don't think it's an assassination...."
~ Jimmy

Early January...
Conditions in the country were worsening more rapidly than ever, as most reserves of water and food stores had drawn thin. Imports from Canada and elsewhere had become the country's primary food source, and tight restrictions on private commerce made access to it even more difficult. Reliance on our food bank deliveries had become critical for the families we supported.

I had just retrieved coins from Amos' provisions and was making my way back to the Root cellar when, once again, a sudden flash interrupted me.

I FIND myself with Chozeq in the office of Bahal's hotel suite. Devlon and Athaliah are standing before him as he sits behind his desk. The room itself seems to reek with a feeling of haunting evil greater than I've ever felt before.

"Did you get it?" Athaliah asks her father anxiously. The devious look on her face telegraphs the intensity of her ill intent.

Bahal grins and opens the top drawer of his desk, lifting out a golden pendant. He lays it on the desk in front of him.

Athaliah moves closer, planting her hands on the edge of the desk as she leans to admire the ancient object. The pendant seems to glow more brightly as she stares at it, causing her eyes to flash yellow with predatory lust. She begins to reach for it, but Bahal places his hand over it and draws it away from her grasp.

"Not yet!" he thunders in a voice that shakes the room. "It is not yet time. Soon… soon, my child," he says with an evil grin.

Devlon is stone-faced, standing beside the others like a warrior at attention. "The preparations are being made as we speak," he reports. "I've called an emergency summit of the world's leaders to be held on the New Moon. None have declined."

Bahal commends him with an approving smile. "The meeting will take place where I instructed?"

"Yes, at the temple, as you ordered. The meeting location is known only to the leaders and their close bodyguards. They've been told that its secrecy is for security purposes."

Bahal smiles more broadly as he clenches the pendant in his hand anxiously. "You have done well, my son. Very well indeed! It will not be long now — our time is close at hand!"

Athaliah and Devlon lift their heads high and draw in a deep breath as if inhaling the words that Bahal has spoken. Their eyes morph and flash brightly with the evil that burns even more intensely within them.

THE ECHO of Bahal's hair-raising declaration was still ringing in my ears as the scene around me abruptly changed, leaving me standing again in the darkened secret passage.

When I arrived back at the house, Uncle Jim was watching the nightly news. It was even more apocalyptic than ever.

"Fires continue to burn out of control across much of the United States," the news anchor explained as footage showed devastated cities and large swaths of suburbs that had been reduced to ashes.

"The unrest over food and water shortages continues to wreak havoc. Scenes such as these have become all too common in the nation's cities."

The footage showed angry mobs battling National Guard troops amid cityscapes that looked like bombed-out war zones.

ELSEWHERE, Frank DeMassi was pouring over research into the ancient pendant.

"Switch off that TV for us, will ya?" he asked distractedly.

He was speaking to Susan, the former bank hostage he'd rescued when the pendant was stolen. She was doing her best to help him with the scattered memories she was able to piece together from her time as a hostage. The trail had grown ice-cold for locating the escaped thieves.

"Are you sure you want to go into this again?" Frank asked her carefully. "I know it was a rough experience for you."

"I'm sure," she assured him bravely. "If there's a chance we can stop them, then I have to try."

Frank showed her some of what he'd uncovered in his research. "This is a picture of the pendant. There are lots of cheap knock-offs of it around, but apparently, the original was worth killing for."

"Poor Mr. McSheffrey," Susan said sadly.

"That would have been you too," Frank reminded her. She looked back at him warmly and touched his hand. Frank cleared his throat and drew his gaze away from her eyes, refocusing on the array of open books in front of them.

"The pendant was used in ritual sacrifice rites for the pagan god Baal during the reign of King Ahab in Israel. It most likely originated in the city of Tyre, in Phoenicia — modern-day Lebanon. That's where Ahab's queen, Jezebel, was from; she brought that particular form of Baal worship with her.

"It was said that immersing the pendant in the blood of a newborn infant during the ritual ceremony of the New Moon could summon Baal Grimoire to destroy one's enemies or give strength in battle."

"Oh, how horrible," Susan gasped.

Frank agreed with a sigh and nod of his head. He pondered the pages silently for a moment, then began to explore an idea...

"...You said they wanted to use the pendant to assassinate heads of state. If any of this is really possible, then they'll have to time the ritual with some event when all these leaders are together."

"And it will have to be on a new moon," Susan pointed out with a dawning realization.

———

A WEEK LATER...

FRANK AWOKE from a sound sleep and sat bolt upright in his bed. He had just experienced the most vivid dream he'd ever seen. In it, he was running along a broad avenue but couldn't tell for sure where it was.

An army of Secret Service Agents blocked the roadway up ahead, diverting traffic, which had tangled into a gridlocked snarl. From the opposite direction, Frank could see the President's motorcade joining a swarm of others with dignitaries from the world's greatest powers.

Suddenly in his dream, he saw Jimmy, who was pointing at something and shouting to him, but Frank couldn't hear what Jimmy was saying or see what he was pointing at. As he strained to hear and struggled to get closer, he suddenly saw an immense light appear directly in his path and heard the voice that had spoken to him in the churchyard. It thundered so loudly that it made the ground shake beneath his feet.

Franklin James,… you are my servant …**go** in the power
of my might!

The shock of it woke him from sleep. It wasn't the voice itself, or
even its thunderous volume, that had startled him the most. There
was something else — some intense urgency that had permeated the
atmosphere, making his heart race and setting his battle instincts on
full alert.

He quickly reached for his 'special' phone… the one that couldn't
be traced… and sent an urgent message.

A COLD WINTER wind blasted against the farmhouse windows. I took a
sip from the cup in my hand to ease the dry scratch in my throat and
glanced again at my phone to see if there was anything new from
Frank Demassi. His early morning text message had said it was
urgent, but I'd received no reply since responding to it. It wasn't like
him to neglect a message, especially if it was something urgent.

While I was still holding the phone it finally began to ring with his
call.

"FRANK, what's up? Your text said it was urgent."

"I had some more checking to do," Frank explained. "I'm more
certain than ever that the threat is real."

"Threat? What is it this time?" I asked.

"I guess I'd better bring you up to speed," Frank admitted.

"Back in August, there was a bank heist. The thieves stole an
ancient Mesopotamian pendant. We've been tracking it since before
Labor Day…."

Frank went on to explain the pendant's connection with Jezebel
and Baal worship and described what had happened with one of the
hostages.

"Wow, Frank, that's awesome!" I said after hearing how Susan had
been saved.

"Well, I can't argue with that. It was pretty amazing, I agree," he remarked sincerely. "Susan is a pretty amazing woman, too."

"Is…? It sounds like you're still seeing her," I observed with a smile.

"You could say that," he admitted. "She's sitting beside me now, as a matter of fact."

"So, how have you been doing…? I mean since the last time I saw you at the old church. Sorry I haven't done a better job of keeping in touch."

"Don't feel bad; we've both been plenty busy from what I've seen! Anyway, we've been going to church, if that's what you mean. We've gotten plugged into a home study group with some awesome believers."

"You're saying 'we' a lot… when's the wedding?" I joked.

"About two months ago — we got married over Thanksgiving weekend."

I wasn't expecting that bombshell…. "Congratulations! I can't believe it!"

"Thanks. I would have invited you to the wedding but figured it might get awkward for you with all those FBI agents around."

"Speaking of that," he said, getting the conversation back on track, "I reached out to you because of something that happened last night. I guess It was a dream, but it felt like more than that. It was the most realistic dream I've ever had. You were in it."

I wondered immediately whether Frank could be a Traveler too. "Was anyone with you? Did you see anyone unusual?" I probed, trying to see if he'd encountered any angels.

"There were huge crowds, actually, but no one I knew, other than you. The President's motorcade was in it too."

As soon as he mentioned the president, I had an uneasy feeling; the pendant he mentioned suddenly made sense.

"That pendant you mentioned… do you know what it looks like? Have you seen it?" I asked.

"Just pictures of it… here; I'll send you one." I could hear him fumbling with his phone for a minute as he forwarded the image from the museum archives. A moment later, my phone chimed.

The instant I looked at the image, I immediately understood the connection — I knew why Frank had seen me in his dream. I had seen this pendant before.

"What did the scene look like in your dream... did you know where you were?" I asked him.

"No, that was just the thing... I couldn't tell where we were. I was trying to get closer — that's when I saw you. You were pointing toward something in the distance and shouting something, but I couldn't hear what you were saying."

"Frank, I think your dream was a vision of something that's going to happen in the future. Maybe soon. And I know where. The President is going to call an emergency meeting with the heads of state of all the world's leading nations. The location is being kept top secret — the leaders will be told that the secrecy is for their protection, but it's a ruse to get them there alone and unprotected. It's going to be at the glass cathedral in Washington DC."

"How do you know all this?"

"Let's just say that you're not the only one who sees things."

Frank was quiet as he took in the information, then we both blurted out a comment at the same time:

"It will be on the new moon/*It will be on the new moon...*" we both said together.

It didn't surprise either of us that we both knew that.

"The question is, which new moon," I noted.

"I think I know," Frank said, sounding more convinced than ever. "That's what I was checking right before I called you back. The weather was cold in my dream — bitter cold. The next new moon is in two weeks, and the weather service predicts a massive cold front. They're saying that it would be the worst blizzard in a decade if not for the drought.

"And there's something else... Susan and I were researching the pendant. It was used during ritual sacrifice rites for the pagan god Baal during the reign of King Ahab in Israel."

"That figures," I agreed.

"The museum archive said that it was believed that performing the ritual of the pendant during the ceremony of the New Moon could summon Baal Grimoire to destroy one's enemies. When Susan was held hostage, she heard them say that they planned to use the pendant to assassinate heads of state."

A SUDDEN OMINOUS feeling came over me, but the idea of an assassination didn't feel right.

"Assassinate? Did they use that word exactly?" I asked. "Did they actually say they were going to *assassinate* them?"

Susan spoke slowly as if searching her memory carefully. "Yeah, I think so, except maybe not with that word exactly. They said they were going to *take them out.*"

"I don't think it's an assassination," I said as the realization struck me. "They don't plan to kill the other leaders; they plan to enslave them."

"Enslave them? How?" Frank asked. "Talk about starting an international incident — that would be World War Three!"

"I don't mean it like that," I tried to explain. "Frank — you remember all those hideous crimes and unexplainable events that happened right after the glass cathedral dedication?"

"How could I forget. We're still seeing 'em happen — those people are pure evil," Frank confirmed.

"Those were all pagan worshipers who were at Bahal's cathedral. They were possessed that night by demons — they were enslaved."

. . .

FRANK AND SUSAN were quiet as the implications hit them. Frank put the pieces together.... "Baal Grimoire... he's the king of hell. The ritual doesn't just call *him*; it calls his demon army!"

"...And then they take control of the most powerful leaders on earth," I said, finishing the point.

⌘

A HEINOUS PLOT

"It will be on the new moon...."

F rank was parked a block away from the Glass cathedral with his engine running. The night was bitter cold and a frigid wind whipped through the streets with biting fierceness. He watched the clock and kept an eye on several Secret Service SUVs that had taken up positions in the distance.

"Have the dignitaries started arriving yet?" I asked him over our three-way conference line. Susan was listening on the other line.

"Not yet, but the Secret Service is in position."

"How far away are you?"

"Close enough," he answered evasively. His training kept him from giving his position away; he wouldn't assume our conversation was private.

"Any leads yet on the baby?" I asked.

"The FBI has issued an alert to all the city hospitals about a credible threat of a possible newborn abduction. They're all on lockdown."

"Something tells me that's not going to be enough," I worried aloud.

A BEEPING on the line signaled that Frank was getting another call. "It's Nyle," he said as he picked it up, adding him to the conference line.

"The package was delivered," Nyle said secretively. It seemed like he, too, was falling back on his prior training. He was talking about installing his wiretap into the temple's security cameras.

"I'm in," I confirmed, bringing up the Temple's security images on my screen in the root cellar. The temple looked empty except for a janitor with a tool bag who was leaving through the back door. Nyle had chosen a good disguise, I noted to myself as I watched him leave.

"Cars are approaching the back entrance," Nyle said suddenly. He had made it around the corner just in time.

"Can you get a look at them?" Frank asked both of us.

"They're just opening the car door now...." I explained as I watched the outdoor security feed. A woman who was being helped out of the back seat looked oddly familiar. As I struggled to place where I'd seen her before, a sudden memory flashed through my mind. I had seen her at the temple ruins in Tyre... she was one of the priestesses of the goddess Anath — sister-god to Baal. When she emerged and stood beside the car, my heart sank — she was very obviously pregnant!

"I think we found the baby," I said, finding it hard to hide my sadness. "One of the temple priestesses is entering the building, and she's definitely pregnant. Probably full term, from the look of it."

More activity on the screen drew my attention back to the exterior cameras.

"More cars are arriving," I said as I watched. "Looks like Bahal and his security team."

The black limousine pulled in front of the door, flanked in front and behind by black SUVs. Armed guards emerged from the escort vehicles and formed a secure barrier on both sides of Bahal's limousine door as his driver opened it. Bahal looked elated as he stood and admired the glass temple. In truth, it was not admiration that gripped his heart but rather an unrestrained lust for power. Power that was now irresistibly within his grasp.

"How are we ever going to stop them? Look at all those guards and guns!" Anna said as she sat beside me, looking at the screen. Her voice was picked up on the speakerphone.

"That's exactly what we were counting on," Frank replied. "As far as the FBI is concerned, Bahal's men are a clear and present danger to the President."

"I'm sending you the camera footage now," Nyle said.

"Got it. The FBI counter-terrorism unit is already on high alert — once I send this to them, we should have a SWAT team here within minutes," Frank explained.

ACTIVITY IN FRONT of the building signaled that dignitaries were beginning to arrive.

"Cars are starting to show up out front now," I alerted the others.

"I see them," Frank said. "Looks like the first of the European contingents."

As more leaders arrived, I scanned the interior cameras, stopping suddenly at one that appeared to be backstage. The priestess I'd seen arrive earlier was wrestling against a group that restrained her; there were tears in her eyes — she was clearly distraught.

"They're forcing her," I said to the others. "They plan to take her baby by force."

"Oh, that poor woman!" Anna cried. "We have to help her! We have to tell the others to pray for her!"

"We can't give away the operation yet," Frank charged, "but going public with this might not be a bad idea when the time comes."

"In the meantime, maybe we can get the Pastors ready to spread the word," I suggested. Anna nodded and began texting PJ and the others - asking them to stand by.

"OK, HERE COMES SHOWTIME," Frank said, interrupting the conversation. "It's the President's motorcade."

On the camera feed, I saw the President's car pull up, surrounded by Secret Service. Athaliah took Devlon by the arm on the entrance walkway, and he escorted her inside.

In the Temple's main auditorium, the world's leaders were seated facing the stage. They all stood as the President and First Lady were announced, applauding as the first couple made their way down the center aisle. Bahal stood in the front row, barely able to conceal the sinister delight in his eyes as he watched the events unfolding according to plan. Athaliah joined him as Devlon rose to the stage.

FROM THE BACKSTAGE SECURITY CAMERA, we could see that the struggling priestess had fallen silent. It appeared that she had been sedated. An arrangement of lights and surgical apparatus made it clear that they intended to perform a cesarean delivery. A medical team entered the room just as Devlon rose to the podium.

"We have to do something!" Anna exclaimed, "we have to stop them!"

"Did you reach PJ and Pastor Wilkes?" I asked.

"Yes. They're spreading the word that we need prayer for something urgent. They don't know what it's about yet."

"We need more time," Frank said, understanding Anna's concern. "It's not time yet."

FEW IN THE audience noticed that Athaliah made her way out of the auditorium as everyone was taking their seats. Devlon approached the podium and began to address the crowd. Nyle adjusted the audio so that we could hear him....

"As all of you know, my country has been under attack for nearly two years. This climate terrorism has been devastating. You have no doubt witnessed its effects in your travels here.

"Tonight, you will learn the full extent of this threat — it cannot be confined to America alone, I'm afraid."

A buzz ran through the crowd as leaders conferred nervously with each other.

A DOCTOR and several nurses had gathered around the unconscious woman backstage, covering her with sterile sheets. Anna shielded her eyes and looked away as the operation began.

DEVLON HELD everyone's rapt attention: "Our scientists have learned that an enemy nation did not carry out these attacks. In fact, they are not from the earth at all."

A collective gasp of surprise was heard through the crowd.

"The enemy that has attacked us is extraterrestrial — not of this earth."

Gasps grew louder. "What evidence do you have of such a claim?" the French president shouted. The others echoed his remark.

"The evidence will be shown to you in due time, I assure you. This news must be kept in the strictest confidence. If it were revealed to the public-at-large untold panic would ensue across the globe."

Devlon shifted his remarks to speak of the importance of banding together against this unprecedented threat. He continued for some time....

"Now..." Devlon finally said as he concluded his lengthy remarks. "It is fitting that we should meet here in this beautiful Temple of Human Enlightenment to pledge our unity as a single human race. This is a Temple for all people, not just the American people. It is time for us to come together as one people — the people of earth. We must now confront this terrible challenge together!"

He turned and waved his hand toward Athaliah, who had entered the stage behind him dressed in her ceremonial robes and horned headdress. She bowed dramatically as spotlights focused on her.

"In honor of this great coming together, my beautiful wife Athaliah — our nation's first Secretary of Unity — has agreed to lead us in a ceremony that reminds us of the common ancient traditions of our many cultures. An expression of the universal yearning that exists in all people, everywhere."

ATHALIAH ROSE to the podium with her hands raised.

"MY FATHER BUILT the gorgeous structure you see around you as a gift — not only to the people of this nation but also to all the people of the world. It is a cathedral of unity, not of division or exclusion. Here we have unified all religions, and tonight we will unify all nations. Together we reflect the human spirit — a spirit that reaches and aspires to attain the greatest longing of our hearts. Peace... acceptance... and the freedom to be what we choose to be!"

THE LECTERN SLOWLY LOWERED INTO the stage floor as she turned and began an elegant dance, spinning and bowing with the graceful movements of a practiced dancer. The crowd was mesmerized by her flowing dance, drawn in by her grace and beauty.

She turned toward the colossal tower of religious symbols and gracefully crossed her extended arms as she bowed to it, dropping to one knee.

AT JUST THAT MOMENT, the cries of a newborn baby could be heard from the backstage security camera as an infant was lifted into the air.

"IT'S TIME NOW!" Susan broke in over the phone line. "The baby has been born — this is where the ceremony of the pendant begins!"

"THE SECURITY FOOTAGE is on its way to Counter Terrorism now...." Frank said, confirming that he understood.

We heard the tires of Frank's SUV spin out wildly as he stomped on the gas and could hear his voice on the radio speaking to the FBI central command.

"There's an impending threat to the President at the Glass Cathedral... I repeat, an impending threat to the President! All units respond immediately to that location. Send SWAT Special Forces to meet me at the Temple's rear entrance; all other units stand by to enter through the front on my mark."

ANNA GOT a call on her phone from Josh... "Josh says the Podcast is live. He sent an emergency SMS alert to all its subscribers — do you want him to Livestream the feed from the temple?"

"Yes! Do it — get everyone to pray! Pray now!" I said anxiously as I felt the urgency in my spirit suddenly surging.

In seconds the podcast was broadcasting the live scenes from the temple — I cut in to explain....

"We need your prayers right now! The world's leaders are in danger, and a deadly threat to the entire world is unfolding as we speak — we need everyone to pray for God's intervention! Forces of incredible darkness are being summoned. It's a ceremony of human sacrifice!"

A SPLIT-SCREEN SHOWED a pair of attendants in priestess robes taking the baby from one of the nurses while Athaliah rose from her knee, holding the golden pendant. It glowed ominously as it dangled from a long chain in her hands. She lifted it above her head and kissed it reverently, then placed it around her neck.

Looking up at the tower of idols, she spread her hands, once again causing the center of the tower to melt open, revealing the golden statue of Baal.

Several leaders in the audience stood to their feet at once in objection.

"What is the meaning of this!" the President of Nigeria exclaimed indignantly.

Before any of them could move, a contingent of Bahal's security forces surrounded the dignitaries. Frantic calls by the leaders to their bodyguards went unanswered.

A flurry of dark forces immediately gathered in the air above them. They streamed above their heads menacingly like streaking shadows, forcing them into their seats.

Athaliah didn't turn to look at the audience. Instead, she focused all of her attention on Baal's image. She bowed her head to it with her palms together, and fingers pointed upward in a praying gesture that touched her forehead. Then she dropped to one knee in front of a small altar that held a golden basin. As she knelt, she raised the pendant above her head and gently placed it inside the golden basin. Its chain was left dangling over the edge.

The priestesses emerged onto the stage with the wailing infant, presenting him to Athaliah.

Anna gasped and broke into sobs as she saw Athaliah lift the child in offering to Baal. The newborn boy's tiny lungs screamed for all he was worth as he shivered in the cold air. The air seemed to be growing even colder as the darkness grew thicker around them.

Athaliah's voice thundered unnaturally as she loudly cried out....

> "Worship the great Ba'al who comes to walk with us upon the earth!"

The priestesses held the baby as Athaliah lifted a golden dagger from the altar.

"FRANK! You have to go in now! There's no more time!" Susan screamed over the phone.

⌘

RULERS OF DARKNESS

"We wrestle not against flesh and blood, but against principalities, against powers, against the rulers of the darkness of this world, against spiritual wickedness in high places. "
~ Ephesians 6:12

All across the world, viewers logged into the podcast in response to the urgent alert. In turn, they contacted their friends and churches as the massive force of prayer warriors grew rapidly around the globe.

AT THE LARGE inner-city church in Harbor City, PJ had interrupted his service with former gang members — now hundreds strong — to join in the urgent call to pray. The podcast was projected onto the main screen.

"God do your miracles! Stop these evil things!" Badrick could be heard shouting in prayer as others earnestly echoed his pleas.

PJ stood gripping the pulpit with his head bowed low, sensing a grave urgency in his spirit as he prayed silently. The spiritual power in the room resonated so greatly that it seemed to shake the walls around them.

THE EVENTS that happened next occurred so rapidly that they were virtually simultaneous....

Doors suddenly burst inward at the front and rear of the building as Frank and his FBI SWAT teams rushed the auditorium. Bahal's men fired on the rushing officers, sending bullets ricocheting off their riot shields. The Heads of State dove to the floor, following whatever emergency protocols they'd been taught, or perhaps just following pure instinct.

At the same instant, Frank rushed onto the stage from the opposite direction with several agents who surrounded the priestesses and wrestled for the baby.

Athaliah seemed unfazed by the chaos around her as she lifted her arms in the air — her eyes were now turned bright yellow. With a voice that echoed in a deep thunderous bellow, she uttered some strange incantation in a language I couldn't understand. All at once, the shadowy creatures that swirled in the air took form — their leathery wings and devilish faces becoming clearly visible. The demon creatures attacked the FBI agents throughout the auditorium, lifting some of them into the air.

AMOS' words rushed through my head without warning:

> "When that day comes, you'll know it's arrived; there
> won't be any doubting it."

That was the instant when a bright flash engulfed the place where I was sitting in the root cellar, and I found myself suddenly standing on the edge of the stage beside Athaliah. Anna looked for me frantically before seeing me in the temple's feed — barely able to believe what she was seeing. She rushed to the chair where I'd been sitting and spoke urgently into the camera, asking everyone on the podcast to storm Heaven!

AN IRRESISTIBLE INSPIRATION filled my thoughts, and I heard myself shouting in a loud voice...

THE LORD OF HOSTS RESISTS YOU!

As the words left my lips, the golden basin was flung off the altar as if it had been blasted aside by the words' impact. It tumbled across the stage, sending the pendant sliding over the floor where it landed at Frank's feet. He quickly grabbed it, just as several agents finally handcuffed the priestesses, and another agent sheltered the baby inside her vest and rushed him to safety.

Athaliah ignored me, still obsessed with regaining the pendant. She pointed toward Frank and the others and shouted to the hellish minions in the air above...

"Bring me that pendant and the child!"

I saw a swarm of the creatures begin to swoop toward them with their deadly talons extended. My shoulder erupted in blazing pain as I shouted at the creatures.... "

STAY BACK, CREATURES OF HELL! **YOU ARE BOUND** IN THE NAME OF THE KING OF HEAVEN AND EARTH — JESUS OF NAZARETH!"

The vicious swarm shrieked loudly as they were immediately consumed in a flash of Hell's roaring fire that sucked them from mid-air.

Athaliah became enraged and lifted the dagger in her hand, clearly intending to kill Frank and everyone near him as she demanded the pendant. Frank looked at her yellow cat-like eyes and felt sudden intense indignation in his spirit. Words repeated loudly in his mind as if being spoken once again:

> *My Spirit goes before you, casting down imaginations and*
> *every high thing that is exalted against the knowledge*
> *of God!*

Athaliah suddenly shrieked in pain as a blinding light struck her. Unbeknownst to Frank, the intense light came from the seal of God on his own forehead. She staggered backward and fell to her knees, momentarily blinded, trying to feel her way across the stage. Overhead, the air in the temple had become filled with Ardent's bright warriors. They struck the demon creatures with fiery wounds, driving them away from the agents below.

DEVLON LEAPED onto the stage in Athaliah's defense, his own eyes now glowing bright red. He began toward Frank and the pendant, shielding his eyes until my shout stopped him...

...MOLOCH!

He turned toward me with a hateful glare and straightened tall.

"**Puny human child...**" he thundered. "**You think you are strong enough to challenge *me*?**" The floor beneath our feet shook as he spoke — it was as if the building itself trembled in his presence.

"**You have been a thorn in our side for long enough. Tonight you will feel my vengeance!**"

AT THAT EXACT MOMENT, the church where PJ prayed with hundreds of former gang members became suddenly engulfed in a mighty move of the Spirit. The unity and urgency with which they prayed shook the church — just as it shook Heaven itself!

I FELT an incredible surge of anointing come over me as I looked at Devlon's demon-filled eyes. I shouted loudly at the creature that possessed him:

"I CLAIM NO POWER AT ALL. IT IS JESUS THE LORD OF HOSTS WHO DECREES JUDGMENT AGAINST YOU TONIGHT!
"...COME OUT OF THIS MAN!"

Like the blast of a hurricane, a wind swept across the auditorium, striking Devlon with enormous fury. The demon-prince was blasted into the air as Devlon's shattered body was thrown backward and slid across the floor.

The demon was hideous looking, with a colossal horned-form and large snake-like eyes that glowed bright red. He stood and stared at me defiantly with an evil glare. "**I serve no king by that name!**" he boasted. At that, he reared his head back and opened his mouth wide with a fierce and terrifying roar that shook the temple's roof and walls violently.

Chozeq appeared at my side as I faced the enraged demon-prince. Words that my angelic friend had spoken to me long ago instantly filled my mind:

> *"We know their weakness. What are they but fallen and powerless creatures? They roar and swell like waves of the sea, foaming out their own shame. Yet when the Lord arises, they fly as chaff before the wind and are soon consumed as crackling thorns in the fire. They are so utterly powerless to do damage to the cause of God that the weakest soldiers in Zion's ranks may laugh them to scorn."*

The huge demon prince reached a hoofed arm toward the idol of Baal above us and shouted a thundering command. Instantly the golden statue moved like a living thing. It stood and then leaped to the stage below, landing with a shattering impact that sent splintered wood into the air. Frank dove from the stage and scrambled for cover as the beastly golden image started toward me, smashing everything in its path. Surprisingly, I felt no fear; instead, I looked intently at Moloch himself.

"You have pronounced judgment by your own words," I shouted. "In denying obedience to your true King, you have sealed your own fate."

A pair of huge golden fists smashed downward directly on top of me — just as I reappeared in a flash on the opposite side of the stage. Splintered wood was thrown into the air from the place where I had just been standing. The sounds of snapping wood continued as the floor beneath the golden beast gave way, sending it tumbling into the basement below. The building shuddered as Baal's image smashed and clawed from below, unable to climb free.

Moloch reached upward toward the wall of idols again, aiming for the statue of Anath. Before he could utter another profane command, I felt the Spirit of the Lord rise up within me. Once again, the words that Chozeq had spoken filled my thoughts…

"Remember that ye are an earthen vessel in which is contained an infinite power and the riches of Heaven itself!"

I shouted the words that the Spirit spoke through me…

"…Be . . . Still !"

Moloch seemed frozen, his voice suddenly silenced. A new look of realized terror filled his face as he stared down at me in shock.

"By the command of Jesus, King of all Kings, your time on earth has ended. You are banished to chains until the day of your final judgment!"

He tried to escape, flailing his wings frantically, while a giant vortex opened in the air behind him, pulling him toward its roaring fire. He thundered in terrified protest as he tumbled backward into the gaping portal and was swallowed up in its burning fire.

The vast portal filled the temple with the terrifying sounds of raging Hellfire and loud screeching of doomed souls as its yawning mouth began to draw in the other hellish beasts. They cried in terror and clawed at one another for escape until their entire number had been swallowed in the raging inferno. Finally, as it drew itself closed, the swirling portal violently shook and twisted what remained of the tower of idols, bringing it crashing to the floor in a pulverized pile of rubble.

Looking around at the scene that remained, I slowly registered the sight. The temple was nearly destroyed, with huge gashes in the floor and crumbling walls. Sections of the roof had large precarious cracks in their glass panes. An army of FBI and Secret Service agents stood staring wide-eyed at me with their mouths hanging open while pieces of paper and debris floated to the ground from the air above.

Coming to their senses, several of them began to drag away what remained of Bahal's security force in handcuffs.

Devlon lay unconscious a few feet away, and several Secret Service agents cautiously approached to check on him. They looked at me with dazed expressions as if they were afraid to come any nearer.

There was no sign of Athaliah or Bahal, who had taken advantage of the chaos to make their escape.

For the most part, all of the world leaders had fled the building, except for a few brave souls who stood staring at the stage speechlessly. Among those were the Nigerian president and the British and Israeli Prime Ministers, who looked at me and bowed their heads respectfully. I bowed mine in return, feeling humbled by their gesture, and then disappeared from their sight.

THE MOMENT I reappeared in the root cellar, Anna shouted my name in surprise and then threw her arms around my neck. A complex swirl of emotions overcame her as she held onto me with all her strength and quietly wept.

⌘

AFTERMATH

"President Sheen is awake.... He asked to meet with you."
~ Obediah

C aden was seated at the anchor desk at WCST TV News reporting on the events of the previous evening. Images from the Glass Cathedral repeated on-screen as she described the extraordinary scenes. News broadcasts worldwide were replaying the shocking footage from inside the cathedral and from news crews gathered outside. They showed clear images of demon-creatures battling with brilliant white angelic warriors, inside and in the sky above the cathedral. Replays of the podcast itself had already topped one hundred million views.

I had to admit that the scenes of Moloch's attack looked pretty terrifying. His golden idol can be clearly seen smashing its way through a blizzard of splintered wood, followed by the sight of the hideous demon prince being pulled into a mid-air vortex and swallowed in Hellfire. The clear recording left most commentators speechless.

"There is no news on the condition of President Sheen," Caden explained on-air. "He is said to be under the care of White House physicians but has not, as yet, regained consciousness. Until his return, Vice President Strident is empowered to discharge the duties of the President."

I couldn't help breathing a prayer for Devlon. In a way, he had been a victim of the plot by Bahal and Athaliah, who used him for their schemes. Nonetheless, his own decisions had led him there. Still, God's love for him was evident — if there were any hope for him at all, it would be by the redeeming hand of God Himself.

"In related news," Caden continued, "First Lady Athaliah Sheen issued a statement early today refuting reports that she had intended to harm the infant. She insists that the ceremony was, I quote, 'a celebration of life that was viciously attacked by rogue factions within our government.'

"The baby has been reunited with his mother, who adamantly maintains that he was forcibly taken against her will. Mother and child are resting safely now at an undisclosed hospital."

MY PHONE's ringing drew my attention — it was Frank DeMassi.

"The pendant is on its way back to Bagdad," he explained. "They've promised to keep it in the bullet-proof glass vault that we shipped it in."

"Thanks, I hope that's enough," I said honestly.

"You and me both," Frank agreed. "If it were up to me, I would have melted it down."

"Thanks for doing what you did last night," I said sincerely.

"No sweat, kid, it's what I do. That was one heck of a ride, I have to admit."

I agreed with his choice of words: "Yeah, you could definitely say that!"

"So, now what? Any clues about what happens next?" he asked.

I glanced over at Amos' journal on my desk and considered his question. "Some," I said carefully, trying not to sound mysterious.

"I get it; you can't tell me," Frank accepted. "I wanna let ya know that you've got a lot of friends now in the Agency. Last night changed everything — nearly everyone who saw what happened has got your back."

ATHALIAH WAS CLEARLY NOT one of those people. It didn't take long before she was back on the offensive. She used Devlon's injury and the so-called terrorist attack at the cathedral as excuses to push through new mandates for attacking 'Terrorist Factions,' which had become her go-to term for churches and synagogues. Vice President Strident seemed all too happy to support the crackdown. Within days a new offensive began, rounding up Pastors and leaders. It quickly began tapping the Legal Defense Fund at a furious rate.

Mr. O. was grateful for the resources to post bail and provide legal defense for thousands of arrested workers. The Defense Fund's legal team was defending cases in all fifty states. Many of those were quickly making their way through Federal Appellate courts.

IT WAS **about a week** after the events at the Cathedral when Devlon suddenly regained consciousness. He immediately made two unusual requests ....

The first one surprised the doctors: "Don't let Athaliah or anyone else other than Obadiah know I'm awake."

The second one shocked them: "Tell Obadiah that I need to meet with the Moretti boy... right away!"

THE APPEARANCE OF THE NAME 'SILAS' on my caller ID didn't particularly surprise me, although it had been a while since we last talked.

"President Sheen is awake," he said after a brief hello. "He asked to meet with you."

At first, I thought Obadiah was kidding with me, although joking was admittedly a little out of character for him. When he didn't laugh, I decided to probe further.

"Do you think that's wise? I mean, I can't really walk into the White House, can I?"

"To be honest, he's not at the White House, and officially he's still in a coma," Obadiah explained, making me even more confused. "Is there someplace where we can meet? I'll explain more when I see you."

I paused in thought... there was no way to be sure it wasn't a trap. On the other hand, I had no reason to doubt Obadiah's good intentions, and God had certainly proved that He can keep me safe if He wants me to be.

"OK, Sure. Bring Agent DeMassi. He'll know the place."

I HAD JUST HUNG up the phone when it rang again. It was Anna this time.

"They've arrested PJ and Reverend Wilkes again," she reported as if it was just another news event.

"I guess that's no surprise," I sighed. "I'll let Mr. O' know that they need help."

"No need. Sheriff Flanagan already spoke to him," she said, bringing me up to date.

"Mom and I will be over soon to help with the food deliveries," she added.

While she was talking, Pete walked in the front door.

"Pete's here now to start packing them. See you when you get here."

FRIDAY NIGHT...

THE WEATHER WAS NOT AS frigid as it was on the night of the temple events a few weeks ago, but it still felt uncomfortably cold as I closed the mausoleum gate and made my way around behind the church.

I sat shivering on the cold stone steps as I waited for Obadiah, finally realizing that meeting out here in the middle of winter wasn't my most brilliant idea.

The solitude in the old churchyard was comforting, however. I thought about the night Frank was saved and the amazing commission he'd received from the Lord here on these steps. The memories inspired a grateful prayer, and I closed my eyes in thanks.

As I did, I was surprised to feel a sudden familiar pull, and seconds later, my surroundings changed in a flash of light.

I QUICKLY RECOGNIZE the dirty basement room in the old tenement building where I'm now standing. Rad is alone - there's no sign of the friends who were with him when I visited here twice before. Both of those visits were on the night that PJ would be stabbed — the night of Chase's execution. From what I can see this time, it looks like a lot has changed since then.

As tough and mean as this older version of Rad appears to be, his eyes are red with a hint that he's been crying. The blood on his knuckles and face are a clue that he's been in a fight, but that's clearly not what caused the tears. Somehow I understand that what has driven him to tears has more to do with the friends who are no longer here. Their absence is ominous — they were the closest thing to a family he ever had.

I watch as he pulls a crumpled paper from his pocket and carefully unfolds it. It's worn-looking and a little yellowed. The creases are wearing thin along the folds from being opened and refolded many times. I recognize it as the letter PJ gave him — the note from his father.

He stares at it, his eyes racing along the lines as he silently reads the words, and a single tear rolls down his cheek.

ANOTHER FLASH INTERRUPTED THE SCENE, bringing me back to the churchyard. I wondered why God had shown me that particular scene, pondering what connection it might have with tonight's meeting with Obadiah.

A short while later, Frank's SUV pulled up the drive. Frank called from his window with an invitation for me to climb in the back. Grateful to get out of the cold, I quickly climbed in and closed the door before looking around.

As I expected, Obadiah was seated in the front passenger seat. I was shocked, however, to see who sat beside me in the back... President Sheen.

"YOU'RE a difficult young man to get a hold of," Devlon said as he offered to shake my hand.

"You're a pretty difficult man to hide from," I answered as I accepted his handshake.

"If I had known that Obadiah and Agent DeMassi could contact you so easily, I may have attempted it sooner. I'm sure you know that they've taken a great personal risk in arranging this meeting. They obviously believe in you."

"I think that shows a lot of trust in you too," I noted. I studied Devlon's eyes for any reason to doubt that assessment — he seemed honestly sincere. "I'm glad you're OK," I added.

"That's what I wanted to talk to you about. Let's just say that I've had time to think in the past few weeks — things have suddenly become much clearer to me."

He sat studying my face for a moment before adding: "I sense a very different... presence... in you than in most men. I suppose that after a man has experienced the presence of evil as closely as I have, its opposite is also plainly seen." There was deep regret in his eyes as he spoke of his association with evil. "The presence I sense in you is, I think... holy." He seemed momentarily taken aback as if the very fact that he was able to make such an observation surprised him.

After a second, he collected himself and bowed his head slightly in a humble gesture. "I wanted to thank you for what you did at the temple. I have to admit; I didn't fully appreciate what had occurred until Obadiah showed me the video of those events."

"It was God who did that. I was just a vessel He used, that's all."

Devlon nodded that he understood, then grew more serious. "Athaliah and her father are very dangerous. There is a level of evil in them that is unnatural — I can see that plainly now. To be honest, I fear what they will do when they learn that I've awakened."

"The evil in them *is* unnatural, that's true," I agreed. "But you don't have to be afraid of them. There's a way to be free of their power — a way that they can't possibly touch you in the way that they did before. You can have the seal of God on your soul."

DEVLON GREW quiet for a moment and looked at me with obvious trepidation.

"W-what did you say?" he stammered.

"The seal of God," I repeated. "When a soul belongs to Christ, it receives the protection of the God of Heaven... He places His seal on us. It's the proof and pronouncement that we are His."

He stared at me with an odd look for a moment, and then he wrung his hands as he looked down at them, explaining.... "That phrase, I've heard it before... I heard it repeated over and over while I was in the hospital. They thought I was unconscious, but I wasn't — at least not all the time. I heard a lot of what was happening around me... and I heard *that*. I'm just realizing now that it was *your* voice, saying what you just said: '*You can have the seal of God on your soul.*'"

I glanced at Frank and Obadiah, and they acknowledged the same thing that I was suddenly feeling — a call to pray. They both bowed their heads in intercession. The Spirit's presence in the car was growing stronger by the moment.

"God brought you here for a reason," I said, stating the obvious. "But it requires a decision on your part. Are you ready to make that choice?"

"I'm not sure it's as easy as that," he worried. "I can't imagine that God wants me — I've been one of His worst enemies." A sudden look of deep sorrow came over him as he said that. He didn't try to explain what he was feeling; he didn't need to. It was clear that whatever had happened to him during his days in the hospital had definitely changed his heart. The rocky ground there had been turned to rich fertile soil. With his conscience suddenly awakened, he struggled to maintain his composure as a lifetime of painful regrets loomed before his eyes.

I MERELY PLACED my hand on his shoulder, and it was as if floodgates were blown open. Devlon bent forward and held his head in his hands as he began to shake. It soon became apparent that he was sobbing.

I started to pray for him silently but had no sooner closed my eyes than I suddenly found myself gone from there in a flash of light.

⌘

SAVED IN TIME

"Are you ready to meet Him?"
~ Jimmy

Rad is still sitting alone, gripping his father's letter. Tears have made streaks in the bloody smudges and dirt on his face. I watch in alarm as he lifts a gun, staring at it as he struggles with the pain gripping his soul. He has started to raise it to his head when he is interrupted by a knock on the basement door.

With a sudden shift in his demeanor from hopelessness to aggression, he grips the gun as he starts toward the door and looks out through the peephole. Then his hand drops loosely to his side, letting the gun dangle as he slowly unlatches the lock and looks out. I'm surprised by the voice I hear from outside. It's a voice I recognize, although slightly older sounding.

"Yo - Rad, mon, I'm sorry to hear it — really true-like I am. Them boys was family to ya, I know it."

Rad just left the door open and collapsed back into a chair. His face again reflects the unsettling mix of emotions swirling inside him — anger, pain, loss, guilt, sorrow....

Badrick pushes the door closed and takes a seat beside him. He glances at the unfolded paper... "What's that, a letter?"

Rad doesn't open his eyes as he subtly points to it. "It was from my father," he manages to say. The words seem to inflict pain as he says them.

"Ah... dat letter. PJ spoke 'bout it. He was thinkin' ya trashed it long ago.... What's it say?"

"Didn't PJ read it? I figured it was him who wrote it for Chase." There's more than a slight trace of sarcasm in Rad's voice.

Badrick knows that Rad wouldn't have saved it all this time if he believed that that was true. "No, mon. PJ said he never read it. He said it was a private letter from a dad to his own son. You know dat's true."

"I never even knew my dad," Rad said, holding his hand against his forehead. "He was never there... my whole life... he never even existed."

"He was in d'prison, mon. How could he be 'dare fer ya? Dat don't mean he didn't love ya."

Rad shook his head, disagreeing. "He had a chance to get out. He coulda been pardoned. He chose to save some other guy instead o' comin' home. He cared more about that murderer than he did about me!"

Badrick waited for the words to fade before quietly responding. "You y'self knows 'bout murderin' — don't ya think he woulda done th' same thing fer you as he did fer dat man?"

Rad's face contorted in sorrow as a pair of tears escaped and ran down his cheeks. He couldn't bring himself to answer Badrick's question.

"I know what y're feelin'— I been 'dare in your shoes. God is doin' somethin' this very night. Th' sorrow y're feelin' is a gift... I know it don't feel like it, but it is. It's God's hand on you — breakin' that hard stone heart. He'll break it all th' way open if y'll let Him. He'll open it so He can get inside and clean up the mess that's in 'dare."

I SUDDENLY FELT DEVLON'S shoulder shake beneath my hand as he shuddered in unrestrained sobs. The transition back to Frank's car was jarring, but I immediately realized that the two scenes were remarkably similar. If I had to choose the two most unlikely candidates on earth to be found in this scenario, both Devlon and Rad would have been at the top of that list — along with Bahal and Athaliah, of course. Still, that was pretty telling company to be in.

"What you're feeling is God's doing," I said to Devlon, admittedly paraphrasing Badrick's words. "It's the Holy Spirit's rending of a heart in order to open and cleanse it. You can't do it yourself — repentance is something that comes when God moves; it's a divine act. It's His knocking on your heart's door.

"There's a decision that we have to make when He knocks... we have to choose whether to welcome Him or harden our heart. Choosing is honestly the only thing He asks us to do — the only thing we *can* do. No other deeds can earn His pardon — no acts that we could ever do are good enough to deserve it. He only asks for surrender.

"If you're willing to do that, then you can go from here tonight with God's seal on your soul — as His beloved child."

The power of God's move in Devlon's soul was palpable — there was a sense of the Spirit's presence that filled the car... and the whole churchyard around us! I could see that Obadiah was wiping tears from his own eyes as the burden of intercession weighed on him heavily. Frank's head leaned against the steering wheel as he urgently prayed — sensing the Spirit's intense concern. Devlon continued to shudder as his remorse broke loose. After a lifetime of being stifled and denied, it suddenly felt to him like an uncontrollable flood.

AWASH IN TEARS, Rad leans over in the chair and drops his head into his hands, letting his gun drop to the floor. Badrick quickly pushes it away, sliding it under a chair out of sight as he places his hand on Rad's shaking shoulder.

Once again, I'm momentarily stunned as I reorient myself to the change in scene but quickly join my heart with Badrick as he starts to pray.

"Oh God, You're a God o' miracles! What yer doin' right now in Rad's heart... it's a miracle, Lord. Break open his heart o' stone an' give 'im a new one... a heart o' flesh that's clean an' in tune with your voice."

"Rad, listen to me, mon. God is wanting' t'save ya t'night. I've been sent fer a reason. This here is yer appointment wit' th' God o' Heaven.

"I know PJ preached to ya all 'bout it. I'm guessin' that yer dad wrote about it in his letter too. He wanted t' see ya someday in Heaven. He's waitin' there for ya."

Rad shook his head with a look of hopeless despair. "I ain't like my dad... I can't be good like he was. God don't want anybody like me."

"Trust me, mon — here's da honest truth... ya can't earn it an' ya don't deserve it. Ya jus' gotta accept it. Jesus did all th' earnin' already. He did it for ya."

THIS TIME the atmosphere in Frank's SUV is like a raging spiritual flood as I'm abruptly re-emerged in it. I can sense Devlon's struggle as I look at him, bowed in remorse. Words begin to fill my thoughts, and I speak them aloud for Devlon to hear.

"Jesus said, 'Come to me everyone who is heavy laden, and I'll give you rest.' He said, 'Drink the water that I give, and it will be a well-spring of joy springing up unto everlasting life.'

"God is right here with us... I know you can feel Him here. He hasn't come to judge you. Your sin was already judged when Christ bore it on the cross. He's here tonight to meet you — to welcome you. He's here to accept you.

"Are you ready to meet Him?"

RAD IS NODDING his head yes in answer to nearly the same question asked by Badrick.

"Come on an' kneel wit' me mon," he says as he invites Rad to turn and kneel beside his chair. Rad's tears are flowing freely now as he drops to his knees. The room has begun to feel like holy ground. I look around me at a group of angelic messengers who have started to arrive, delivering answers to a lifetime of prayers from Chase and Rad's grandmother, as well as the prayers of many others.

Rad's brokenness is a stark contrast to the bitterness and pride I had seen before. He is openly weeping as he struggles to pray along with Badrick.

DEVLON WAS SHAKING his head hesitantly in answer to my question. It seemed the path for him would not be as straight as Rad's. Devlon struggled as though his heart and soul were entangled in a tremendous conflict. A battle was raging inside him — a war for his soul.

A sudden awareness stirred within me as I sat beside him. There was another presence with us — something evil, and it seemed to be growing stronger.

I BREATHED a prayer for help and immediately found myself rising from the seat. At least, that's what it felt like. I quickly realized that 'I' wasn't moving at all; in fact, no one was. It dawned on me what was happening... I was 'traveling' in the same space as my physical body. I was moving outside of time while my body and the others around me remained within it — frozen in place.

The scene immediately brought to mind a similar experience that I'd had several years before, on the day before the tent was raised. That time, I recalled, everything in the natural world stood frozen in time, but the bat-winged hoards and angelic armies — the supernatural things — moved freely.

The implication became clear. I searched for the evil presence that could still be felt, scanning the car and Devlon himself. That's when something caught my eye — there was some kind of red mist oozing from his coat pocket. However, as I watched, I realized that the mist wasn't coming *from* his pocket but rather moving *toward* it.

I followed the mist's trail, which stretched like long smoky tendrils to Devlon's side door. I moved upward, passing as I expected, through the solid roof of the SUV, just as I'd done dozens of times in travels with Chozeq. The source of the evil assault became apparent as soon as I emerged into the night outside.

A few yards from the car, I saw a strange distortion — a breach in time. I recognized it because I'd seen it before — it was a swirling vortex, a whirlwind in time.

I could see through it to what was on the other side... and what I saw nearly made my blood run cold. It was Athaliah herself.

She appeared to be engaged in some kind of divination ritual. There were candles burning and ritual implements, and her ancient book was lying open. An image on the book's open page caught my eye — I knew I'd seen it somewhere before. Then it struck me — it was a picture of another pendant that I'd seen being worn by Athaliah's brother — the pendant of Moloch. The image in the book seemed to glow with an eerie red aura as she spoke her strange incantations over it.

IN A FLASH, I was back at Devlon's side with a sudden understanding of what I needed to do. Reaching into his coat pocket, I pulled out the pendant. It glowed red as I held it by its chain.

"This is the pendant of Moloch," I said to Devlon as he looked at it in surprise.

"H-how?" he began to ask... "I was wearing it at the temple," he recalled as it came to him. "They must have put it there at the hospital... in the coat pocket." He looked at me with concern... "When Athaliah placed that around my neck...."

"That was when Moloch entered you," I finished his sentence. "Moloch is gone, but Athaliah is using this to cloud your mind. We have to destroy it."

"Destroy it? How?" He asked, anxiously agreeing.

"I have an idea," I said, climbing out of the car. I was praying that the sudden idea that had just entered my mind was inspired. It honestly seemed crazy as I thought about it — I was pretty sure that the others would have stopped me if I'd told them what I planned to do.

EVERYONE JUMPED out of the car to watch as I ran a few yards further up the old dirt drive and used my best pitching arm to let the pendant fly high into the air — far out into the empty field behind the church-yard. The glowing red disc was still airborne when a colossal bolt of lightning struck it in midair, vaporizing it without a trace. At the exact moment that it exploded, a vision rushed through my mind of Athaliah's book bursting into flames.

The tremendous peel of thunder was still reverberating as Devlon collapsed to his knees in the middle of the dirt driveway. There was no longer any sign of hesitation as he willingly bowed his head. The rest of us knelt on the ground around him and placed our hands on his shoulders as he anxiously surrendered his heart to Christ, right there on the dirt drive. The newest soul to be redeemed on that old church's sacred ground.

⌘

AWAKENING

"How do I undo the damage?"
~ Devlon

D evlon sat at the ceremonial desk used for signing important Bills and Proclamations. Cameras and reporters filled the room in front of him. His sudden reappearance at the White House just an hour earlier had surprised everyone, including the First Lady. The two of them had not spoken since the night of the new moon, three weeks prior.

Aside from Obadiah, no one on the President's staff had even known that he'd awakened from his coma — not even Vice President Strident. The Press was scrambling to get the story. Questions abounded over his part in the events at the temple. Athaliah awaited answers most of all — she'd lost all connection to Devlon since Friday's events at the church when her ancient book of occult spells mysteriously burst into flames and was reduced to ashes.

Devlon signaled that he was ready to begin, and the room fell perfectly silent.

. . .

"I'M sure that many of you have questions about my absence since the events at the temple. I'm thankful to report that I am fully recovered and feeling well. As you have undoubtedly seen from the video footage, those events were dramatic proof that dark supernatural forces have been at work in our country. I'm here to confirm from first-hand experience that that is true."

Athaliah bristled with outrage as she listened.

The President continued, "Those events — and especially their aftermath — have opened my eyes to that reality. It has become undeniably clear to me now that the true cause for our nation's terrible calamity is not terrorism. Rather, as our young prophetic friend has said, it is due to our turning away from God. I regret my part in that turning, and I am urging every American to turn back again to the God in whom we have trusted for generations. I urge all of us to pray for our nation and for God's mercy upon us.

"As a first gesture of that reconciliation, I am here today to sign a full executive pardon to James Moretti." Devlon read from the proclamation:

"By virtue of the power and authority in me vested by the Constitution, and in the name of the sovereign people of the United States, I do hereby proclaim and declare unconditionally, and without reservation, that James Matthew Moretti and any who have provided aid and comfort to him or indirectly participated in the acts that had been deemed criminal or treasonous against the United States are hereby pardoned with the restoration of all rights, privileges, and immunities under the Constitution and the laws which have been made in pursuance thereof."

Most of those in the room could not see Ardent's imposing figure standing beside Devlon, drawing his flaming sword in the president's defense. Except, that is, for Athaliah and the gathering hoard of shadowy imps who filled the room, hovering above the reporters' heads.

His protection quickly discouraged any thought of an attack by those dark forces. In angry frustration, Athaliah stifled the rant of curses that filled her heart and abruptly left the room, taking her sulking minions with her.

IMMEDIATELY FOLLOWING THE CEREMONY, Devlon asked Obadiah to join him in the Oval Office.

"Please arrange to have my things moved to the Lincoln Bedroom and have a guard posted at the door," Devlon requested. "If Athaliah could have breathed fire just now, she certainly would have. I dread the thought of being in the same room."

He settled into his chair behind the Resolute Desk... "Gather together all of my executive orders. We'll need to rescind most of them."

Obadiah nodded and took a note.

Devlon restlessly stood again and walked to the window, looking out over the National Mall. The huge reflecting pool in the distance was empty and dry; small whirlwinds of dust flared up here and there like faint Tasmanian Devils in the cold, dry air. The surrounding lawns had long ago withered and died.

"How do I undo the damage?" he asked half under his breath, to no one in particular.

"The country is severely wounded," Obadiah agreed. "Its healing will take time."

"What was it that Jimmy said?" Devlon queried, "...that night outside the temple — when the drought first began. He said something about God healing the country again."

Obadiah didn't have to search far for the recording — it was a saved link on his phone. He played the clip as Devlon watched it attentively.

"Remember, on the day that you turn back to Him, he will accept you, as a father loves his child. Then He will open the Heavens and refresh your land, and will have mercy upon your nation and heal your hearts."

"On the day you turn back to Him...." Devlon repeated thoughtfully. "The country has grown bitter and cynical. Do you really think they'll turn back to God?"

"There are many who never left Him," Obadiah assured him. "I have a feeling that there are more believers now than when all this started."

ATHALIAH, meanwhile, wasted no time in calling a meeting of her top staff, including the heads of all the nation's security agencies.

"You heard the president's remarks," she said disdainfully. "It is obvious that he still suffers delusions from his injuries at the temple. I'm afraid that his judgment is gravely impaired. However, this may work to our advantage. The Moretti boy is now likely to emerge from hiding; that will be our opportunity to deal with him once and for all."

"Deal with him?" the Attorney General asked. "What do you mean, exactly? The President's pardon carries the weight of law. We can no longer arrest the boy."

Athaliah dismissed his objection with a wave. "Use your imagination, man! The boy can no longer be charged with *treason*... but I'm sure that a group as smart as all of you can come up with something else." She sneered at them across the table as smoky black shadows became visible against the ceiling. The unnerved officials began to sweat as the hideous creatures moved menacingly above their heads.

IN HER WEEKLY radio address later that day, Athaliah called on her loyal followers to... "support the president in his time of illness." Her remarks were a thinly-veiled assault on Devlon's credibility, openly casting doubt on his mental fitness.

REPORTERS WERE CRAMMED into the signing room again at ten o'clock the next morning. Devlon sat this time with a stack of his previous executive orders and began to draw from the pile, rescinding one after another.

Prohibitions on religious expression were the first to go, followed quickly by restoring tax-exempt status for churches. He eliminated requirements for religious organizations to report their membership and revoked civil penalties for 'divisive' statements. Finally, he struck the requirements for schools to teach courses promoting Ancient Religions, Paganism, and the Occult.

ONE LARGE PROBLEM REMAINED. The ordinances that had been cleverly sprinkled into budget measures and other Bills were now law. Those could not be rescinded as easily. Thousands of church leaders were now defending themselves against violations of those laws in court battles throughout the country. At least a dozen of them had already reached Federal Appellate courts.

ATHALIAH WAS beside herself with rage over Devlon's actions on the executive orders. She stormed into Bahal's office at his Royal Suite, atop the Four Seasons Hotel.

"Everything we've worked for is ruined!" she angrily protested. Her hands were clenched in the air as if she was pulling her hair out. "How is this possible? He was ours!" She reared her head back in rage: "The *world* was in our grasp!"

Bahal's eyes were dark with a sinister glare. Even in his silence, his hatred for what had happened could not have been proclaimed any more loudly.

"It was the boy," he snarled through his clenched teeth. "He has grown stronger than we imagined. Our enemy has not raised up a servant with such power in quite some time."

He stroked his chin as he considered his own words. "Still... he *is* a man — and a young one, at that." He looked at Athaliah intently, "We must learn more about the boy. Who are his closest friends?"

"He has been like a ghost - we know little about him!" Athaliah snapped.

"How can that be?" Bahal asked thoughtfully. "Millions know him on that podcast of his. He has been interviewed on television. We have even had his house to search."

"His mother is dead," Athaliah noted cruelly. "His closest friend died of cancer three years ago. There are those others at the tent meetings, but they haven't seen him in two years."

"Haven't they?" Bahal challenged. "Who is helping make those video recordings? Who works with him on those podcasts?"

Athaliah considered his question silently. "Another girl appeared on his podcast the night of the temple ritual; we hadn't seen her before."

"Find her..." Bahal said coldly.

I ANSWERED MY PHONE — happy to see Ward O'Malley's name on the caller-ID.

"Your friend Silas has been a great help to us in our legal challenges," he shared gratefully. "He has given us background on how the Administration targeted faith-based organizations. We're preparing a brief to the Court challenging all of them on Constitutional grounds."

"That's great, Uncle Ward! Silas has been a big help to me too."

I thought about revealing Obadiah's role in the President's conversion but decided against it. Something told me that his secret identity still needed to be preserved.

"So, what are you going to do now that the President has pardoned you?" Uncle Ward asked.

"I'm not sure," I admitted. "Something still doesn't feel right about venturing out just yet."

"You've been in hiding for two and a half years — it will be an adjustment, I'm sure," he said, assuming my hesitancy was emotional.

"It's not that. I just don't think this is over yet. Athaliah and her father are still out there — I don't see them giving up so easily. Besides, it's not like I have anywhere else to go."

"We'll follow your wishes, whatever you decide," he assured me. "Things are about to heat up on the legal front — I have a feeling the Supreme Court will hear our case soon."

THE SUPREME COURT...

MR. O's instincts were right about the legal case. Just days later, the Supreme Court announced that they would hear the case. The atmosphere in the country seemed more divided and hostile than ever — at least, the Administration's supporters were more hostile than ever. It was clear now that they had really been Athaliah's supporters all along.

ON HER RADIO address and social media posts, Athaliah seemed to be doing all she could to stir up even more division. She was now directly calling on her 'Enlightened Friends' to oppose the President's efforts 'by any means necessary.' They organized protests in front of the Supreme Court, demanding that the new laws be upheld.

Meanwhile, a resurgence of violent attacks on churches was breaking out all over the country. Our weekly podcast became a global prayer meeting as Christians worldwide banded together in prayer. The powerful move of God's Spirit continued to intensify the more that persecution increased.

. . .

ONE OF THE most dramatic changes was the transformation in President Sheen. He had suddenly become an avid supporter of religious freedom, not to mention an outspoken believer. His own Cabinet members were baffled by the change, which represented a complete about-face in nearly every position he'd previously held. Support for him among believers grew exponentially as a result, while his former supporters became violently opposed.

***

IN HARBOR CITY, PJ looked out over a packed auditorium of former gang members as they sang together in thundering worship. The large church was filled to the point where extra chairs crammed the ends of every row of pews, and even the choir loft was filled with them. In every service, testimonies were told of lives that had been dramatically transformed. He couldn't help breathing a grateful prayer for God's amazing work!

Tonight they were dedicating a team of urban missionaries — the first to be commissioned from the ranks of the former gangs. Badrick was among them.

PJ made his way down from the platform as he called the team forward and was joined by leaders from the city's local churches. His heart swelled with praise as he stood in front of Badrick and the others with him and anointed his forehead.

> "Lord, tonight we honor the great act of redemption that
>   you have performed in the lives of these who stand
>   before us. We pray that the transforming work
>   you've done in them will spread to all of those they
>   touch. Use these servants mightily to save and
>   redeem — to seek and save those who are lost.
> We anoint them tonight to send them forth in your
>   power, for the glory of your name and ask now for
>   your Spirit's anointing upon their lives.
> Father, may they be mighty warriors for your kingdom
>   in these closing days of time!"

Hundreds of their peers — long-time friends and former enemies alike — gathered around them, praying for God's blessing on their lives.

AFTER THE SERVICE, PJ congratulated Badrick. "God has his hand on you. Give it time," he counseled. "God will show you where he wants you, soon enough."

"I know where I'll be goin'," Badrick immediately replied. "I'm goin' t' Bushwick, Brooklyn… that's where He's callin' me. I know it, sure as can be."

⌘

28

CHOOSING SIDES

"We're calling on believers everywhere to storm Heaven...."
~ PJ

Devlon tossed and turned as he tried to sleep. Thoughts of his dealings with Athaliah and Bahal haunted his mind — along with his own despicable actions over the past two years. He clearly recalled the sight of Athaliah's cruel yellow cat's eyes and thundering voice. The memory triggered thoughts of his enslavement to Moloch and the terrible defiance and fury of that demon prince. Most troubling of all was the memory of Governor Taylor's assassination. He couldn't blame Moloch entirely for that decision; there had been enough greed and lust for power in his heart to have done it on his own.

There was no question that he would have to confess to his involvement — his newly-awakened conscience insisted on it. He knew, also, that the longer he waited, the more Athaliah and Bahal could use it against him. His greater struggle was with the consequences of turning the country over to Bo Strident — his lightweight vice president would be little more than a puppet for Athaliah and her shadowy minions to control.

The wake-up alarm he'd set on his phone roused him from his groggy stupor. He'd been awake for half the night, and his eyes struggled to focus on the time that his phone displayed: 5:00 AM.

Devlon felt a deep unction to begin the morning with prayer for the first time in his life. Not just a simple 'good morning God' prayer, but a serious time of prayer. Maybe it was the influence of being in the Lincoln bedroom, recalling Lincoln's own clear reliance on divine help. Whatever the inspiration, he knew that he needed to call upon God for wisdom — he needed to seriously pray!

He dropped to his knees beside the bed and began to call out to God.

THE WIDELY PUBLICIZED events at the temple weeks earlier, followed by Jimmy's pardon and the rescinding of so many executive orders, had shaken the already-fractured country to its core. Athaliah's supporters were entrenched and emboldened; they quickly doubled down on their agenda. Federal Agencies were now packed with activists who paid lip service to the President's new orders while effectively ignoring them.

In addition to the stepped-up prosecutions and organized mob violence, the chaos that pervaded the country was also growing. It seemed like evil was spreading more quickly than ever, like a terrible disease.

Calls for help were coming into the Blaze message board from churches around the country at a volume not seen before. Violent attacks were on the increase, and the Legal Defense Fund was juggling a massive caseload that continued to grow.

The conditions were reaching a boiling point as the date for the Supreme Court trial drew nearer. Athaliah's Homeland Security resources were further enabling the violent protesters. Thankfully, Frank was leading a covert task force of agents within the FBI who were countering those efforts with the support of the President.

"THANK YOU, Governor. These people really need our help."

Devlon spoke to the governor of a large Midwestern State, encouraging the deployment of National Guard troops to protect churches. It was his fifteenth call today to governors around the country — all except one of them had pledged their support. It would not be as easy to convince some of the other governors.

Devlon pushed back from his desk in the Oval Office and stood to stare out the window. His heart was still heavy with the decision that he knew he would need to make soon. The more he had pondered and prayed over it, the clearer it became and the heavier it weighed on him. He closed his eyes and breathed yet another prayer for wisdom. With a sigh of resignation, he finally pressed the intercom with a call to his Secretary.

"Margie, can you please contact Obadiah and ask him to see me right away? Thank you."

DEVLON WAS STILL STANDING at the window when Obadiah knocked ten minutes later.

"Please, come in and have a seat," he invited him. There was a degree of humility in his voice and manner that Obadiah hadn't seen before. It was clear that something was seriously weighing on him.

"I've come to a decision that will have large repercussions for the nation and myself personally."

Obadiah's brow wrinkled with a worried expression. He had an idea of what Devlon might be about to say. The thought troubled him as much as it did Devlon.

"What I must do is certain; there is no shrinking from it. Regarding the manner in which it is done, however, I would greatly value your advice." He turned again and gazed out the window as he continued.

"Let's say, hypothetically, that a sitting President was to confess to a serious crime. Would he be tried while serving as the President?"

Obadiah considered the question silently before answering, then cleared his throat uncomfortably. "The Constitution is silent on whether a president can face criminal prosecution in court, and the Supreme Court has not directly addressed the question. However, the Justice Department has affirmed a policy that a sitting president is "constitutionally immune" from indictment and criminal prosecution. It has been concluded that criminal charges against a president would "violate the constitutional separation of powers.""

Obadiah shifted in his seat and cleared his throat again before continuing.

"That is not to say that he could not be removed from office. The Constitution allows the Congress to remove a president for high crimes and misdemeanors, using the impeachment process."

Devlon nodded acceptingly; Obadiah had confirmed his own understanding.

"I presume that the Vice President would assume the Presidency in that case?"

"Yes, I'm afraid so," Obadiah conceded before considering it further. "That is unless the Vice President is also impeached. If, for example, the Vice President was also implicated in the President's crime, then Congress could very well impeach them both. In such a case, the Speaker of the House would be next-in-line to the Presidency."

"I see," Devlon acknowledged thoughtfully. "What would become of the Cabinet officers in that case?"

"The Cabinet serves wholly at the pleasure of the President. They can be replaced at any time by the new President — you can replace them at any time yourself, as well."

Devlon straightened and turned to look at his Chief of Staff. For some reason, he hadn't seriously considered that possibility.

"How well do you know the House Speaker?"

"I've known him for many years. He's a man of principle and a good friend," Obadiah replied.

Devlon thoughtfully made his way back to his desk with an earnest gaze and sat down. They had some detailed planning to do.

"HER NAME IS ANNA MIRABELLA, 55 Jessica Street, Center Springs." The UEA computer nerd seemed pleased with himself for locating Anna so quickly. "A facial recognition search picked her image out of recent High School photos."

"Where is she now?" Athaliah asked, studying Anna's picture carefully.

"We're not sure," the agency head answered. "It looks like she's still living at home. We're dispatching agents to watch the house and confirm. Do you want us to bring her in?"

"Not yet," Athaliah answered with a cunning sneer. "She can lead us to the boy. Just don't let her out of your sight."

FOR THE NEXT SEVERAL DAYS, the agents watched Anna, recorded her daily routine, and then gathered again to report their progress to Athaliah.

"She spends most days at an old farmhouse where she is helping with food distribution and caring for a pair of goats. No sign of the boy," they reported.

Athaliah grumbled in frustration. "Keep on her... he's bound to show up sooner or later."

THE SUPREME COURT soon announced a trial date for the landmark case — giving the parties 30 days to prepare for opening arguments. As a result, the camps of supporters on both sides began to ramp up their efforts in earnest.

Athaliah quickly called upon her followers, encouraging Pagan ceremonies and occult rituals worldwide.

. . .

"HAVE YOU SEEN WHAT'S HAPPENING?" Anna said, standing beside me in the root cellar.

The agents who were tracking her were safely out of earshot. With the fields now as barren as Death Valley, they had nowhere to hide and were forced to conduct their surveillance from out on the road. It wasn't the agents she was talking about anyway - it was something much more incredible.

"Churches everywhere are having prayer meetings about the Supreme Court case — they're praying around the clock. Churches in other countries are doing it too. They're calling for a month of global fasting and prayer — worldwide!"

The enthusiasm in Anna's voice echoed the feeling that was growing inside me as well. It felt like something significant was about to happen that Christians everywhere could sense together. It was as if the ear of faith could hear the approaching thunder of a mighty delivering army.

"WE'RE CALLING on believers everywhere to storm Heaven," PJ said to millions on our podcast's global prayer chain that week. "This is the time for us to seek God for deliverance — the time has come to ask Him to unloose the armies of Heaven — to glorify Himself before all the world."

AS THE TRIAL DATE APPROACHED, supporters gathered in force outside of the Supreme Court building. Police barricades had to be erected to separate the opposing groups of demonstrators, while more arrived each day on both sides. Large crowds soon overflowed onto the lawns of the Capitol Building and the Library of Congress. They blocked the roads in all directions.

Athaliah's supporters shouted obscenities and threw garbage at their opponents while performing ritual dances dressed in strange robes and headdresses. Many of them beat themselves with sticks or metal bars as they called out to their 'Universal Deity' or openly invoked the name of Ba'al-Melqart — ruler of the gods.

Meanwhile, their Christian rivals knelt together in a massive prayer vigil that stretched across the Capitol lawn. They could be heard praying for those who would be their enemies and asking God to restore unity to the nation.

ON THE NIGHT before opening arguments, the crowd at the Center Springs tent grounds overflowed into the surrounding fields, more than 10,000 strong. News crews moved among the peaceful masses, broadcasting the moving scenes of worshipers as they called out to God with tear-streaked faces.

Large groups gathered in other major cities as well, filling open spaces with praying throngs. News broadcasts showed images from around the country and shots of massive rallies across the globe.

I watched the amazing scenes on the TV, noticing how angels had camped out around the gatherings in every city. These were warrior angels — Heavenly battle groups. It was clear that they were preparing for a monumental battle that would soon stretch around the world.

I made my way out onto the darkened farmhouse porch and scanned the night skies. The sight of the massive crowd at the distant tent grounds, surrounded by glowing defenders, was breathtaking. My heart was drawn to join them in prayer, breathing a plea for God's protection over all of them.

It seemed clear that God's timeline of events was quickly coming to a head — it had now been nearly two years since the drought began. There were only a few entries in Amos' journal that hadn't happened yet, including one here at the tent grounds that had driven him to tears.

THE VIBRATING of my phone's silent ring drew my attention. I was surprised to see Ward O'Malley's name.

"Hi, Uncle Ward. I figured you'd be busy preparing for tomorrow," I said as I answered it.

"If we're not prepared by now, we never will be. What we really need now is prayer."

"There's a lot of that going on," I said, watching the massive crowd in the distance. "Have you looked at the TV?"

"Yes. I suppose that's what made me want to call. I really appreciate all that you've done to help make that happen. It's truly remarkable."

"I can't claim any credit for it. The Lord is the one moving people's hearts. I know I don't have to tell you all that's at stake — this battle is the Lord's."

"I've certainly had that feeling. It's reassuring to hear you say it," he admitted appreciatively.

At his request, Uncle Ward and I spent a few minutes praying together for the trial and God's hand on events over the coming days.

"Just remember," I offered as we said goodbye, "this is God's battle. He's the one who will not only do *something* but will do *everything*."

⌘

29

BATTLE JOINED

"Michael and his angels fought against the dragon, and the dragon fought and his angels."
~ Revelation 12:7

I watched live coverage from the Supreme Court the next morning as Mr. O'Malley arrived with a world-class team of high-powered trial lawyers. They all had volunteered their services to be part of this historic case. They were escorted inside by a wide ring of security guards as Athaliah's supporters hurled insults and anything else they could find. The Government's defense lawyers arrived soon afterward, receiving cheers from those same supporters.

Proceedings were closed to the public, and recordings were not permitted. The ongoing TV coverage relied on frequent reports from journalists, who took turns making their way outside with updates. Both sides appeared to make strong points in their opening arguments.

. . .

ON THE EVENING after the first day of hearings, prayer vigils worldwide saw their crowds swell larger than ever. The enemy opposition was more active and agitated as well. Mobs of pagan worshipers filled temples, fields, and beaches, stirring their followers with hate-filled rants and calls for Believers to be silenced — *once and for all.*

Each day that passed saw their ire rise to higher and higher levels. By day three, violent attacks were breaking out against the praying crowds. In reality, the violence reflected the monumental spiritual battle now being fought across the globe. In travels with Chozeq to many of these scenes, we could see the tremendous conflict that raged in the skies over every gathering.

IN HARBOR CITY, a mass of Believers, thousands strong, had gathered in the city's center. It was led by a team of church leaders from throughout the city. The simulcast of other global prayer vigils from around the world was projected onto giant screens.

"Lord, hear our cry — defend your people and restore justice!" the pastor from an inner-city church called out.

His prayer was suddenly interrupted by the loud shouts of a surrounding mob. They screamed profanity and hurled rocks and bottles at the gathered crowd. The closer they drew, the more threatening and violent they became. Chief Fernandez and his officers intervened to stop them but were quickly overwhelmed.

All at once, from within the peaceful crowd — as if they had all heard a simultaneous call — an army of young men began to emerge. They gathered in orderly lines, surrounding the Believers like a defensive barrier. Then, as if on cue, they all spread their arms to shield the crowds behind them. They had once seen PJ do the same thing on the day that he stopped a barrage of bullets — that was the day they had all been saved. The invisible guardians who stood directly in front of them spread their wings, blocking the shower of rocks.

A single wave from one of their defenders' invisible hands sent a shockwave outward, knocking the attackers off their feet and into a disheveled pile against trash cans, buildings, and cars. A legion of angelic warriors gave chase to the dark forces in the air, driving them back in retreat.

ON THE FOURTH day of proceedings, attorneys for the Legal Defense Fund dropped an earth-shattering bombshell when they called their final witness. There were gasps of shock and surprise as Devlon Sheen stepped to the witness stand.

"President Sheen, thank you for your testimony here today," the Defense Fund attorney began. "Are you familiar with the group of laws collectively known as the SFBI Act?"

"Yes, I am."

"Can you tell the court what those initials stand for?"

"It stands for: 'Stop Faith-Based Indoctrination.' Its laws were created to single out and arrest religious leaders for their beliefs."

"Was there a particular reason these laws were hidden in budget measures passed by Congress, rather than being clearly identified?"

"It was felt that they would not be passed on their own merits."

"You mean, the Congress would not have approved them if they'd known about them?"

"That's right."

Devlon's testimony continued for two hours, in which he divulged the process by which the laws were conceived and then hidden inside a package of budget measures more than 20,000 pages long. He explained how a financial crisis was engineered to force Congress to pass the bills quickly as a tactic to prevent the hidden laws from being discovered.

By the time he finished, it was impossible for the government's lawyers to refute that Congress never intended to pass the SFBI laws and would not have if they had known about them.

"One final question, Mr. President. Why was your Administration so sure that Congress would not pass the measures on their own?"

"It was obvious," Devlon answered with a regretful look. "We knew that the measures were discriminatory and clearly unconstitutional."

The Government's defense team was rendered speechless and

rested without cross-examination, hoping to avoid any further damage to their case. With that, the Justices retired to Chambers.

Tensions were high on all sides as the day ended, still awaiting a decision by the Court.

THE FLASH that interrupts my evening prayers is not surprising. I'm watching Athaliah pacing around the room in an angry tirade as she complains to Bahal venomously.

"I should have killed him at the temple when I had the chance!" she seethes. "Now we can't touch him — not with that horrible seal on his soul." She angrily pours herself a strong drink and takes a gulp. Her eyes flash with fury as she turns back to Bahal and makes a fist, waving it in the air. "How could this happen — how did the enemy get to him?"

"Need you ask that question?" Bahal spits his reply. He looks as if it pains him to explain what should already be evident to Athaliah. "When the boy freed him from Moloch's service, it engendered within him the seeds of conscience. Once a man's spirit has awakened, the battle is already lost to us."

Bahal walks across the room and joins her in pouring himself a strong drink. His face is set in an angry scowl as he stands staring out the window, plotting his next move. His expression is as venomous as hers as he speaks.

"The time has come to rid ourselves of the boy once and for all, along with those who support him — those followers in Center Springs. We must cut off the head of this movement." He turns from the window, his eyes narrowing.

"What have they discovered from tracking the girl?"

"Nothing useful," Athaliah says in frustration. "The boy is nowhere to be found."

"We mustn't expect him to be seen walking in plain sight," Bahal counsels irritably. "Where is she spending most of her time?"

"She volunteers at an old farm, distributing food or some such nonsense."

"Show it to me," Bahal barks as he moves to his computer. She retrieves the address from her email and reads it to him as he plugs it into a search, bringing it up on a map. His eyebrows lower as he studies the location solemnly — something about it is familiar. Still seeking the connection, he switches the map to the satellite view. From over his shoulder, Athaliah gasps as she sees what he sees — there in the farm's north field is a tent surrounded by an enormous crowd of people.

Bahal continues to stare at the screen as he issues his adamant instructions through gritted teeth. "Send all you have. Search the farm... and cut down that tent!"

ATHALIAH'S TEAM has just finished planning the logistics for their raid as news of the Supreme Court's decision comes over the airwaves. The Court overturned all of the arrested pastors' convictions and ordered the immediate return of children to their families. Every one of the SFBI laws was struck down as unconstitutional, and all pending cases were dropped.

Athaliah erupted in rage....

"Make sure you get him," she demanded. "No excuses this time!"

"What about the girl and the old man?" the team's commander asked.

"Casualties," she answered heartlessly. "Leave no witnesses. Begin the attack! Go at once!"

The hint of an ominous thundering in her voice sent those in the room running for cover. None of them dared to correct her choice of words as they silently questioned them: shouldn't it have been 'raid' rather than 'attack?'

I WAS WATCHING news reports of the Supreme Court's decision when my phone rang with a call from Agent DeMassi. He didn't wait for me to say hello - speaking urgently the moment I answered.

. . .

"LISTEN CAREFULLY... we've just learned that Athaliah's agents are planning a raid on the farmhouse!"

His words are not a surprise; I've been expecting them.

"They've apparently been watching Anna for weeks and must have figured out a connection. I'm not askin' if you're anywhere near there, but if you've got any friends there, you'd better warn 'em."

"WH-WHEN ARE THEY COMING?" I stammered, concerned about Anna and Uncle Jim.

"CAN'T SAY FOR SURE... it'll likely be right after Anna arrives. They'll need to put the two of you together to make their case."

"THEIR CASE? What about the President's pardon?"

"THAT'S THE KICKER... that's actually how my unit caught wind of it. They're invoking a conspiracy charge that's not connected to the Treason pardon — conspiracy to hoard food rations."

"WHAT? THAT MAKES NO SENSE."

"EVERYBODY KNOWS THAT, but it doesn't matter — they just need the charge to justify the raid. Look, Jim... I've seen how this can go down. If people get hurt during a raid, they can claim there was resistance. If I had to guess, I'd say they have no intention of taking you in alive, and they won't leave any witnesses around either."

There was a short pause as Frank chewed through the logistics. "What time does Anna usually get there?"

. . .

"AROUND EIGHT O'CLOCK, I GUESS."

"THAT'S NOT MUCH TIME," Frank said with genuine concern. "I'm mobilizing a team now, but it'll be tight. Don't call her phone; they'll be monitoring it. I'll be there as soon as I can."

I STARED at the phone after he hung up — my mind was racing. Finally dropping it into my pocket, I rushed into the kitchen, catching Uncle Jim.

"Frank... agent DeMassi just called — UEA agents are on their way to raid the farmhouse!"

He looked startled by the news but wasn't thrown by it. It looked like he'd been expecting it for months... maybe for years. The questions in his eyes quickly resolved as I explained everything Frank had just shared.

"Yer best bet is the secret passage — go get it open an' ready so you can get straight down there as soon as Anna arrives."

"What about you? You have to join us!"

"I ain't gonna be much good down there. Somebody needs t' stay an' hold 'em off. I'll keep 'em busy until Frank gets here."

I GLANCED AT MY WATCH... if I was right about Anna's arrival time, I didn't have long to prepare. I rushed back into my room and grabbed Amos' journal along with mine, stuffing them into my backpack. Heading quickly down to the root cellar, I soon had the secret door opened and had stashed the backpack, laptop, and other podcast equipment inside. Finally, I folded up the old desk and unplugged the lamp to look like they'd just been stored there.

As Uncle Jim and I waited in the living room, the memory of what happened to mom came to mind once more. I quickly called Uncle Mike...

"Uncle Mike, whatever you do, don't come near the farmhouse or the tent grounds today! Stay away! Make sure Anna's mom stays away too — it's important!"

I had to repeat the plea several times before he finally agreed. My heart was pounding when I hung up the phone.

ANNA'S VOICE at the door a moment later brought a new rush of adrenaline. The sound of her 'hello' changed to a surprised yelp as I grabbed her hand and pulled her inside. She struggled in confusion as I half-dragged her toward the root cellar. Once inside the pantry, I rushed to explain....

"Frank called to warn us — agents are on their way right now — they're raiding the farmhouse!"

While I was still speaking, the sound of helicopters suddenly echoed outside. There were more than one..., and they were landing.

The shocked look on Anna's face turned to confusion as I stepped through the hatchway to climb down. "W-what are you doing? Where are you going? They'll find you there!"

"Trust me!" I begged, dropping to the dirt floor. "Quick! Follow me!"

She reluctantly followed, ducking her head awkwardly as Uncle Jim dropped the hatch above her and covered it with the rug. I held the lit lantern and waved my hand toward the secret door. Her eyes grew large in surprise.

"W-what is that? Where does it go?"

⌘

30

BRAVE

"Be braver than a lion, for God is with you."
~ Chozeq

"**H**urry and get in!" I urged, pulling her by the hand. Once she was safely inside, I threw the lever, closing the door behind us. Just moments later, we heard the muted sounds of commotion upstairs. It sounded like they broke in the back door and turned over the kitchen table. An army of heavy footsteps could be heard on the staircase and down the cellar steps as they roughly searched the house.

Above the commotion, I could hear Uncle Jim's voice shouting in objection from the kitchen above our heads.

"Now, hold on there! This ain't no way t' treat a citizen... I ain't even seen a warrant an' you've near wrecked my house!"

The commander's voice replied with blatant disregard for Uncle

Jim's complaint. "You're suspected of harboring a fugitive wanted by the Federal Government. The warrant is right here."

"This don't say nothin' 'bout a fugitive... it's some nonsense 'bout illegal food storage."

"Does that food stored in the barn belong to you?" the commander barked accusingly.

"Food? It's for the food pantry... it goes t' needy folk 'round here."

"You're under arrest for illegal hoarding of food rations in time of national emergency," the commander decreed.

"Now wait one minute! That don't make a spark o' sense. Since when is givin' away food the same as hoarding it? I'm gonna have t' ask you t' leave my property plain'n simple."

The commander yelled loudly as we heard shuffling and a chair being knocked over. "Where are the girl and the Moretti kid?"

"The Moretti boy?" Uncle Jim asked. His voice was unsteady, as if he was being restrained. "How should I know 'bout him? Besides, I heard the President pardoned him."

"Not for this, he hasn't," the commander insisted. While he was speaking, one of his men interrupted.

"THERE'S a trap door in the next room, sir... it looks like a hiding place."

We heard the hatch being flung open as Uncle Jim explained what it was.

"That ain't no hidin' place; it's a root cellar. Ain't you people ever seen an ol' root cellar before?"

The stone wall muffled most of the sound in the room beside us, but we could vaguely make out the sound of men searching it. We heard their voices as they reentered the kitchen above our heads.

"It's empty, sir, looks pretty much unused."

"I told ya'" Uncle Jim replied.

We heard more shuffling, and something was banged roughly against the kitchen wall.

"Where is he?" the commander shouted angrily.

Uncle Jim didn't answer. The commander repeated his question, and we heard another thump against the wall.

SOMEONE ELSE COULD BE HEARD reporting... "We found these in one of the upstairs bedrooms. It looks like someone else is living here."

"It's jus' a farmhand, that's all," Uncle Jim started to explain, but the sound of a loud slap cut him off mid-sentence.

Just as the commander was yelling renewed threats, we heard one of his men yell from the back door.

"CHOPPERS INCOMING, SIR. IT'S FBI."

The commander shouted to his men: "Let's move out! Round up the evidence; we'll take it with us."

There was a flurry of loud footsteps as men exited the house. Then I heard Uncle Jim yell out briefly like he'd been hit, followed by the sound of someone hitting the floor hard. A single set of footsteps then exited through the back door, and it closed with a slam.

WE WAITED IN AGONIZING SILENCE, listening carefully, but there was no movement upstairs.

"Uncle Jim is hurt," I said to Anna urgently. "I need to help him."

"Wait!" she urged. "What if it's a trap?"

The memory of Frank's words replayed in my mind:

> *'If I had to guess, I'd say they have no intention of taking you in alive.'*

I was just about to tell Anna how to reach the Mausoleum without me when we suddenly heard new voices above us. One of them was Uncle Mike's — he was shouting in an urgent tone.

. . .

"Jim! Mr. Van Clief! Can ya hear me?"

A second set of footsteps and the sound of a police radio hinted that Mike wasn't alone — the Sheriff was with him.

I immediately threw the lever, rolling open the stone door, and rushed out, bursting through the hatchway.

The pantry was a mess, with half the shelves emptied onto the floor. The kitchen table and chairs were toppled, and contents of the cabinets were strewn around the room. Uncle Jim was lying in the middle of the floor.

As I quickly knelt beside him, I could tell that he was breathing unsteadily; blood was running from a wound on his head, and he held his heart with one hand. When he saw me, he took my hand with the other. He labored as he spoke in half a whisper:

"I DONE THE PAPERWORK Jim," he gasped out the words. "The farm is t' be yours now. I ain't got no other kin… you're the closest thing t' kin I got."

I felt tears welling up in my eyes as I listened.

"I wanna thank ya' fer what ya done, Jimmy. I never would'a found forgiveness if it hadn't been fer you. I wouldn't be headin' home to Heaven." He closed his eyes as if listening to something that thrilled his soul. "That music sure is beautiful! Ain't it the most beautiful ya ever heard?"

His eyes opened, and he looked up toward the ceiling with a peaceful expression, but it seemed clear it wasn't the ceiling that he was looking at.

"Clorinda…" he whispered in a breathless voice. A sudden well of tears filled his eyes and trickled down the sides of his face; then, he was gone.

I felt his hand go limp, and my own eyes filled with tears. The Sheriff knelt and gently closed Uncle Jim's eyes; then, he laid his hand on my shoulder. Uncle Mike did the same while Sheriff Flanagan quietly led us in prayer.

ANNA STOOD beside me on the front porch an hour later as the ambulance drove away. Frank stood in the barnyard a short distance away, talking on his radio as he watched his team and a company of National Guard troops comb the tent grounds in the distance. The tent was no longer standing.

Uncle Mike ran to meet Lena as she pulled up the drive. She was crying as she embraced him, and they made their way to us. Anna's eyes were as red as mine from crying as well. After Anna and her mom hugged emotionally, they looked together toward the tent grounds, swarming with soldiers and investigators.

"What happened?" Lena asked.

Uncle Mike and I shared a knowing glance. Rather than answering, I handed her the journal that I held in my hand, open to the entry we'd just been reading — the one smudged with Amos' tears. I pointed to the place to begin reading.

~ April 26, 1871, ~
We found ourselves standing in the North field looking over a sorry sight. The large tent had been toppled and shredded — its ropes cut. Chairs lay strewn over the field, along with scattered possessions — shoes, jackets, and Bibles everywhere. Evidence of bloodstains could be plainly seen, some still glistening wet in the afternoon sun.

WE WERE GATHERED a few hours later in the living room. The furniture had been straightened and the shelves reorganized. Despite its restored appearance, the old house didn't feel the same — not without Uncle Jim. I couldn't help expecting him to come walking through the front door at any minute, tired from a day's work.

The TV news reported the day's events, beginning with the Supreme Court decision and then repeating scenes of the tent grounds. While we watched, the programming was suddenly interrupted with a special address by the President.

Devlon looked somber as he faced the camera from his desk in the Oval Office. Obadiah briefly leaned in and whispered something in his ear and then quickly disappeared off camera.

DEVLON BEGAN.

"I am coming to you tonight to express my sadness over the events today in Center Springs. Our hearts are grieved over those who tragically lost their lives, and our thoughts and prayers are with those who lost loved ones.

"In response to those events, I am announcing significant changes in my Administration.

"One of my first acts when I became President was the creation of a new Federal Agency, the Unity Enforcement Agency. That, I now realize, was a grave error. I have been made aware that this Agency was behind today's terrible attack in Center Springs. I promise that a full investigation will be conducted, and those responsible for criminal acts will be prosecuted.

"Moments ago, I informed the Congress that I am immediately disbanding the UEA. Its directors and personnel will no longer hold authority in any capacity or within any other agency of the Federal Government.

"Further changes in my Cabinet will be forthcoming in the next twenty-four hours."

Devlon paused as he considered what he was about to say next. When he continued, it was with a humble expression and deep conviction in his eyes.

"Events in recent days have opened our eyes to the true

struggle surrounding us. Two years ago a young man delivered what was clearly a supernatural message to this nation and to me. He warned us then of the drought that has since devastated this country and told us that on the day that we, as a nation, turned back to God, he would accept us once again, as a father loves his child.

"God's message that night promised that then He would open the Heavens and refresh our land and would have mercy on our nation and heal our hearts. Tonight it is my sincere hope that all of us, as a nation, will heed that call. I am calling on you to join me tonight in asking for God's forgiveness and mercy. May He meet us here in our weakness so that we may once again be a nation unified in faith and worship — one nation under God.

"Please join me in a moment of silence for those lives that were lost today. If you will, please also join me in praying for God's forgiveness and mercy on our nation."

The camera remained on Devlon's face as he sat with his eyes closed, catching the image of a tear as it escaped and rolled down his cheek. He finally looked into the camera once again with a humble nod.

"Thank you, my friends, and may God bless you."

THE REACTION TO Devlon's heartfelt message was more profound than anyone expected. Within the hour, churches around the country began to ring their bells and opened their doors for impromptu services. News reports repeated the President's short address, with astonished newscasters appearing at a loss for words.

Online forums exploded with reactions that overwhelmingly supported the call for a return to God. It seemed as though the country was growing more unified after all — this time in admitting its need for repentant hearts.

———

LATER THAT EVENING, I sat at my bedroom desk writing a record of the day's remarkable events. Even with obvious victories, it had been a tragic day. My heart felt heavy, despite a profound sense that an even greater victory was approaching.

The look on Uncle Jim's face when he said Clorinda's name had etched itself in my mind. It was a look of genuine peace and pure joy. Despite that assurance, I felt an ache in my heart. That familiar emptiness haunted me once again; the pain of losing someone I loved.

Tonight there were a dozen other families feeling the same sense of loss after the day's events at the tent grounds.

I laid down my pen and leaned on the desk, holding my head in my hands. Almost immediately, the soft glow from Chozeq's wings brightened the room.

The first words from my mouth surprised me, expressing the concern that was really troubling me beneath all the others. Chozeq's arrival had a way of inspiring my deepest honesty.

"THEY'RE NOT GOING to stop, are they?" My remark was a conclusion rather than a question. "Athaliah and Bahal will keep on coming for me. How many more will be hurt? Why me?"

Chozeq seemed to expect the question. He settled to his knees and leaned back on his heels — his counseling pose, as I'd come to welcome it. His voice was quiet and understanding.

"EVIL MEN HAVE a fear of true saints. They hate them, but they also fear them. Remember that Haman trembled because of Mordecai,[1] even when he sought the good man's destruction.

"In truth, their hate arises out of a dread which they are too proud to confess. The name of the eternal God is named upon you. You hold the protection of all the legions of Heaven. You have omnipotence as your guardian, and God will sooner empty heaven of angels than leave a saint without defense.

"Pursue the path of truth without the slightest tremor. Fear is not for the Believer but for those who do ill and fight against the Lord of hosts. Be braver than a lion, for God is with you.[2]"

⌘

31

FACEOFF

There is none like God... Who rides upon the heavens for your help.
~ Deuteronomy 33:26

"Early the next morning, news programs were buzzing about a flurry of announcements from the White House. Throughout the morning, one Cabinet member after another had been replaced, along with the head of the NSA and several other top posts. In such a divided political atmosphere, the people chosen to replace them were equally surprising. They were well-qualified and respected experts from *both* political parties.

Devlon's choice for Chief of Staff had not changed — Obadiah remained by his side. Most of the new Cabinet selections, in fact, were Obadiah's recommendations. The President had also announced that he would hold another press conference at noon when he promised to make an announcement that 'would have large repercussions for the nation.'

I'D FINISHED MILKING the cows and stood in the kitchen listening to the news reports. Uncle Jim never liked to have the TV on before breakfast, but the stillness in the old house was a little too much for me.

Thankfully, Anna was on her way over for breakfast, along with her mom and Uncle Mike. I kept myself busy whipping up Uncle Jim's French Toast recipe in a large bowl. I was slicing the last loaf of his homemade bread as Anna entered the front door.

She greeted me with a kiss. "How are you doing?" she asked insightfully as she looked me in the eye.

"I'm ok," I said, offering a smile. "How about you guys," I added as I welcomed her mom and Uncle Mike right behind her. "Looks like you had a late night."

Uncle Mike explained. "We were at the church — First Avenue. PJ opened it for anyone who wanted to come. It was really packed; we stayed pretty late."

I was surprised that I hadn't heard about it and had to remind myself that I was still technically in hiding.

"That sounds great," I said, unable to hide the longing and disappointment in my voice. I turned back to the griddle and flipped a few slices.

The others grew quiet, and Anna offered a gesture of comfort, massaging my shoulders for a few seconds, then came alongside me.

"What can I do? I'll slice the bacon if you want?" she offered.

Wow, I knew she hated touching uncooked bacon. I chuckled and smiled at her gratefully as she picked it up and started cutting off thin strips, trying her best to hide her displeasure.

A few of my first slices were either over-or-undercooked. Uncle Jim had been the griddle master; this was my first attempt at the job. I seemed to get the hang of it after a while — the slices at the top of the pile were almost as good as his.

Mike and Lena finished setting the table and then sat watching Anna and me as we juggled spatulas side-by-side. From the looks on their faces, it was apparently great entertainment.

With our platters finally full, we presented them on the table and sat down to a shower of compliments. Uncle Mike offered to ask the blessing, and we took each other's hands, bowing our heads.

HE HAS JUST BEGUN PRAYING when a flash carries me to a familiar setting, yet despite its familiarity, it doesn't look as I expect. I'm standing in front of Pastor Jerome's Calvary Hill Church, but the building is larger than before, and the shrubberies have changed.

As I watch, waiting to see why I've traveled here, the church doors open, and Pastor Jerome emerges, followed quickly by three others who I recognize easily. Not surprisingly, Pastor Jerome looks older, with a thorough dusting of gray hair.

The first one to follow him out is Radison. He is clean-cut and neatly dressed; the change in his appearance makes it hard to tell how old he is.

Badrick is the next one to emerge. It takes me a moment to recognize him; his dreadlocks are gone, and his hair is cut short. He wears a neatly-trimmed beard.

The last of the three is the biggest shock yet, as PJ walks through the door. He's a middle-aged man, fit and healthy-looking. It occurs to me that this is *after* the night he met Ardent. The night he was stabbed.

I'm reminded of the words that I heard Ardent speak to him in the emergency room on that night:

> *"He has chosen to anoint thee with a portion of faith that has been seldom known to the earth. Ye shall be a powerful witness to this land in the closing days of your mortal time."*

AS THE SCENE ENDED, Ardent's words were still swirling in my mind, and I found myself back at the kitchen table. I saw Anna look at me suddenly as if she'd been startled by something. I looked at her apologetically and acknowledged Uncle Mike's prayer, closing my eyes to rejoin him.

"What was that?" she said to me quietly, leaning closer as Uncle Mike finished.

"What was what?" I answered evasively.

"That. It felt like your hand wasn't there for a split second, and then it was back."

"Really?" I didn't have to fake my look of surprise; her question honestly shocked me. It occurred to me that I'd never traveled before while holding anyone's hand.

"Sorry... never mind," she said after studying my face for a moment. "I don't know what I was thinking."

"Well, *I* think this breakfast is awesome," Uncle Mike chimed in loudly as he poked his fork into the pile.

I stood in the barn an hour later, watching Anna feed Elroy and Rosie. Her love for the two goats hadn't dimmed since the day Uncle Jim presented them to her as gifts. They were babies then, not the 170-pound giants now in front of us. They still loved her back the same way they did when they were young kids — she literally had them eating out of her hand.

I leaned against the stall's gate, happily watching them together. Anna was easy to watch.

We worked together the rest of the morning packing food and loading cars for the day's food distribution.

The TV was on as we entered the living room around noontime. Uncle Mike waved for us to sit as he pointed to Devlon getting ready to start his press conference.

Devlon stood at the small lectern in the Press Briefing Room, quietly looking down at his notes. The room grew eerily silent as the audience watched the somber expression etched in his face, building in anticipation.

. . .

"No doubt you have heard by now the announcements regarding changes in my Cabinet. Those changes are effective immediately — the new Agency Heads were already sworn-in this morning in a private ceremony at the Capital.

"As I said yesterday, I am deeply saddened by the events in Center Springs. Our thoughts and prayers remain with those who lost loved ones.

"I have called this briefing today for another reason. As a result of recent developments in my own life, and in light of yesterday's events, I have resolved to publicly acknowledge today something that weighs heavily on my conscience." Devlon released a deep breath — it seemed clear that it was not a nervous sigh, but instead revealed his deep regret.

"I am deeply sorry to admit that my Administration was complicit in the assassination of Governor Taylor and Congresswoman Jackson. I will be turning myself over to law enforcement authorities immediately following this briefing."

AN ARRAY of surprised gasps and expressions of shock could be heard throughout the room. Devlon waited for the disturbance to die down and then continued.

"The bomb was planted by members of a private security force belonging to Bahal Ebezej, my father-in-law. Additionally, Vice President Strident was fully aware of this action and played a central role in coordinating the events himself. He also was responsible, with my approval, for placing evidence at the bomb site containing DNA belonging to James Moretti. This DNA was gathered from the Moretti home by agents of my Administration after it was unjustly seized."

"I regret my actions in these matters and confess them with great remorse. I owe an unfathomable debt to society and, most especially to the Taylor and Jackson families. I realize that no amount of remorse or apology can repay what is owed for the innocent lives that were taken."

DEVLON HUNG his head in shame as he stepped back from the podium. Obadiah came alongside him and gently directed him toward the door behind them. Reporters were shouting questions in a loud, chaotic chorus, all of which remained unanswered.

*

The broadcast cut back to the studio, where the news anchor could be seen listening to instructions from the control room and then quickly explained to the camera....

"We're getting a report that Athaliah Sheen, the First Lady, is preparing to give a statement in the Rose Garden at the White House. Here is the First Lady...."

ATHALIAH IS STANDING at a lectern on a low stage. Seated on the platform behind her are members of Devlon's former Cabinet and other ousted Department Heads. Secret Service agents stand at all sides, guarding the group, and several of Bahal's private security agents stand close by. In front of them are rows of reporters.

Athaliah flashes a charming smile to the cameras, assuming a sympathetic gaze as she begins.

"I regret that it has come to this — our family had hoped to keep my husband's condition from public view. My husband, you see, has been suffering severe mental difficulties since the traumatic events several months ago. After the terrible assault that he suffered at the hands of the terrorist, James Moretti, he has frankly been plagued with delusions and hallucinations.

"Today's unfortunate announcements are the result of his medical incapacity. I have directed the White House doctors to sedate him and provide him the help that he needs in a suitable mental-treatment facility.

AS I HEAR what she is saying, a sudden indignation rises within me, and I hear Chozeq's words repeating in my mind:

Be braver than a lion, for God is with you!

ATHALIAH CONTINUES HER COMMENTS, grinning as she explains.…

"So, you see, all of this nonsense about returning to God and seeking mercy and so forth — it is nothing but a delusional rant. We know, of course, that there is no supreme being who decrees droughts and judgments. Such superstitions were dismissed by intelligent people a century ago. Thankfully, we are now informed by science and not superstition."

Few seemed to notice the gradual gathering of Rolling black clouds as they began to form over the crowd.
Athaliah continued, weaving her deceitful account.

"As we have known for the past two years, this terrible calamity is the fault of the Moretti boy and his cult of fanatics. Now this group's influence has been allowed to spread across the country and throughout the world. The laws that we had put in place are needed in order to stop this cancer from spreading further. I pledge to you that, while my husband is getting the help he needs, I will work with Vice President Strident and the rest of the administration to restore these needed measures and stamp out this disease of religious extremism once and for all!"

MY HEART IS POUNDING INSIDE me as I sit on the edge of my seat in the farmhouse living room. Then the voice I've been expecting suddenly echoes loudly in my spirit with a familiar command:

You are my witness to this defiant generation. Speak the words I give you boldly and without fear. NOW... STAND!

THE FLASH that engulfed me when I jumped to my feet was more shocking to Anna and the others than it was to me. I could feel my resolve set like granite as I stood directly in front of Athaliah, in the midst of the seated audience.

My voice nearly thundered as I shouted, drawing the attention of the stunned crowd seated around me.

"IT'S YOU WHO ARE THE DISEASE!
IS IT BECAUSE THERE IS NO GOD IN HEAVEN THAT YOU HAVE
INQUIRED OF BAAL-ZEBUB, THE GOD OF YOUR FATHER?
IS THERE NO END TO YOUR LIES AND POISONOUS WORDS?
BECAUSE OF THIS, GOD'S HEART IS HARDENED AGAINST YOU, AND
HIS FURY IS GREATLY INFLAMED!"

ATHALIAH BECAME enraged as she saw me — bristling at the decree that God had spoken to her.

Her face contorted in rage, and she pointed at me — her words thundered unnaturally and stretched out into a long wail as she screamed to the agents surrounding her:

"Kill...... Him......!! ......Now!"

BEFORE ANY OF them could react, the black clouds overhead erupted in a blinding flash, brighter than the noonday sun. **The massive lightning bolt struck Athaliah** directly in the heart, obscuring everything nearby with its brightness. The force of the powerful strike and its enormous concussion sent people tumbling in all directions as chairs toppled off the platform, and the audience was knocked backward.

ATHALIAH WAS GONE in a split second.

Climbing from the ground, agents cautiously approached the place where she was standing, finding only the bony charred remains of her hands, still clinging to the lectern, along with what was left of her feet, and something smoldering on the floor between them. It was just the top of a blackened skull.

Members of the audience slowly rose from the ground where their toppled chairs had tossed them and stood awestruck in total silence. Several of the Cabinet members who were seated on the platform scrambled to their feet and ran away in terrified disbelief.

A few of them, however, began dropping to their knees. Their spontaneous reaction spread as more and more joined them, even among the security agents.

"THE PRESIDENT WAS RIGHT," I said, lifting my voice in invitation. "He didn't lose his senses; he came to them. God is ready to welcome you today if you'll open your heart to Him. He stands ready to forgive your sins right now. Repent and turn to Him, so your sins can be wiped out — so that times of refreshing can come from the Lord.[1]"

Tears could be seen on many of their faces as they knelt with their eyes squeezed closed. Soon sobbing could be heard from several in the crowd. For those who were willing to join me, I prayed with them the sinners' prayer, welcoming dozens of newly redeemed souls to the Kingdom.

FINALLY, looking back to the blackened platform, words from the book of Second Kings came ominously to my mind...

"...they found no more of her than the skull, and the feet, and the palms of her hands."

~ The fate of Jezabel ~ 2 Kings 9:35

⌘

32

DISTANT THUNDER

"And it came to pass... that the heavens grew black with clouds and wind, and there was a great rain."
~ 1 Kings 18:45

Anna leaped from the couch and held me gratefully as I reappeared at the farmhouse. The newscast had captured the entire event on live television. Anna's mom had tears in her eyes as she looked at me in wonder over what God had just done. Uncle Mike just held his hands against his head and kept repeating, "Praise the Lord," over and over.

Within minutes my phone started to ring. Pete was first to call.

"Bro... I'm in total awe!"

"I guess that makes two of us," I admitted uncomfortably.

"You're like an international phenomenon, man. You should see what everyone's saying! People are even collecting copies of your wanted poster from the Post Office."

I laughed aloud. "Grab me one of those; that pretty much sums up my last two years."

"Hey, seriously, though," he said more soberly, "I'm glad you're alright. That was pretty scary, I have to admit."

I'm reminded of Chozeq's words from last night: *Fear is not for the Believer but for those who fight against the Lord of hosts.*

"I really never felt afraid," I confessed honestly. "Unfortunately, Athaliah is the one who should have been afraid. She was going up against the God of the Universe; that's what's terrifying."

"Yeah, that's definitely true," Pete agreed. He was quiet for a second and added in a sympathetic voice: "I heard about what happened to old Mr. V.; I'm sorry, man, I truly am."

"Thanks," I said quietly. "He's missed. The old place isn't the same, ya know?"

"Yeah, I do," he answered sadly. "If there's anything you need, just say the word."

"I appreciate it. I'm probably gonna need some help with the fields... that is when we finally get some rain."

"Aren't you the guy who stopped it in the first place?" he joked. He quickly added, "Just say the word, and I'll be there for whatever ya need."

I HAD JUST SAID goodbye to Pete when the phone rang again — it was Uncle Ward this time.

"Jimmy, I'm sorry for not calling sooner — after everything at the Supreme Court, I had things to finish with the other lawyers, then I was in the air and traveling...."

"It's OK," I assured him. "Congratulations on winning the case; you guys did an awesome job."

"Thanks, he said quietly... and thanks for your prayers." After a short pause, he added, "I heard what happened to Jim Van Clief. I'm really sorry, Jimmy."

"I know," I said sincerely. "Thanks."

The line was silent for a moment as he waited before changing topics. "What can I say about this afternoon at the White House? That was... that was like something right out of the Old Testament."

"Actually, that's true — more than you know," I agreed.

"Are you going to come out of hiding now? It looks like the ones who tried to get you are gone."

"Bahal is still out there," I said. "But you're right; the government's search is over. I guess I might venture out now." I glanced over my shoulder at Anna as her eyes lit with a gleam of excitement.

NYLE WAS the next to call, followed by PJ and Pastor Wilkes, then Mr. Giovanni from Carmine's Diner. Finally, Sheriff Flanagan called to check in and see how I was doing.

HOURS LATER, things seemed to settle back to some degree of normalcy. Frank called with news that warrants had been issued for Bahal's arrest, and most of his security force had already been captured. He also let me know that Obadiah assured him the President would not be going to any mental facility.

This was further confirmed when the news began reporting that impeachment proceedings for Devlon and Vice President Strident would begin immediately. In addition, newly emerged evidence of serious voting abnormalities were triggering calls for a new special election.

ANNA and I sat alone as Mike and Lena prepared dinner. She could tell that something was troubling me and gripped my hand tightly as if to keep me from suddenly vanishing again.

Her insights were pretty good. My mind kept going back to the scene I'd visited during breakfast — seeing PJ with Radison, Badrick, and Pastor Jerome. Ardent's words to PJ kept replaying in my mind: *Ye shall be a powerful witness to this land in the closing days of your mortal time.*

It seemed that there was something more to that meeting. There was something else I was expected to see. As I'm struggling with it, the familiar flash of swirling time signals another jump.

It DOESN'T SURPRISE me that I'm standing once again in front of Calvary Hill Church. The four men are seated on the church steps, having what appears to be a serious conversation. I walk closer to see if I can hear what they're saying, never imagining that the closer I walked, the more visible I'd become.

Rad is the first to notice me. He stops talking suddenly and stares wide-eyed in my direction. The others follow his gaze and quickly assume frozen expressions as well. In a few more steps, I'm fully visible and am standing right in front of them.

The look on PJ's face is not shock; it's more a look of realization as if a hundred mysteries are being suddenly answered in his mind.

Realizing that they can see me, I nod uncertainly to PJ and then look to the others, deciding to introduce myself.

"Hello, Pastor Jerome; I'm Jim Moretti." The Pastor shakes my hand and nods at me slowly; his mouth is hanging open in a speechless gape.

"Badrick..." I say with a friendly nod as I shake his hand. "It's good to meet you finally."

Looking at Rad, a flurry of images from his life rush through my mind. "Hello, Rad," I say as I offer him my hand.

"I don't use that name anymore... it's just Radison," he corrects me as he tentatively takes my hand. The instant that our hands touch another flash obscures the scene.

THE SURROUNDINGS ARE strange and unfamiliar this time — I'm in a foreign country. To my surprise, Radison is with me. At first, I assume that I'm sharing one of his memories, but then he looks at me, obviously as disoriented as I am. He clearly sees me.

"W-Where are we... what's happening?" he asks me in astonishment. The implication of what's happening dawns on me. Amos' own words from the first day we met suddenly come to mind, and I repeat them to Radison in explanation....

"The Bible is full of people like us — travelers. They're more commonly known as Prophets." A smile crosses my face as I consider what God is doing — in fact, it's what God *has been doing* all along. "It looks like you and I may be spending some time together. Do you have a notebook? It'd be a good idea to start keeping a journal."

WHILE WE'RE SPEAKING, a boy on a bicycle rushes toward us, passing right through both of us. Radison gasps in shock and stares down at himself as he catches his breath. I reassure him with a grip on his shoulder and begin to explain: "The first thing to know about traveling is...."

WE WALK along the old stone-covered road as we talk. I share some of my experiences with him and recount the unforgettable night when he and Devlon Sheen were saved together.

"You guys are connected somehow...," I begin to explain. While I'm speaking, my eyes fall on the face of someone I immediately recognize, and that connection becomes crystal clear. It stops me in mid-step, and mid-sentence.

The man is sitting in a sidewalk cafe right beside us. His face is as cruel and ruthless as ever — the distinctive smell of his cognac-soaked cigar permeates the air. There's more gray in his hair, but it is Bahal, without a doubt. We hear him speaking to the man seated across from him.

"The money will be deposited in this account when you have successfully completed the job," Bahal says as he slides a handwritten note across the table.

"How do I know I can trust you?" the man challenges.

"You don't. Others will gladly take your place if you wish to change your mind."

The man stares at the amount written on the note in front of him: fifty million US dollars are not easy to dismiss. He places his hand on the paper and slips it into his pocket. "Have arrangements been made at the museum?" he asks.

"The guards have been duly compensated," Bahal confirms. "The pendant will be unguarded, and its case left unlocked."

Turning to Radison, I point out Bahal and his companion, explaining the history. It's pretty apparent what pendant they're talking about.

Glancing around us, I try to identify our surroundings. "It looks like he's in Europe this time," I note. As soon as those words come out of my mouth, words from Revelation chapter 13 suddenly echo in the air around us:

> *'...and they worshiped the beast, saying, Who is like unto the beast? And who is able to war with him? There is given to him a mouth speaking great things and blasphemies; and there is given to him authority[1]....'*

Radison's face reveals the same stunning realization; it is clear that he has heard it too. We both look back at Bahal with a shared understanding of who he really is. Then, just as quickly as it had begun, the scene fades from sight in a flash.

RADISON and I find ourselves back at the church steps, shaking hands once again. We share a glance that acknowledges what we have just experienced together. Radison swallows nervously — his eyes open wide in surprise.

He glances at the others, unsure what he should share. "Wow! ...I mean, you being here... that's, like, wow. I-It's good to meet you." He says awkwardly. I nod back, sensing that this will not be our last meeting.

After releasing his hand, I look at PJ, who is watching me with a curious smile. "What's going on?" he asks innocently enough.

I'm considering my answer when I'm reminded of a conversation with Amos.

"How much time is left?" I'd asked him
"You can rest assured that His coming won't be a clock's tick late, and it won't be a tick early either. When the last soul to enter the kingdom has found safe refuge in Christ, that's when time will be up for the church."

The answer to PJ's question seems suddenly clear. There are a lot more souls who still need to find refuge; the country's return to God will buy them some time.

In *this* time, however — *the time I'm visiting now* — that delay is nearly over.

"**Things are about to get mighty interesting in the world,**" I tell him. Glancing back at Radison, I see him swallow and nod in agreement.

PJ doesn't question the comment. I get the sense that my words are just confirmation of something he already knows. He looks at Radison with an approving glance, then watches me as I take a step back.

"Say hi to Anna and the kids for me," he says, just as I'm fading from sight.

———

'ANNA AND THE KIDS....' PJ's words reverberated, leaving even more of an impression than the experience with Radison.

Anna was still gripping my hand, and she turned to look me in the eye with the same scrutinizing expression she had at breakfast. This time she didn't question me. Instead, her eyes softened into a secretive 'I'm glad you're here' mien, and she just hugged my arm, laying her head against my shoulder.

'Anna and the kids....' PJ's words repeated in my head once more.

———

AFTER AN EARLY DINNER, Anna and I cleaned up the dishes together. Then Anna joined Mike and Lena in the living room while I excused myself to visit the bathroom upstairs. As I stood in front of the mirror, I thought about all that had happened in the past three-and-a-half years — since that night when Anna first walked into the Sub Shop. I thought of mom's advice and how she had come to love Anna like her own daughter. The degree to which Uncle Jim had grown to love her was apparent, too — he treated her like close family. He treated us both that way. My heart was warmed as I even remembered Kelly's selfless approval: *"she seems really nice."*

A thousand memories of days together with Anna swirled in my mind, washing over me and then receding like waves in the ocean, making room for the next barrage. The look in her eye this afternoon, after she sensed my traveling revealed a degree of trust and acceptance that I doubted could exist in anyone else's heart except hers.

I realized that PJ's words had not surprised me — they had only served to bump my already teetering resistance the final inch until it had finally fallen and shattered on the ground in a million pieces.

I tugged on the gold chain around my neck, retrieving the ring I'd worn on it since the night I arrived at the farmhouse. Mom's ring. It wasn't a big diamond, but it sparkled like crazy.

I washed it until the gold gleamed like new and admired it one last time, then nervously placed it in my pocket.

ANNA and I stood together on the farmhouse porch a short while later. We watched the sunset until the western sky turned light pink and stars began to peek through in the East. The sound of early spring crickets could be heard from the farm's open fields.

Anna sensed my nervousness and squeezed my hand, "What's wrong?"

I didn't answer her question. I cleared my throat and looked into her eyes — those eyes that were like magnets for my soul, always drawing me in.

"Anna, there's something I have to ask you. It's the most important question I've ever asked." She looked at me and nodded - I could see the hint of tears as her eyes misted.

"The past three years have been pretty unbelievable; I don't know how I would have ever gotten through them without you. You've been here by my side every day, even when you knew it was dangerous. You've been a true partner in everything I've done — the Blaze podcast has been amazing; that was all you.

"I guess what I'm trying to say is that I can't even imagine living without you. I'll never find anyone like you in a million lifetimes. This year especially has made me realize that I don't have to get older to know that you're the most important person in my life, and you always will be."

I watched a tear escape and run down her cheek as she listened. I knew that it was now or never. I nervously slid a hand into my pocket, collecting the ring in my fist, and then dropped to one knee. Looking up into her misty eyes, I presented the ring to her, holding it up for her to see.

"This was the ring that my dad gave to mom. It's been my dearest treasure, next to you. I'd be honored if you'd be willing to wear it.

"I-I guess what I'm asking is... if you'll have me... will you marry me?"

She burst out crying as she shook her head yes, over and over, unable to form words. I slowly placed the ring on her finger, feeling relieved that it fit her so well. She held it in front of her face and choked back tears as she looked at it.

When I stood to hug her, she wrapped her arms around my neck, giving me a kiss that lit the eastern sky; it made me tremble inside. I picked her up in my excitement and spun her around, knocking over one of the porch rockers as she squealed and screamed in joyful celebration.

LENA AND MIKE came running out onto the porch to see what was happening, and Anna ran to her mom, flashing the ring. Soon Anna and her mom were crying and screaming as they hugged each other.

"Nice work, kid," Uncle Mike said as he slapped me on the back and then took me into his arms. "Told ya she was the one."

"Yeah, you did," I freely admitted. I hugged him again, grateful for all he had been for me over the past few years.

Anna finally made her way back to me, wrapping me in her arms. Her mom smiled and nodded for Mike to come inside, leaving us alone on the porch once again.

I'M NOT sure how long we stood there together. The sky grew dark, and the night air felt electric. Gradually a gentle breeze began to blow, carrying a moist coolness that we hadn't felt in a long while. We could hear the faint rumble of distant thunder in the night sky.

Anna nestled closer under my arm as we stood together. I looked out over the old farm's fields and released a deep breath. Uncle Jim's old pickup truck was parked nearby, along with Bessy, the tractor he loved. A glance toward the dark and abandoned tent grounds brought a complex mix of emotions as a wave of memories flooded my mind. Kelly..., Mom..., now Uncle Jim.

Anna seemed to sense my thoughts with remarkable intuition. I felt her hug me and lean her head against my chest. Soon I felt the vibration of her voice as she began to sing — quietly at first. Unlike me, she had a beautiful voice and knew how to use it to stir the soul. I'd heard her sing the song before; it had been a favorite for both of us over the past few years.

> *"Why should I feel discouraged*
> *Why should the shadows come*
> *Why should my heart feel lonely*
> *And long for heaven and home...."*

Her voice grew a little louder as she squeezed me reassuringly...

> *"When Jesus is my portion*
> *A constant friend is He*
> *His eye is on the sparrow.*

And I know He watches over me...."

She looked up at me as she paused; her eyes reflected a deep understanding of what was swirling in my heart. I accepted her kiss gratefully and hugged her closer. Her gentle reminder had been the perfect encouragement. After a brief silence, I felt a thankful prayer surging up inside me; it flowed out naturally.

"Lord, You are our strength; God is our song. God, Himself is our salvation.

"Lord, You've shown us what kind of God You are — You've shown the world! We've seen that You are a fighter, through and through. Just the way Pharaoh's chariots and army were dumped in the sea, and wild waters poured over them; they sank like a rock in the deep sea. Your strong right hand, God, shimmers with power; your strong right-hand shatters Your enemies.

"In your mighty majesty, You smashed those who made themselves Your enemies. When You let loose Your hot anger, they were destroyed. They pursued us; they hunted us down; they chased us ceaselessly. You blew on them, and waves covered them. They sank like a lead weight in Your majestic waters.

"Who compares with you, Oh God? Who compares with you in power, in holy majesty, In awesome praises, wonder-working God? You stretched out your right hand and swallowed them up. But the people you redeemed, you led in merciful love; You guided them under your protection.

"You have brought us and planted us in the land of Your heritage, the place where You live, the place You made, Your sanctuary that You established with Your own hands.

"You rule forever, Lord, for all eternity![2]"

. . .

WE STOOD TOGETHER in an emotional silence for a moment, and Anna offered a heartfelt amen. After a minute, she looked at me with a smile.

"I recorded that," she said happily. She quickly hit send, forwarding the impromptu voice recording to Josh. Knowing him, it would be posted worldwide within the hour.

UNCLE MIKE suddenly burst through the screen door onto the porch....

"It's raining! They're showin' it on th' TV — heavy rains have started over in th' Northwest and are spreadin' fast across th' whole country. It's dousin' fires that've been out o' control for months."

He was still speaking when a loud crack of thunder and lightning shook the air, and the skies overhead opened with a downpour that hit the ground like a massive, warm shower. Uncle Mike held his head in his hands in joyful amazement as Lena rushed to his side. He grabbed her and spun her around on the porch in a spontaneous dance of joy.

A MOMENT LATER, Lena tugged his hand and ran down the porch steps, where they began to spin and dance in the rain together.

Before I realized what was happening, Anna had pulled me into the muddy barnyard. We laughed hysterically at each other's awkward moves in the slippery mud, unafraid of looking ridiculous. We held onto each other as we danced, dancing hand-in-hand, whirling and splashing in the refreshing rain.

WE DANCED IN JOYOUS ABANDON... we danced and danced!

⌘

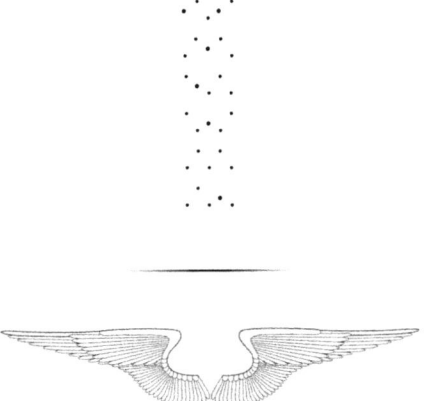

THE END

AFTERWORD

C.S. Lewis introduced 'That Hideous Strength,' the third book in his famous Space Trilogy, by saying,

"This is a 'tall story' about devilry, though it has behind it a serious 'point.'"[1]

His description fits Jimmy's story as well, although that fact is admittedly the closest this story will ever come to being compared to Lewis' work.

The inspiration for Jimmy's adventure grew from personal experiences that deepened my understanding of God's view of suffering. Central to that understanding was the truth that suffering is the result of evil and that God does not create or use evil, but He can use the pain caused by it to shape us.

The source of evil is clearly identified in Scripture. "Your adversary, the Devil," is the roaring lion who seeks to devour us. This is just as true today as when Peter wrote those words, perhaps even more so as we draw nearer to the end of the age.

The power of engaging stories is their ability to spur our imagination, allowing us to experience their events, almost as if we are a part of them and living them first-hand. Jimmy's adventure brings this epic conflict with evil to life so it can be 'lived' and not simply described metaphorically. It's important to note that this story's fictional account is not an attempt to describe actual prophetic events closely. Nor does it imply any political allegory or reference to real-life events.

In illustrating the epic conflict between good and evil, it draws upon one of the Bible's most dramatic and fascinating contests, the story of Elijah and the wicked queen Jezebel. Bahal and Athaliah embody those notorious characters who represented a time in Israel's history when Ba'al worship was at its worst. Athaliah was, in fact, the name of Ahab's much younger sister, the daughter of King Omri, Ahab's father. She was an evil queen in her own right who slaughtered the royal line of Judah to seize the throne for herself and eventually met her own violent end.

While the battle with evil is the story's backdrop, its deeper message is about God's faithfulness and willingness to use unlikely people who may feel they have little to bring on their own.

Within and Without Time is, more than anything else, an object lesson in ways God can use ordinary people and weak things to accomplish the most extraordinary work.

In essence, Within & Without Time remains a story about the shocking contrast between human frailty and an infinitely powerful and sovereign God. A God motivated by love as immense and immeasurable as His power.

⌘

THANK YOU FOR READING!

PLEASE TAKE A MOMENT TO LEAVE A REVIEW.

BOOKS BY

D. I. HENNESSEY

Available on Amazon

"www.amazon.com/gp/product/B09DFDM364"

NOTES

3. MOONLIT GRAVEYARD

1. Philippians 1:21
2. Matthew 11:28
3. Ephesians 1:7

6. VIGILANCE

1. The Resolute Desk is a double pedestal partners' desk made from the oak timbers of the British ship HMS Resolute. In 1880, Queen Victoria gifted the desk to President Rutherford B. Hayes.

    https://www.whitehousehistory.org/questions/what-is-the-resolute-desk-and-where-did-it-come-from#:~:text=The%20Resolute%20Desk%20is%20a,exceptions%20being%20Presidents%20Lyndon%20B.

16. DARKNESS AND LIGHT

1. (understand?)
2. (the ranking member of the group)
3. (a policeman?)
4. (tell the truth or you'd better run.)
5. (you don't really believe what you're saying, because I don't!)
6. weak
7. Dance — meaning fight
8. Hey you 'From the race' - Chicano
9. Where You From? Is a way of asking if he's a member of any gang.
10. Are you a Policeman?
11. Leaving the gang.
12. Rifan, Rifamos! - we rule, reign, control!

18. FULLNESS OF TIME

1. Galatians 4:4
2. Spurgeon, Morning & Evening, Feb 9th.

20. STAND

1. Isaiah 41:10
2. 2 Chronicles 20:17

21. DRAGON'S FOE

1. Jimmy's words are inspired by C. Spurgeon, Morning and Evening, Nov 30th

30. BRAVE

1. Esther 3:6
2. Chozeq's words are adapted from Spurgeon, Morning & Evening, April 7th

31. FACEOFF

1. Acts 3:19

32. DISTANT THUNDER

1. Revelation 13:4-5
2. Adapted from Moses' song in Exodus 15:2-18 (The Message Bible)

AFTERWORD

1. Lewis, C. S.. The Space Trilogy, Omnib. HarperOne.

CHOZEQ

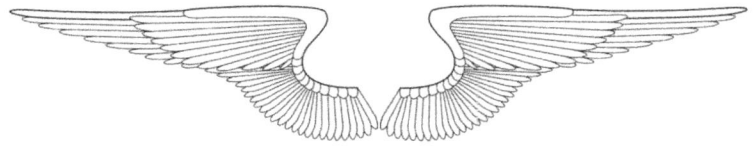

Hebrew **kho'-zek**, qzx

Noun Masculine: strength, power, powerful one